the women of hearts book one

MARCI BOLDEN

HIDDEN
HEARTS

Cover design by Okay Creations
Book layout by Lori Colbeck

ISBN-13: 978-1-950348-23-7

the women of hearts book one

MARCI BOLDEN

HIDDEN
HEARTS

PINK SAND
PRESS

PROLOGUE

Julia Fredrickson pushed her cart toward the exit of the local food mart. As the tinted glass doors parted, they admitted a burst of summer sunlight and the sounds of cars navigating the parking lot. A siren wailing in the distance.

Leaving the grocery store shouldn't be a fear-inducing event, but a jolt of terror rolled through her like an electric shock. She felt her throat tighten as she forced herself to swallow. Breathing became a chore almost too hard to manage.

Now that the tall glass door had opened, she felt exposed. She was standing in the lobby of her neighborhood grocery store, but she might as well have been standing on a stage in full view of the world. As it had so many times over the last few weeks, the hair on her nape stood and her nerves came alive. Though she couldn't see any danger, she felt peril down to her bones.

Someone was watching her.

Someone was waiting for her.

This wasn't the first time Julia had suspected she was being followed. Actually, this sensation was becoming much too familiar. She couldn't explain the feeling or pinpoint exactly why she felt so vulnerable. But she *knew* it. Someone was watching her.

She wanted to turn around. Go back inside the security of the store where the staff knew her by name. Maybe she would have if she hadn't spent so much time sorting through the pile of organic tomatoes that the manager had come to see if she needed assistance. She had smiled and selected two bright red Romas that were not on her list. Her husband didn't eat tomatoes. She would likely throw them away before Eric could ask why she'd wasted money on them.

She didn't tell the manager that picking the produce had been an excuse to linger in the store. Being surrounded by shoppers and staff was better than being alone. No. Not alone. She was *never* alone anymore.

Eric said she was becoming paranoid and suggested she go to the doctor. He said maybe her hormones were out of balance. Ever since she'd had a bout of baby blues after their second child was born, he attributed *everything* to her hormones. Never mind that was over twenty-five years ago. Other than that one brief postpartum spell, she had never been prone to anxiety or blowing things out of proportion. She'd been a stay-at-home mom and hoarder of bandages for scraped knees and bike accidents. But she'd never been paranoid.

Julia faced her parking spot—eight spots down the far-left row. She'd made it inside the store in less than a minute. But that was before she had a cart of groceries. She counted the reusable bags she'd filled. Six. She could carry six bags.

She again scanned what she could see of the parking lot from where she stood inside the store. After finding no immediate danger, she hefted the bags onto her forearms and then forced herself into the sunlight.

Damn it.

She'd been so preoccupied with checking her surroundings, she hadn't dug her sunglasses out of her purse. The midday sun was blinding as it filled the sky and reflected off windshields. She also realized she hadn't pulled her keys from the outside pocket of her purse. They were within easy reach there, but the handles of the overfilled market bags pressed hard into her forearms, limiting her movements. She would have to put them down to free her hand enough to secure her keys.

Quickening her steps, Julia rushed toward her car. The bumper sticker boasting that she was a proud volunteer at the local dog shelter was like a beacon. She was almost there. Almost safe. The soft soles of her tennis shoes didn't make a sound as she rushed, but she was certain anyone close enough would hear her labored breathing. Sweat broke on her brow as she stopped at her trunk. Dropping the bags from her left arm without a care for the contents inside, Julia dug in her purse pocket and snagged the loop of her keyring with a finger. The relief she felt at having the keys in her hand was immeasurable. And ridiculous. She was a grown woman terrified of being alone in a parking lot. In broad daylight.

Maybe Eric was right. Maybe she was becoming paranoid.

Using the button on the fob, she released her trunk and then set her groceries inside. Taking a moment to exhale a long breath, Julia made the decision to call her doctor. Something was off with her. Having this kind of fear every day without reason was not normal.

Julia rested her fingertips on the trunk lid hovering above her head. Before she could pull it down, the lid slammed, startling her. Jumping back, she held her breath. A tall man stood between her and the sun. With his face silhouetted by the light, she needed a moment to recognize him.

She smiled when she did. She really was being paranoid.

HOLLY AUSTIN PACED in front of the room-length white-board. She ignored the photos of cheating spouses and suspected scammers and skimmed over her barely legible notes. Once again, she wished she had better handwriting. Squinting to make out a word as she walked, she cursed when she accidentally kicked a chair. Shoving the obstacle under the table, she continued her pass along the board.

The HEARTS Investigative Services conference room looked like a war zone. Colorful sticky notes, uncapped highlighters, and unstapled pages from police reports covered the table where the team staged cases. While some of her co-workers kept their notes in neat piles and color-coded notebooks, Holly worked best in chaos.

She turned her focus to one of the photos on the wall. The picture captured the woman's blue eyes and bright smile at the moment a breeze blew her long golden hair off her shoulders. Julia Fredrickson clung to her husband's arm. The sunlight sparkled off a large diamond on her left ring finger, as if to tell the universe these two people belonged together.

Julia and Eric looked so happy. In the photo, dark glasses hid his light eyes, but Holly easily recalled the pain that had filled his entire face as he'd begged her to help him.

Two days after this picture was taken, Julia vanished. She'd been missing over a month. The more time that passed, the less likely it was that she would be found. Eric knew that too. That was why he'd come to HEARTS when the police continued to imply that Julia had probably needed time away and would be in touch with him soon.

Over the last week, Holly had dug through the Fredricksons' personal lives, bank accounts, and social media pages. Seven days of asking friends intimate questions, watching Eric Fredrickson just in case he wasn't being completely honest, and trying to discover if Julia had a lover who might have whisked her away to start a new life.

Well over fifty hours spent hitting the same dead ends the police had run into. That wasn't sitting well with Holly. Every minute she spent looking for Julia added to the weight of dread in her stomach. She knew better than most how quickly the world and the people in it could change. She'd learned very young how unfair life could be. Though Julia's children were adults, Holly didn't think they had learned that lesson until their mother's disappearance. They had the kind of naiveté that came with being raised in a stable home, sheltered from the ugliness of the real world. That reality had been thrust upon them without warning.

Holly rubbed her thumb over the simple silver heart charm she wore around her neck. She needed to start over. Go back to square one. Start again.

Closing her eyes, she visualized the security-camera footage the store manager had copied for her. A man approached Julia as she put her groceries in her trunk. They spoke for just a few moments. And then she followed him to somewhere out of range of the only working camera in the grocery-store parking lot.

What had he said? Why would Julia go with him?

What the hell am I missing?

Someone gripped Holly's shoulder without warning, startling her. She grabbed the wrist attached to the offending hand, elbowed the solar plexus, and had the owner of all of the above face down on the floor with her knee in his back in seconds. The dark-haired man pinned beneath her grunted.

Samantha, the newest member of her team, laughed. Sam usually sat around munching on breath mints and sharing celebrity gossip no one cared to hear. She was brilliant at searching the Internet and finding people's darkest digital secrets. Holly didn't even want to know all the private databases the little sneak could access. Too bad Sam also had a warped sense of humor. The grin on her thin face made her appear far too pleased with the situation.

Leaning against the conference room doorjamb, she smirked at the scene before her. "I told him not to touch you while you were deep in thought. He didn't listen. Did you, Detective?"

Holly looked at the man she still had immobilized against the charcoal-gray commercial-grade carpet. The set of his jaw and deep lines around his eyes as he winced indicated he was in pain, but she was more focused on what Sam had called him. *Detective?*

He wheezed before saying, "I have some questions about Julia Fredrickson."

Sam chuckled as the man struggled against Holly's hold on his wrist and the steady pressure she kept on his back with her knee.

"This isn't funny, Sam," Holly chastised. "I could have hurt him."

"Uh, Ms. Austin," he said, "you *are* hurting me."

"Shit. Sorry." Holly pulled him with her as she stood. After years in active-duty service, her kneejerk reactions still got the better of her at times. Being both a woman and a soldier required finely tuned self-preservation skills. Even now as a civilian, she didn't always take time to measure her response when she was startled. Life-saving habits died hard.

An awkward-sounding laugh—the kind suspects used when trying to act casual—left him as he looked at her with wide, almost-black eyes. He quickly looked away and focused on stretching his shoulder. His moves didn't seem sincere. He seemed nervous. His hands trembled as he brushed his suit.

She tried to read between the lines of his behavior and suspected he was there to tell her to back off the Julia Fredrickson case. Though Holly did her best to stay on the good side of the police department, this wouldn't be the first time an officer had stopped by to warn her that she was treading on his turf. She hadn't backed off once, and she didn't intend to now. If that was his purpose in showing up at her office, he was wasting his time.

As she scrutinized him, the detective's dark skin changed from ashen to an interesting shade of maroon. She didn't see many men in the heart of the Midwest who had the sepia skin tones she'd seen so often in the Middle East. Though his nose was a bit long for his thin face, she thought he was handsome. She didn't usually notice those things, but she supposed her adrenaline was rushing as much as his, clouding her mind.

Turning her attention to Sam, Holly fought the urge to body slam her receptionist to wipe the grin off her face. "We'll talk about this later."

Sam's pink-tinted lips twisted into a deep frown. "Sure." She turned on her too-high-to-be-practical heels and left them alone.

The detective swiped at his cheek, but a few bits of gray carpet lint and a tiny scrap of neon-orange paper stuck to the black hairs of his short-trimmed beard.

Holly pressed her teeth together but couldn't stop the words from tumbling out. "There's still a little... Right there." She pointed and then watched the debris fall away as he moved his hand over his chin. "Got it."

The detective shrugged and pulled at his black jacket as if to shift the material back into place and then straightened his tie. Finally, with a huff, he met Holly's gaze again. This time, though, he didn't look so shaken. She actually thought he looked amused.

"So. Next time I should wear a cowbell?" He grinned, showing off a dimple in his cheek that inexplicably drew her attention. She stared until he cleared his throat.

Holly didn't embarrass easily, but a sense of mortification built in her chest as heat spread throughout her body, settling in her cheeks. Another sensation she wasn't used to. Not that her assault on him was unwarranted. What kind of cop surprised people? He certainly would have been trained better than that.

She planted her hands on her hips, attempting to push her unexpected discomfiture down and regain control of her emotions. "Don't ever grab me without warning, Detective. Unless you enjoyed that." Her breath caught as soon as the words left her, and his eyes darted to hers.

That sounded wrong. Very wrong. She wanted to look away, but she wasn't about to let this situation get the better of her. His smirk twitched and drew her attention to his lips. Seeing another shred of paper trapped in the whiskers on his chin, she ran her finger under his full bottom lip to knock it away. She jerked her hand back when she realized what she'd done. "Sorry. I'm sorry. Are you okay? Did I hurt you?" The words rushed out, blending together in a barely intelligible strand.

Damn it. She was acting like a fool, coming across just as he probably expected a female private investigator to. A silly, stumbling girl dressed up to play private eye.

He made a show of flexing the arm she'd twisted. "I'm good. My pride is beat to shit, though."

"Don't take it to heart," she said. "I've practiced martial arts since I was a kid. My father wanted to make sure I could take care of myself."

"Well, you can." He reached into his pocket to pull out a black wallet and then flashed his credentials. "Detective Jack Tarek."

Though he lowered the badge quickly, she grabbed his wrist—without the intent of overpowering him this time— and lifted his identification for closer inspection. "*Jakeem* Tarek."

He shrugged. "Jack makes me stand out a little less. You know, besides all this." He waved his hand in front of his face. She suspected he meant the distinct combination of features and skin tone that implied his ethnicity rather than the fact that he was handsome enough to make her want to bat her eyes and giggle.

The word *swoon* came to mind, and Holly very nearly acted on it for the first time in her life. Instead, she released his wrist and held her hand out to him. "Holly Austin."

"Yes, I know."

He accepted her offer with a firm grip. Men who gingerly clasped her hand as if they could break her tended to see her as female first and as investigator a distant second. Tarek's greeting let her know he saw her the other way—an investigator who happened to be female. Of course, having just pinned him to the ground likely gave him an idea that she preferred men not handle her with kid gloves, despite her current state of rambling and apparent blushing.

He did, however, hold her hand longer than necessary for the customary greeting.

She begrudgingly slipped her palm from his and balled her fingers, a futile attempt to stop the feel of him from escaping her skin. Yet another response she didn't fully understand but couldn't control. "Sam said you're here to pick my brain?"

"I was hoping to cross-reference my case with yours. Have you found anything new on Julia Fredrickson's disappearance?"

She stared at him, careful to keep her face neutral. And not only because she was hyperaware of the man before her. Police seldom wanted the help of PIs working a case when there were still fresh leads to be investigated. Julia Fredrickson hadn't been missing long enough for the police to consider her case cold. His request surprised her. Holly didn't like surprises. Nor did she trust them. Surprises rarely ended well.

"I'm not here as a cop." He lifted his hands as if to show her he was innocent of any wrongdoing. "Not officially, anyway. My mother's neighbor has gone missing. Have you seen the news reports on Penelope Nelson?"

Holly nodded. There were similarities that had piqued her curiosity. She was keeping a close eye on the news, hoping to catch updates that might connect the latest missing woman to Julia.

"She's a sweet lady who sure as hell wouldn't just walk out on her life," Tarek said. "Something has happened to her, and I promised my mom I'd look into it."

"I get that." Holly wanted to believe him, but she couldn't help feeling he was baiting her. The police department had shut her out cold. They wouldn't give her the tiniest morsel of information on Julia's case. Eric Fredrickson had been giving her as much information as he could on the investigation. "What I don't get," she continued, "is what you need from me."

"When the department found out this was personal, they limited my access to the case and put the biggest asshole they could find as the lead detective, knowing he'd never give me information. I can't work on this through the force, but I can't *not* work on this, either. The woman is my mom's friend."

Tarek gestured to a file on the table that she hadn't noticed. He must have put it there before she dropped him. She opened the folder and scanned the eight-by-ten photo inside. Just to confirm what she already knew, Holly glanced over her shoulder at the image of Julia—a petite forty-three-year-old blonde with blue eyes and a perfect smile. She took the picture from the file and held it next to Julia's. "They could be sisters."

Tarek joined her at the whiteboard. Through her

peripheral vision, Holly noticed him looking over her face. "You look like her. Like *them*. Only younger."

Holly frowned at his observation. "There are a lot of blue-eyed blond women out there, Detective. I'm one of many."

He didn't seem dissuaded by her explanation. "Her husband hired you, knowing that you look like a younger version of his missing wife?"

She cocked a brow as she faced him. "Her husband hired my *team*. I took the lead by choice. *My* choice. The fact that I look similar to his wife has nothing to do with why he hired this agency, nor does it impact my ability to work this case."

He opened his mouth as if to object but then seemed to think better of it and pointed to the photo she was holding. "That's Penelope. She disappeared from outside a strip mall yesterday. We pulled the surveillance, of course. A man approached her as she was putting bags in her car. He talked to her for exactly eighty-three seconds before she followed him and got into a car. She hasn't been seen since. I looked into recent missing persons cases and came across Julia's. These cases have way too many similarities." Tarek scanned the pictures taped to the wall. "Are all these cases related?"

"No. These are from various things we're working on now. We like to bounce ideas off each other, but I'm the lead on the Fredrickson case. Julia disappeared six weeks ago from a grocery-store parking lot on MLK. Just like Penelope, she vanished in the middle of the morning from a high-traffic area, but nobody noticed a thing. The manager of the grocery store where Julia disappeared gave me a copy of the surveillance recording." She gestured to a fuzzy screenshot she'd printed. "The quality isn't clear enough to make an identification, but the man she left with was Caucasian, approximately six feet tall. She appeared to go with him willingly. We suspect she knew him or his cover story was convincing enough to get her to trust him."

"Or he had a weapon," he said.

"He didn't appear to be holding one in the video. Of course, the quality wasn't that great."

"Any evidence she had a lover? Maybe she ran off with him."

Holly shook her head. "Her life was about as perfect as it could get. I've looked in every dark corner I can find. There is no evidence of an affair, let alone one serious enough for her to leave her husband."

"Yeah," he said. "That's what I'm running into with Penelope, too." He pointed to another printed still from the low-quality security footage. "That his car?"

"The cops are stonewalling me—"

"Don't take it personally. They can't compromise their case."

She pressed her lips together, taking a moment to temper her immediate response. "Yes. I know that. I may not be a detective, *Detective*, but I understand procedure and would never risk compromising a case or losing a suspect to protect my pride." She let her words sink in before continuing. "Julia's husband has been feeding me information. From what he says, this car was reported stolen earlier that morning and found outside town the next day. They found a print inside that matched Julia's. This was likely the vehicle used to abduct her. And I say abduct because despite what looks like her seeming to willingly go with this man, I don't believe she did." She eyed Tarek. "Unfortunately, I don't have much more to go on than that. Mr. Fredrickson has been an open book, but we just can't find any leads. The evidence is starting to point to her being a victim of opportunity. Which means she could be anywhere."

Tarek shook his head. "I would have thought that as well, but look at them. Two women, almost identical in appearance and age, taken in almost identical circumstances. He chose Julia, just like he chose Penelope." He faced Holly. "You know, if by chance Fredrickson did this—"

"He didn't."

"He may have you in his sights," he finished as if she hadn't spoken.

"He doesn't. And if he did, I'd knock the wind out of him and pin his ass to the ground before he knew what was happening."

Tarek laughed. "Gotcha."

"He told the police she thought she was being followed."

"And what do the police think?"

Holly stared at him. He was a cop. He knew exactly what the police thought. That Fredrickson was throwing false leads to distract them. "He suspects they don't believe him. And we both know why. The first suspect is always the husband."

"Is he a suspect?"

"Aren't the spouses always a suspect? That doesn't make them guilty."

Tarek responded by giving her the same flat stare she'd given him. When she didn't budge, he lifted his hands in a show of surrender. "Look, my boss told me to butt out, but I can't. I don't know Penelope well, but she means something to my mother, so I'm going to do my damnedest to find her. Besides." He shrugged. "I never was very good at following orders."

Holly lifted her brows. "Well, that's good to know before we get into bed together." Her eyes widened—she didn't mean for them to; they just did—as she realized what she'd said. *What the fuck, Austin?*

Tarek smirked.

"I didn't mean—"

"I know what you meant," he said. "I'd like for us to work together unofficially if we can."

"Unofficially?"

"Unofficially. Because I'm not *officially* on this case."

She stared into his eyes, gauging if she could trust him. Trust didn't come easy for Holly. Life had thrown her a few curveballs, and her line of work tended to show her the ugly side of people. But something about Jakeem Tarek made her *want* to trust him. Finally she narrowed her eyes. "This goes both ways. You hear something, you let me know. Julia Fredrickson has been missing for six weeks. I *need* to find her."

"Same for you."

She weighed his offer. He would be able to find out more information on the official investigation than she could, and that could help her move the Fredrickson case forward. Julia's husband was growing frustrated, but no more so than Holly. He'd given up on the police ever finding his wife and dumped a huge amount of money into HEARTS to see progress that wasn't happening.

HEARTS had blanketed the area with posters, had gone door-to-door, and had come back empty-handed. Sam had worked her magic to gather traffic-cam and security footage. Holly had interviewed dozens of people over the last week. And she still had nothing.

Given how much time had passed since Julia had gone missing, a dark cloud hovered over the case. Holly wasn't stupid. The likelihood of finding Julia now was even less than it had been a week ago when she took the case, but failure was not an option, most especially when a woman's life was on the line.

"Was Julia's case the only one that flagged in your search?" she asked.

"Yes. I only looked locally, but no other cases matched the victimology."

"Okay," she said. "Let's widen the search to a fifty-mile radius. See if we can find other missing women who fit this description."

"A hundred. Just to be safe."

"I'll get Sam on this right away. She does a lot of our research." She started for the door and then stopped and turned toward him. "I'm guessing you do have information to share that we just haven't gotten to yet?"

"Don't worry. I have information to share."

"Good." She crossed the lobby to the reception desk.

Sam's cocky smirk suggested she was still pleased with the outcome of her latest round of mischief. "You look mighty good on top, Hol."

Holly deepened her frown. "Not funny. You shouldn't have let him surprise me."

"I tried to stop him."

"Clearly you didn't try hard enough."

Sam leaned back and tapped her pencil on the desk. "I told him you didn't want to be disturbed at the moment, and he got snippy with me. You know I hate that."

"So you let me nearly break his arm?"

Sam shrugged as her grin reappeared. "The way you had him pinned was sexy as hell. I think he was turned on by it. He's probably into S&M. Most of the cops I've dated have been. It's an authority fetish."

Holly lifted her hand to stop her. Once Sam got going on her sex life, ending the flow of information was nearly impossible. "I could not possibly care less about your fetishes, Sam. I need you to run a search for me. Any missing women in a hundred-mile radius who fit Julia Fredrickson's description. Except Penelope Nelson. That's the case Tarek brought in." Holly started toward the conference room.

"Hey," Sam called.

Holly turned back, knowing she'd regret it. Sam didn't seem to take anything seriously. Probably because she'd never been in the field. She'd never seen someone die. She'd never pressed her hand to an open wound and promised someone they'd be okay, knowing damn well they wouldn't. Holly envied Sam's innocence sometimes, but most of the time the naiveté just annoyed the hell out of her.

"Check out his butt," Sam whispered as she held up her hands and motioned as if she were cupping melons. "Very nice."

Holly spun away without reacting. Any other of the HEARTS probably would have at least given Sam a thumbs-up, but Holly wasn't amused.

JACK HADN'T STOPPED REPLAYING THE HOUR OR SO HE had spent with Holly since he left the HEARTS office. After returning to the station, he sat at his desk and glanced around as if he were about to do something incredibly wrong. Which, to some extent, he was. The police databases should never be used to gain insight on someone for personal reasons, but there wasn't a man or woman there who hadn't done a little background check on someone for reasons other than solving a case.

He wasn't surprised to find Holly Austin's police record was clean. He let out a low whistle, however, when he brought up her family history. Mother deceased. Father lucky to still be alive, based on the number of DUIs and stints in the local jail. With a father like that, he didn't have to think too hard about why she had such a tough outer appearance.

She'd likely had to work more than others to separate herself from whatever lifestyle she'd had growing up.

He had saved the link to HEARTS Investigative Services' website when he'd first found out one of their agents was working a similar case. He'd researched all six of the private investigators, but now that he knew Holly was the one leading the search for Julia Fredrickson, he clicked on the About page and reread her bio. Two tours in Afghanistan, a black belt in jiujitsu, and a long list of marksmanship badges to prove her skill with a gun. Holly Austin was definitely not a woman to be crossed.

She was tough. She was sturdy. She was someone who had spent so much time looking out for herself that she didn't seem capable of stopping, even for a moment. Women like that had history. Stories.

Baggage.

Jack sat back, wondering why that word had popped into his head. A subliminal warning? If so, it was one he intended to ignore. Even if he wanted to deny that he had been instantly enchanted with Holly Austin, he couldn't. Not just her physical attractiveness, but her boldness, her dry humor, her dedication to her job. Everything about her spoke to him on some level no woman had ever reached before.

He wasn't scared off by her or her past. He was intrigued. He wanted to pick her apart bit by bit to see what made her tick so he could better understand why he had felt such an immediate and intense connection to her. He was even more impressed now that he had experienced her skills firsthand. And there it was again—the memory of her pinning him down that was going to be permanently embedded in his mind. He expected his fantasies were going to get a lot of mileage out of the time he spent with her.

Staring at her professional headshot on the website, Jack was considering how the image didn't do justice to the soft curve of her jaw or demanding blue eyes when his phone vibrated. He didn't have to wonder who it was. His mother had been calling him about every three hours or so, checking to see if he had any new information on her friend.

He connected her call as he left his desk. The last thing he needed was someone at his office to overhear him reassuring her he was doing all he could to find Penelope Nelson. "Mom," he said, putting the phone to his ear. "You okay?"

"Have you found her?" his mother asked, her heavy accent laden with worry.

He let his breath out slowly as he stepped into the bathroom and glanced under the stalls. He was alone. "Not yet, Mom. These things take time. I keep telling you—"

"She's in trouble, Jakeem."

"I know, Mama. I'm trying. I met with a private investigator today. She's going to help me."

His mother hesitated. "*She*?"

He let that fall. Her inquisitive tone could mean two things: she didn't approve of a female private investigator *or* she was going to press to find out if this private investigator could possibly be the soulmate she'd been praying for so her son could settle down and give her grandchildren. Since she was becoming more and more accustomed to the role women played in American society, he'd guess it was the latter.

He didn't want to get pulled into either conversation, so he said, "I can't talk now. I'm at work."

"This isn't work?"

"Yes, but it's not something I can discuss right now." He closed his eyes when she sighed a long, slow breath. "I'll find her. Are you okay otherwise? Need anything?"

"No. I'm okay. Will you come by for dinner, *babba*?"

He couldn't say no, not when she was so upset, but he wasn't a fool either. He was going get grilled on the PI he'd mentioned. Since his mother could read him like a book, he had no doubt Holly Austin was about to become as much of a fascination for his mother as she'd become for him.

Crap.

[2]

HOLLY FROWNED when Sam entered her office just after the workday started. Sam eased a cup of coffee onto the desk, but Holly kept her focus on the papers in front of her.

Holly hadn't asked for coffee, and Sam didn't act like the administrative assistant that she was hired to be unless it suited her. Oh no, Sam wanted something. And Holly knew exactly what that was, but she wasn't about to delve into the gushy girl-talk Sam was hoping to get from her.

After a few moments of being ignored, Sam said, "That detective was here for a long time yesterday."

"Yep."

"Make any headway?"

"Nothing concrete. How's that search going?"

"Scanning some databases now. I'll let you know."

"Thanks."

Sam didn't take the hint Holly was giving with her short, clipped answers. Instead, she picked up the business card Jack had handed Holly before leaving and stared at the plain text on the front. Holly knew it was plain because she'd stared at it, too.

"Do police often come to PIs for help?" Sam asked.

"No."

"So why did he?"

"His mother's friend is missing. He told her he'd investigate it, but his department shut him out since the case is personal. He thinks our cases could be connected, so working with me is the next best thing to being on the other case."

"Do you? Think the cases are connected, I mean."

"Yes." Leaning back, she drew a deep breath as she nailed Sam with a hard stare. She didn't intend to engage in the same topic Sam was hoping to discuss, but Holly did have a thing or two to say. "He heard you, Samantha."

Sam widened her eyes and held her hands up to cup imaginary melons again. Holly nodded one decisive, unamused nod. She didn't admit that Sam had been right. That Jack's ass looked perfect in his slacks.

Sam started to grin but quickly cleared her throat and wiped the smirk from her lips. "Whoops."

"Yeah. *Whoops.* Don't do that again. HEARTS is just getting off the ground. You could get the entire agency in trouble, and I'll be damned if one person sinks this ship over something stupid. Understand me?"

In a rare show of humility, Sam dropped her hands and bit off any attempt at sarcasm. "It won't happen again, Holly. Promise." The moment passed, and she smiled. "But he does have a great ass. Tell me you noticed, because if you didn't, I'm going to have to start believing the rumors about you being dead inside."

Holly drew a breath and let it out slowly as Jack's face—and his perfect...*everything*—flashed through her mind.

"Oh my God! You're blushing!" Sam clapped her hands together as she tossed her head back and laughed. "You *did* notice! I bet his ass looks fantastic in a tight pair of jeans."

"Whoa!" Alexa called as she passed the doorway. Backtracking, she stuck her head in, her dark eyes practically dancing and her lips in a big smile. "Whose ass are we talking about?"

"*Nobody's*," Holly insisted, snatching Jack's business card from Sam's manicured fingers.

Sam's bright gray eyes widened as she spun toward Alexa. Despite Holly's warning, Sam dove right back into sexually objectifying Tarek all over again. Not that Holly hadn't been doing the same in her mind since the moment she'd pulled him to his feet.

"This super-hot detective stopped by to see Holly—"

"About a case," Holly clarified before Sam could deliberately taint the truth.

Sam continued as if Holly hadn't attempted to deflate her enthusiasm. "The pants he was wearing perfectly accentuated his tight little behind. I wanted to take a bite out of him. But"—she let the word linger as she turned to Holly—"the way he was looking at the boss lady, well, let's just say I bet he wouldn't mind if *she* were the one doing the biting."

"What did we just discuss?" Holly chastised.

Sam exaggerated a frown before looking at Alexa. "Apparently I whisper too loudly. He heard me make a comment or two about how scrumptious he is."

"Dipshit," Alexa muttered.

Sam shrugged. "I can't seem to help myself when there's man candy around. I just wanna..." She made a show of smacking her straight, overly whitened teeth together, making a loud chomping sound, and then growled.

Alexa gasped and put her hand to her chest as if she'd never seen such a display.

Holly scoffed at her dramatic response. "Oh, please. You aren't much better. You're lucky the bartender at the pub hasn't filed a restraining order against you yet."

Whenever the team went to lunch at their favorite burger and beer spot, Alexa requested they be seated in the back right-hand corner of the building. Then she smiled and batted her eyes at the bartender all during lunch. And got free beer. Holly pretended to be irritated that Alexa would misuse her feminine wiles to get a free drink, but in all honesty, she was a bit jealous. She'd never learned how to be a carefree flirt like Alexa and Sam.

No. She was a blatant "I'll show you mine if you show me yours" type. That might get her a one-night stand on occasion, but rarely did it get her free drinks just for walking into a place.

"I know when and where to make inappropriate comments, and a lobby that amplifies every single noise isn't the place. Remember that," Alexa said, pointing a finger in Sam's face.

Holly sighed. "Sam, get back to that research I asked for. If there are more missing women out there who we can tie back to this suspect, we need to know."

Sam gave a limp salute before leaving.

Holly leaned back. "She's such a handful."

"She's getting better."

"Is she? It's a damn good thing Detective Tarek laughed off her comments."

"I'll talk to her again."

Holly shook her head. Everyone at HEARTS looked to Holly for leadership, except Sam. Sam seemed to need a surrogate big sister more than a leader. Alexa did well in that role. She had a much more tender approach than Holly's no-nonsense attitude. Holly wasn't so great at tender. "I don't think my expectations are too high. I just need some professionalism out of her."

"Your expectations are reasonable. She's just got some growing up to do."

"I'm not trying to be a bitch, Lex. But we can't afford our reputations to be tarnished because she's lacking common sense." Holly grabbed the mug Sam had brought to her.

Alexa was quiet for a moment. For too long. Clearly she was analyzing what Holly had said. Or how she'd said it. Or her facial expressions. Or blinking patterns. Or some other crazy shit Alexa had the ability to notice that no one else seemed to.

One of the benefits of having an agency filled with women was that they all looked out for each other. But that was the downfall as well. Holly was a loner. She looked out for her team, noticed the smallest of changes in them, and knew when something was off. Unfortunately, they all held those same qualities. They'd each been trained in some branch of military or law enforcement, so their instincts were sharp. Too damned sharp sometimes.

Holly didn't get away with nearly as much internalizing as she used to.

Finally, Alexa used the soft tone she utilized to gain the confidence of witnesses and asked, "Are you okay?"

"Why wouldn't I be?"

"You think we haven't noticed how much time you're putting in lately? Because we have. And we're all getting a little worried. It's only been a week since we took on this case, and it's already breaking you down."

"A week in a missing person's case is a very long time. You know that."

Alexa's older sister had been kidnapped twelve years ago. She knew better than most the reality of the ticking clock and what the passing time meant for the victim. "She was missing for almost a month before he brought her to us."

Holly winced, hating the bitter truth Alexa was trying to serve her. "Are you trying to soften the blow of this being a recovery rather than a rescue?"

Alexa tilted her head, and the pencil holding her long, caramel-colored hair in a haphazard bun slipped free and bounced off the black vinyl captain chair beside her. She bent, disappearing behind Holly's desk for a moment before standing again. She put the pencil between her red-painted lips and muttered around it. "The odds are not in her favor. You know that." A moment later, she tucked the pencil back into the mass of hair. "You need to prepare yourself and the Fredricksons for the worst while hoping for the best."

"I know. The detective was here because the woman he is looking for matches Julia's description. She was abducted last week in the same manner." Holly let her shoulders sag. "I didn't say it to the detective, even though I'm sure he was thinking the same thing, but I think she's a replacement for Julia."

Alexa stopped messing with her hair. "You think he's killed Julia and needed a live victim to take her place?"

Holly looked at the photo of the smiling woman staring up at her. She'd spent far too much time the last week entranced by the bright blue eyes captured in the image. "I can't think of any other reason he'd take a woman who was basically identical to her. Can you?"

Putting her palms on Holly's desk, Alexa stared straight at her. "If Julia is dead, that is *not* on you, Holly. You have done everything you can to find her."

"I know."

"Do you?"

"Yes, I do." She exhaled heavily. "But I don't think that

will offer much comfort to her family." Holly lifted her hand when Alexa took a breath. "Don't start on me."

"You're too close to this."

"I'm not."

"You are. You should reassign this case. Let me take it."

"Because a missing person isn't too close to you?"

Alexa gestured to the photo Holly kept on the shelf behind her desk, but Holly didn't turn around. She understood the point Alexa was trying to make.

"My missing sister looks nothing like Julia Fredrickson, Holly. Your mother, on the other hand... You think I haven't seen the way you look at Julia's photos? The photos of her and her daughter."

"I'm fine." Her proclamation sounded as false to her ears as she knew it to be. She had stared at those photos, part of her envying the time Julia and her daughter had spent together. Wishing she knew what growing up with a mother felt like.

"You're connecting with a victim on a level that you have no business reaching, Hol," Alexa pressed. "Julia Fredrickson is probably dead. She was probably dead before you got this case. The likelihood of any other outcome is slim in this case."

Holly shifted as Alexa's words poked at things she didn't want touched. "I know that."

"If you don't find her alive, you're going to carry that with you."

"And you won't?"

"Not like you will. Not like you've been carrying your mother's death on your shoulders all your life."

Holly ground her teeth together and glanced at the frequently traveled hallway outside her office. Lex was the only one privy to the details of Holly's mother's death. One night too many drinks and too much guilt had loosened her tongue, and she'd regretted it since. Leaning forward, she met Alexa's determined gaze with her own. "And what of your lifelong guilt? Hmm? Will bringing Julia home—alive or dead—help put your sister's ghost to rest?"

Alexa blinked as if she'd been slapped and then stood upright. "No. It won't."

"We all have things in our past that pushed us to be where we are now. We can't hide from them forever."

"I know."

"So let me do this. Let me find Julia. And deal with whatever emotions that stirs up. I'm in too deep to hand this off. If, by some miracle, she is alive, she doesn't have time for you to learn everything I know about her case just to save me a little hurt."

Alexa nodded. "Okay. But if this starts getting to you, I'm here. I'm happy to help."

"I know that. Thank you."

Without another word, Alexa left. Exhaling, Holly turned her chair to look at the picture behind her. Alexa wasn't wrong. Julia Fredrickson did look like her mother. And seeing the images of Julia and her daughter had stirred something deep within Holly. A kind of personal sadness she didn't indulge often. She was eight when her mother died. They'd never had the kind of bond Julia had with her daughter. She'd never seen her mother age. She'd never been able to seek out the advice only a mother could give.

Holly fondled the pendant on her necklace for a few moments before tucking the little heart into her shirt and turning back to her desk. She didn't have time to think of her loss. She had to do what she could to stop the Fredricksons from facing their own.

JACK SLOWED HIS STRIDE AS HE ENTERED THE conference room later that afternoon. Holly was standing stone still, as she had been the day before. Lesson learned—he wouldn't sneak up on her again. But he would certainly take a moment to appreciate what he hadn't the first time he'd seen her. She didn't quite reach his chin, but she had proven she was fit and agile. Her physical strength had been a stark contrast to the subtle vanilla scent that had filled his nostrils when she'd pinned him to the floor. She said she had trained in martial arts, but that kind of natural defense instinct had come from being in the line of fire for too long.

Sergeant Holly Austin had done two active-duty tours in the Army. He guessed that explained the haunted look in her eyes when she'd helped him off the floor. She'd undoubtedly seen some shit he'd only viewed through the censored lens of television media.

Skimming over her, as her admin had suggested she do

to him, Jack noticed how her suit was fitted but loose enough to allow her to body slam a man without restricting her movements. The jacket she wore hid the gun he knew was on her hip but stopped short of hiding the delicious curve of her ass.

"You going to stand there all day?" she asked as he took in her long legs.

"I was debating the best way to approach you without being physically assaulted."

She faced him, and that odd sensation he'd been feeling every time she crossed his mind hit him right in the gut. Her smile—her *genuine* smile—was beautiful. She was gorgeous without it, but seeing her blue eyes brighten with amusement made him want to slide his hand into her long hair and taste her lightly tinted lips.

He imagined her slender body would fit perfectly against his as he pulled her in to kiss that smile from her face. She wore makeup, but just enough to highlight her features. She didn't hide behind a mask of blush and eyeshadow. He liked that. He liked that she was confident enough in her beauty that she didn't feel the need to falsely enhance it.

She bowed her head slightly. "You may enter."

He did, stopping at her side to look at the pictures she had been examining. She'd added copies of his photos of Penelope Nelson to the wall right below the images of Julia Fredrickson. The similarities between the two struck him again. Which reminded him once more how much Holly reminded him of both. He couldn't stop himself from looking at her to again confirm the resemblance. A primal need to protect her took root deep in his stomach. She might deny the danger of a man who hired a PI who looked eerily similar to his missing wife, but Jack wasn't going to.

Holly cleared her throat. "Any progress last night?"

He glanced in her direction but couldn't look at her long. The only real progress he'd made was imagining her leaning over him again but without her knee planted in his back. The fantasy flashed through his mind—her light hair hanging down as she moved her lithe body over him. He forced his breath out and the image from his mind along with it. *Focus, Tarek.* "I dumped the description of the man on your video into the photo lineup database. From what little we can make out on the videos, I wasn't able to nail down a photo. We need more information. I was thinking we should interview the families again. Maybe you'll catch something I missed and vice versa."

She nodded. "Let me call Fredrickson. He's not enthusiastic about working with the police these days, but maybe I can convince him this could help." She pulled her cell phone from her pocket but stared at it for a moment before looking up at Jack. "We danced around something yesterday that I think we need to face."

Jack's breath hitched. He had already figured out Holly didn't like to pull punches, but was she really going to call out the fact that there was definitely a spark between them?

"If this is the same suspect—if the same guy took Nelson who took Fredrickson—the likelihood is that he was replacing her. Julia is probably dead. I have to let her husband know that, but until we find evidence otherwise, we are treating this like a rescue mission. We're going to reassure him of that. That we're trying to save her, not just find her remains. Got it?"

He nodded. "Yes, ma'am."

"Ma'am?" She smirked and focused on her phone. After tapping the touchscreen a few times, she turned her back to Jack and put the phone to her ear. "Mr. Fredrickson, it's Holly Austin." She listened for a moment. "No, but I would like to stop by with a detective. He's working a similar case and may have some insight."

She ran her hand over her hair, and Jack had to clench his hand to stop himself from doing the same. When she pulled her hand free from the golden strands, she left them a bit of a mess. He couldn't quite determine if he wanted to soothe the strands back into place or hold her hair in his fist as he pulled her to him. Either way, he was using all his restraint not to touch her.

"I know you've lost faith in the police," Holly said, "but Detective Tarek is working on this case from a different angle. He'd just like to hear your side of the story. I don't want to put you through this again, but working with him really could be very helpful."

She dropped her hand to her hip and nodded as if the man on the other end could see her. "Thank you. We'll see you in a few minutes." Ending the call, she turned to Jack.

The surprise on her face and slight quirk of her brow made him take a step back. He hadn't even realized he'd moved closer—so close he was unintentionally violating her personal space.

"Uh." She licked her lip and broke from his gaze. "He's waiting for us. I'll drive."

He fought the urge to grin. Of course she'd drive. She was the most alpha female he'd ever met, and he doubted she ever fell back for anyone—especially a man. He wanted to disagree just to see how she'd react but instead gestured for her to lead the way. She grabbed the file off the table and headed to her office, where she opened a desk drawer and snagged a pair of keys. As she did, he took a quick glance around her office. Clean, neat, and completely impersonal. She had two photos behind her desk. One was a group of women he assumed to be her co-workers, since they were standing in front of the sign in the lobby. The other was older and appeared faded. As he moved closer to take a better look, she rounded her desk and nearly pushed him out of her space and back into the hallway.

As they entered the lobby, the women there—Sam, the naturally tan blonde who had unnecessarily sown the seeds of his attraction for Holly, and a brunette who skimmed over him with obvious distrust—stopped their conversation.

"Detective Tarek and I are going to interview our victims' families to see if we missed something."

The woman blatantly looked him over as if memorizing his appearance. "You wearing your tracker?"

"She never does," Sam sang like a child telling on her older sibling.

Holly looked from one to the other. "I have my phone. You can trace that if you need."

The woman glanced at Jack. "Everybody knows to toss the phone first. If it were that easy to track a missing person, wouldn't Julia Fredrickson be home already?"

"I'm going to be with a police detective, Rene. I'm confident between the two of us, we can handle anything that comes our way."

"Leave addresses of where you'll be."

Holly grabbed a pen and piece of paper off Sam's desk. While she jotted down addresses, the woman continued assessing Jack.

Sam smiled when he cleared his throat. "Detective, since Holly doesn't have a lick of manners, this is Rene Schwartz. She's one of our investigators."

Jack held his hand out, and Rene stared at it for a moment before accepting his greeting.

"Nice to meet you, Detective," she said with an accent that held subtle hints of Brooklyn.

Jack was sensitive to where people came from. He knew better than most those roots couldn't be altered. Growing up a Middle Eastern Muslim in a midsized predominately white Midwest city had taught him that.

"Likewise, Ms. Schwartz."

She pressed her lips together as if she didn't believe him before looking at Holly. "You want backup?"

Holly shook her head. "I trust the detective."

Sam gasped dramatically. "Holly trusts someone? Has hell frozen over? Are pigs flying? Is it the twelfth of never?"

Holly did that brow lift she seemed to have perfected. The silent warning was enough to make Sam snap her mouth shut.

Her teasing smile disappeared as she muttered, "Sorry, Hol."

Jack cleared this throat again, this time as a reminder to the women that he was still standing there, but they all seemed content to ignore him.

Holly slid the paper to Rene as she asked Sam, "Find any additional cases?"

"No. Should I expand my search?"

Holly didn't bother to check with Jack. "No. But keep checking and let me know if anything pops up. Joshua is monitoring the morgue for me just in case someone fitting Julia's description finds her way to him."

"Don't let Eva hear that," Rene warned, tucking the addresses in her suit pocket.

"Eva may not like it, but her ex-boyfriend is an asset the agency can't afford to lose just because their relationship didn't last. I'll be back before the afternoon briefing." Holly headed for the door.

Jack took a moment to look between the women at the front desk before following Holly out into the morning sun. "Want to enlighten me on Mama Bear?"

She pushed the button on a remote, and a sleek black sedan chirped in response. "Rene was with Witness Protection until last year when she lost a team member. She resigned from her unit right after. Blamed herself."

He nodded. "It's hard losing a team member."

Holly opened the car door and slid in behind the wheel. "She was responsible, and she knows that."

"Well, that's—"

"The harsh reality of being the leader." She started the car and gripped the steering wheel. "You're accountable for your team—the good and the bad."

He watched her as she backed out of the spot. "You're speaking from experience."

She didn't answer. She didn't need to; he could see the guilt play across her face.

3

"FREDRICKSON IS ANGRY," Holly said as she drove across town.

"It would be faster to take Fourth Street," Tarek offered, motioning toward the upcoming intersection.

She smirked. The section of town where the Fredricksons resided was a hotspot for locally owned restaurants and other businesses, which made the population multiply like fruit flies during the lunch hour. "No, it wouldn't," she simply stated.

"Yes, it would."

"No. It wouldn't. Fourth is bumper-to-bumper this time of day. It's faster to go around. As I was saying," she continued when he didn't argue. "He's angry and rightfully so. He was hoping to see results by now, and I haven't been able to produce anything more than the police have. He's just reacting to the situation. Tread lightly and show him some patience and understanding."

Jack creased his brow. "Good plan, Austin. Maybe I'll even ask him some questions related to the case. You know I'm a cop, right?" he teased. "I've actually made it all the way to detective. Now, it doesn't happen often, but every now and then, the department even lets me interview people."

She laughed quietly. "Sorry. I do respect your skills and experience, *Detective*."

"Good to know. I respect your skills and experience as well, *Private* Detective."

"Investigator. Just investigator. And I'm just making it clear that Fredrickson's been on edge."

"Why do you think that is?" The suspicion in his voice was clear.

"Probably because his wife of twenty-plus years is missing."

"Think he had anything to do with it?"

The clouds started to clear from the overcast sky, letting the sunshine through. Holly smirked as she opened a compartment in her console and pulled out a pair of dark sunglasses. "You've asked me this already, Tarek. No. I don't think he had anything to do with his wife's disappearance. But I do think he's closing in on his breaking point. He's taking this hard."

"Sometimes when people take things hard, it's because of guilt."

"I've looked into him, but you're welcome to do so again. Just not to his face." She glanced at him, cementing her warning with a stern look before sliding her sunglasses over her eyes.

"I'll do that." Jack reached into his interior jacket pocket to produce his own tinted glasses. "Why go into investigating instead of police work?"

She was a bit thrown by the change of subject and took a few moments to answer. "I considered a lot of options when I left the Army. The private sector seemed to be the best fit for me at the time. I wanted to use my skills to help people, but I wanted to do so on my own terms."

"And now? Are you happy with what you're doing?"

She considered his question. "I spent an awful long time trying to keep my team alive in one volatile situation after another. Some people are cut out for that kind of responsibility. I started to question if I was, and when you start to question yourself, you make mistakes. Mistakes could get someone hurt—or dead—so it was time to leave. Now, I'm right back there—being responsible for people who could be put in dangerous situations. At least now, the situations are fewer and much further between."

"Are you questioning your abilities now?"

"No."

Despite her firm and instant answer, he pushed. "You sure?"

She scowled before answering. "I'm a strong leader, but having that weight day in and day out can be a hell of a curse. When I came back, I decided to go into business for myself. I started out wanting to do private security, but there isn't much call for that when you are of the female persuasion. Most people—men in particular—don't think women are capable of protecting them. Before long, I was doing investigative work, but I needed help, so I brought on my old friends Eva and Alexa. Rene walked in one day last year, on a whim she said. But she fit. We brought on Tika and Sam to help with the admin side of things a few months ago. Tika is a natural at reading people and helping with investigations. Sam...well, you met Sam."

He chuckled. "Yeah. I met Sam."

"She's smart as a whip on the research end of things. Seriously lacking on the common-sense side. Now I have a whole team to look out for. Again."

Jack sat quietly, as if processing everything she'd said, before rapping his knuckles on the dash. "HEARTS. Holly, Eva, Alexa, Rene, Tika, and Sam. It's an acronym. I didn't get it until now."

She turned down a tree-lined street, leaving the small brick buildings that had stood for decades. The houses on either side of the street were small but had large yards, indicating they'd been built before the city population had grown. In a few blocks, the yards would get smaller and the houses larger.

"Not my idea," Holly said, "and trust me, I was not thrilled when it passed the vote. As people come and go... well, we can't keep changing the name. But in my attempt to not feel solely responsible for them, I insisted we all be equal and come up with a name to reflect that. After some brainstorming, Austin Investigative Services became HEARTS. It seems so...feminine."

"God forbid a business owned and operated by women exude any kind of femininity."

She glanced at him, not at all surprised that he didn't see how having a team solely comprised of women could be seen negatively by some clients. "We aren't hired to be feminine. We're hired to find missing family members or clear people's names when accused of crimes or catch people cheating the system."

"Spy on philandering husbands?"

"Unfortunately, that accounts for a huge number of cases we see. So, yes, spy on cheating *spouses*. Women commit adultery, too. Those cases are pretty easy to wrap up. Most people distracted by the possibility of sex don't see much else around them." Once again, she'd said something that could be misconstrued. She glanced at him before clearing her throat and returning her focus to the road. "Overall, we work the cases where we feel we can offer the most help."

"Well, that's not true."

She pulled up to a stop sign and took the opportunity to give him more than a passing glance. "What does that mean?"

"This is hardly a decades-old cold case that no one is looking into now. You took this on because Fredrickson was feeling lost and, as you pointed out earlier, needed to hang on to his last bit of hope. I mean, that is assuming you aren't doing it just for the cash flow."

She ground her teeth together before answering. "Of course not. We're not shysters. We all work hard to solve our cases and make sure our clients are protected and taken care of."

"I don't doubt that."

"Every one of us—"

"Holly," he stated. "I believe you're a good PI. You don't have to prove it to me."

She pressed her lips closed. "Sorry. Let me take the lead when we get in here," she said as she parked behind a trailer with the ramps down. A man in a dark-green, long-sleeved uniform rode a mower across the Fredricksons' front yard while another trimmed the box bushes along the front. The way the sun was beating down, she thought they had to be burning up in those uniforms, even though they were likely made of cotton.

"Lawn care when the wife is missing?" Jack asked as he removed his sunglasses.

Holly released her seat belt. "The grass doesn't stop growing for our personal convenience, Jack." She tucked her glasses back into the compartment so she knew exactly where they would be waiting for her. "Listen, Eric Fredrickson is in a bad place right now. Take it easy in there."

"Sure thing."

Holly stopped at the sidewalk, waiting for Jack to join her so they could walk as a united front to the door. If Eric peered out the window, she didn't want him to have any doubt that she was working with the man at her side. He'd expressed his frustration with the police more than once, but she needed him to trust Jack. If she took too strong of a lead or fell too far in the back as they approached the house, Eric might read more into it.

As Jack joined her, he jerked his chin toward the house. "You've got an admirer."

Holly glanced back in time to see the man who had been tending to the box bushes lower his face and turn away. "Aw, honey," she said with sarcastic sweetness, "don't be jealous. He might have been looking at you."

Jack chuckled as he followed her to the house and, when they reached the front door, stood with his hands on his hips.

"Stand down, Detective," she ordered after knocking.

"What?"

"Ease up on that defensive cop pose you have going. He's already frustrated with the police. Let's not add to his agitation."

He looked down before heaving a sigh and shaking the tension from his shoulders. "Sorry. Habit."

"And it's a good habit, but he's a client, not a suspect. Lighten up."

"Yeah. I'm going to take pointers from you on lightening up." He snickered at his own joke.

She cocked her brow, opened her mouth, and then clamped her lips shut as the door opened. Every time she saw this man, the distress in his eyes seemed to have grown tenfold from the last. Her heart ached for the pain she saw plainly written on his face. "Mr. Fredrickson," she said softly, "thank you for letting us drop by on such short notice."

"No problem," he said to Holly, but his attention fell on the man beside her.

She gestured to Jack. "This is Detective Tarek. I told you about him on the phone."

"You have another case like Julia's?"

Jack nodded. "I'm afraid so. I know you've been through this what probably seems like a hundred times, but I'd like to hear what happened from you."

Mr. Fredrickson stepped aside, and Holly entered a living room that reminded her of a magazine cover. The cool blues and grays stood out against the white trim and crown molding, and everything seemed to have a place. Fredrickson gestured to the gray cloth sofa, and Holly sat. Jack took a moment to finish assessing their surroundings before easing onto the sofa. She would have chastised him, but that was actually a smart thing to do. Walking into someone's home, even someone she trusted, could always pose a danger. She had come to trust this family, but she could understand that Jack was being cautious.

Fredrickson dropped into a chair across from Holly. "I can't really tell you anything that I haven't already."

"That's okay." Holly's tone was firm but understanding. She was familiar enough with the man to know how to handle him. She wasn't exactly submissive, but she intentionally eased up on her usual assertiveness. "Detective Tarek may think of something no one else has. Tell us about the last time you saw your wife," she coaxed.

He exhaled loudly. Leaning forward, he planted his elbows on his knees and gripped his hands together. He blinked several times before meeting Jack's gaze, but he quickly looked at his hands again. "I woke up late. I was pissed that I wasn't going to have time to shower before heading out to work. I was short with her. It wasn't her fault, but I snapped at her anyway. It wasn't until after my first meeting, around eleven, that I calmed down enough to realize I'd been an ass. I called to apologize. She didn't answer." He glanced at Jack and then lowered his face. Clearly he was still struggling with the guilt he felt that the last moments he'd spent with Julia had been filled with anger. "I tried again before leaving work at about six. I was going to offer to take her out to dinner, but she still didn't answer. I thought she must have really been pissed at me, so I stopped and bought some roses on the way home. The police have the receipt. I guess they needed proof I was where I said." Lifting his gaze, he once again looked at Jack.

Holly did as well.

The detective nodded and appeared sympathetic on the surface, but Holly saw through the act. He was filing away clues, trying to pin this entire thing on the man sitting across from them.

"Anyway," Fredrickson said, "I got home, and she wasn't here. I thought she was still blowing off steam. Making a point or something. So I reheated leftovers and watched some TV. By nine, I started getting worried. I started making calls, but no one had seen her. I called the cops around midnight." He stared at his hands as he shook his head. "I should have known something was wrong the first time she didn't answer. She doesn't hold grudges like that. She would have answered and told me I had been an asshole and then let it go. I should have known."

Jack gave him the standard reply. "This isn't your fault."

"So I've been told."

"She was taken from a grocery store. Is that the store she usually shopped at?"

"Yeah. And she always went on Tuesday mornings. She said there were never lines on Tuesday mornings, and she volunteers pretty much every other morning. Kids and animals," he said with a slight smile. "She thought they were the last innocent things in the world."

"Tuesday?" Jack glanced at Holly. "She only shopped on Tuesdays?"

The spark in his eye let her know that something had fallen into place for him. She had missed something. Goddamn it. She wanted to know what but wasn't about to ask in front of her client.

"Yeah. She walked dogs at the shelter in the morning and then went to the grocery store. Every Tuesday."

Jack returned his focus to Fredrickson. "She was familiar with the surroundings, then?"

Fredrickson nodded. "Yeah. We've lived in this house for eight years. That's the only grocery store she shops at. She says they have the best produce."

"So if she were agitated or nervous, do you think the staff at that store would notice?"

He shrugged. "They might."

Jack made another note, and Holly's heart dropped to

her stomach. What had she missed? Tuesday at the grocery store? Clearly that was important, but she couldn't put her finger on why.

"Did you watch the security video?" Jack asked. "Did the man who took her look at all familiar?"

Holly lifted her hands when fury flashed in her client's eyes. Shit. She should have warned Jack about this particular trigger. Using her most soothing tone, she said, "It's just something we have to eliminate."

Fredrickson jumped to his feet, pointing his finger at her. "I told you Julia didn't leave me. She wasn't cheating on me."

Holly stood as well, her legs shoulder-width apart with her left hand up and her right hand low—not on her gun, but she was ready to reach for her holster if necessary. Not that it would be, but her training overrode her knowledge that Eric Fredrickson wasn't a threat. "That's not what he's implying."

"The hell it isn't," Fredrickson boomed as he took a step toward her.

Jack bolted to his feet and put himself between Fredrickson and Holly with his right hand closer to his gun. Jack took the same position Holly had taken, but he was clearly more on edge than she was. She stepped to the right, and as soon as Fredrickson's gaze followed her, Jack again placed himself between them.

What the fuck?

"Ms. Austin has made it clear to me your wife isn't suspected of adultery," Jack said, using the kind of sympathetic tone a hostage negotiator would use to diffuse a volatile situation, "but that isn't the only reason she could have gone with him. He could have been a friend or an associate. We just have to consider whether she may have known him, as that might lead us to figuring out who he is. One way to figure out whether she might have known him is to ask if *you* recognize him."

Fredrickson stared at him for another moment before backing down. "I didn't recognize him." He ran his hand over his hair. "Look. I don't know anything. I wasn't there when she was taken. I haven't heard from her since I left home that morning." He looked over Jack's shoulder at Holly, but this time his eyes were filled with sadness. "Where is my wife?"

"We're doing everything—"

"Don't give me that shit," he demanded. "You sound like the cops. I hired you to find Julia. Now..." Gesturing toward Jack, he narrowed his eyes. "Now there's someone else missing. Clearly you think this is tied to Julia's disappearance somehow, or he wouldn't be here. What the fuck is going on?"

Holly held her breath, preparing to dance around the truth.

Eric licked his lips and took a long breath before saying much more calmly, "Tell me what you're thinking. I'm *paying* you to tell me."

Her stomach twisted with the stress of what she had to admit. "Mr. Fredrickson. Often in cases like this, where there's been a second victim...it's because the first victim has perished."

She kept her voice gentle, a balm against her words. Even so, Fredrickson flinched like he'd been punched.

"Perished?"

"Oftentimes," she said softly, "the second victim is...a replacement."

Fredrickson inhaled and let the breath out slowly as he gave Holly a cold stare that didn't sit quite right with her. Clearly Jack was once again set on edge, because he stood a bit taller, and from the corner of her eye, Holly saw him move his hand an inch or so closer to his gun.

The oxygen seemed to have vanished from the house, sucked out as the atmosphere filled with tension. Fredrickson darted his eyes at Jack but only for a moment before settling his frigid stare on Holly again.

"It's been nearly five weeks since my wife disappeared, Ms. Austin," he said. "If you can't help me—"

"That's not what she said," Jack insisted before Holly could respond.

Fredrickson nodded. "If I think of anything, I'll let you know, but right now... I've told her everything."

"Mr. Fredrickson—" Holly started.

"Go. Get out. Both of you." His order was soft, buried under the weight of her suggestion that his wife might have died.

"I'm sorry we upset you." Holly tugged at Jack's arm as she headed for the door.

JACK FOLLOWED HOLLY BACK TO HER CAR, TAKING long strides to match her determined gait. She climbed into the driver's side and slammed the door. Once he was in the passenger side, with much less stomping and slamming, he intended to comment on how frustrated he was, too, but she turned and glared at him. The fury on her face cut his words off before he could say them.

"Don't you *ever* do that again," she said through clenched teeth.

Whoa. Wait. What? She was mad at *him*? "Do what?"

"Defend my goddamned honor, Detective. I can stand up for myself. I don't need protection, and I don't need *you* telling *my* client that I'm doing everything I can."

"I wasn't defending you. I was..."

"What?"

"I had your back, Austin. There's a difference."

"Bullshit." She shoved the key into the ignition. "You put yourself in front of me because you were implying that I am weak. That I couldn't take care of myself if needed. Would you do that with a man?"

He leaned across the console and grabbed her hand before she could start the engine. "I wasn't implying a damn thing."

She knocked his hand away. "The hell you weren't."

"Hey, as far as I'm concerned, while we're working on this case, we're partners. And nobody is going to get in my partner's face and accuse her of not doing her job."

"Your *partner* can take care of herself. That man is hurting, and he needs someone to blame. If pointing his finger at me alleviates some of that pain, I can take it." She started the ignition.

"There is something off about him," Jack warned.

"Yeah. His wife is missing."

"No, Holly. It goes deeper than that. He's disturbed."

She shook her head. "No. He's upset. And he has an alibi. Rock solid."

"Maybe he does. Maybe he didn't hurt her. *That* day."

"Are you implying he abused her? There are no indications—"

"There rarely are. Did you check her hospital records?"

"Yes."

"His police records?"

"Yes. I also interviewed her family and close friends; I even asked them about her marriage, Detective. Just like a *real* investigator." As soon as she said the words, she pressed her lips together and her cheeks tinted pink. She glanced around before asking, "What was it about Tuesday that tripped your trigger?"

Jack huffed out a breath. "He said Julia always went shopping on *Tuesday*. Do you know what day Penelope Nelson was kidnapped?"

Holly exhaled much as he had done, and some of the stiff anger eased out of her posture as curiosity edged out a bit of the fury in her eyes. "Tuesday?"

"Tuesday."

"That could be significant."

"Could be. I think we should look into that. Don't you?"

She returned her attention out the window. "Yes, I do."

"Me, too."

"I'll reach out to the store manager and see how far back his footage goes. Maybe Julia was being followed."

"And maybe he wasn't quite as careful in the weeks leading up to her kidnapping," Jack said. "Hey," he added in a more neutral tone when she put the car in gear. "I'm sorry if I offended you. My instinct as a cop—as a man," he admitted, "is to protect my partner. I didn't mean to imply you can't handle yourself. You body slammed me a little over twenty-four hours ago. I *know* you can handle yourself. I'm sorry."

She nodded, and he assumed she was appeased by his apology, but when she looked at him, the scowl remained on her face.

"Are you done being mad at me?"

She seemed to contemplate his question for a moment. "Are you done treating me like a princess?"

"You're no princess, Princess."

Fire lit in her eyes.

And he loved it.

"Asshole," she muttered, and he laughed as she pulled away from the curb and around the lawn care truck.

"I want to do a stakeout. I want to watch him."

She groaned. "He did not beat, kidnap, or murder his wife, Tarek. I've checked into him. Thoroughly."

"I believe you. *I do*," he said when she opened her

mouth. He skimmed her profile, taking in her straight nose and thin lips. He could see how some men wouldn't take her seriously. When she relaxed the seemingly permanent stress on her face, she looked soft and tender. Not the type of woman who could body slam a man without straining. "I really didn't mean to imply that you can't take care of yourself."

She nodded. "I know. I'm sorry. Men tend to underestimate me. It pisses me off."

"Which again makes me wonder why Fredrickson hired a female investigator to find his wife. He doesn't come across as some new-age modern thinker to me. He's an executive, and they tend to be a bit more old-fashioned. More of the a-good-wife-knows-her-place type. The kind who don't trust a female to perform as well as a male in this field. So why hire someone he, by nature, expects to fail? Does he not want to find his wife?"

"Jack—"

"Stereotype or not, that kind of guy has been trained by society to view women as inferior. His wife has been missing for five weeks, and instead of going out and finding the most manly male detective he can find, he hires an agency of females. Don't act like this exact thing hasn't crossed your mind."

She pressed her lips together before sighing loudly. "Yes. When he first came to HEARTS, I found it odd that he would seek us out. *But*," she stated before he could comment, "after questioning his family and friends and discovering that Julia was the decision-maker and caretaker in their home, I deduced that he came to us because he's used to women solving his problems."

"Speaking of their home, did you notice that nothing was out of place? Not even a photo of Julia. Everything was perfect."

"He has a maid that comes in once a week."

"What day?"

Holly bit at her lip for a moment. "Thursdays."

"Today is Wednesday. It's been six days since the maid was there. In six days, he didn't once pick up a photo of his missing wife and stare at her image, wondering where she is?"

She shook her head firmly. "He lives in that house. He knows how to set a frame back to the right position."

"Or maybe he isn't as concerned as he wants everyone to believe. Maybe—"

"Maybe he killed his wife and buried her in the basement and I'm just too stupid to figure it out?"

He glanced at her. "That's not what I'm saying."

"That's what it sounds like you're saying." She stopped at a stop sign and turned to stare at him instead of checking to see if the intersection was clear. "It sounds like you're still convinced that I can't put two and two together. Did you see the pain in his eyes? Did you see his soul shatter when he realized that I was telling him that his wife might already be dead?"

"Maybe it wasn't his soul shattering, Austin. Maybe it was fear that you'd figure out he's a very bad man."

"Jesus," she said under her breath before checking for cross traffic and pulling from the stop.

"Something is wrong with him, Holly. Something is very wrong with him. You're just not seeing it. Maybe he didn't kill Julia and bury her in the basement, but there's something going on inside him that isn't sitting right with me. I'm doing a stakeout. With or without you."

She let out a long breath. "You're so freaking impossible."

Jack grinned. "You have no idea."

4

The Nelsons' house was nothing like Julia and Eric's. The Fredricksons bordered on upper middle class. The Nelsons' small house was a bit rundown, but they clearly took pride in their home. Though the vinyl siding could have used a power wash, the yard was immaculate.

Jack pointed to the nearly identical house next door. "That's my mother's place."

A strange sense of warmth touched Holly's chest. "You grew up there?"

"Just high school. She couldn't afford to buy a house until I was older."

"It's nice."

"She worked hard for it."

The pride in his voice made her turn toward him. "I'm sorry I snapped. I just don't like being coddled. By anyone, but most especially by men."

"I'm sure being a female in the Army made that a sore spot."

"I appreciate you considering my safety."

Jack chuckled. "I'd believe that if you sounded the least bit sincere when you said it."

"I am sincere. Now let me return the favor. You're not supposed to be on this case. If you go in there, Mr. Nelson could tell the lead detective you paid him a visit and get you in trouble. Let me handle this."

He looked at the Nelsons' house and let out a long breath. "I promised Mom—"

"I know you did. But she wouldn't want you to get written up. Would she?"

A wistful smile caused his dimple to deepen. "She'd probably try to ground me for a month."

"Well, we wouldn't want that."

"I'll take the risk. We're a team, Austin. We're doing this together."

"Not if it costs your job." She looked at his mother's house. "Is she home?"

"She will be soon."

"Go wait for her. I'll come over when I'm done." She didn't give him a chance to argue before climbing from her car and heading toward the three steps that led to the porch. She knocked and stepped to the side, waiting for an answer. A tall, thin man opened the door. She recognized Gary Nelson from the photo in Jack's file.

The stress of the last week was evident in the sadness in Mr. Nelson's eyes and the disheveled brown hair sticking out in every direction. Just as with the houses, the contrast between the husbands was stark. Fredrickson was so well put together on the outside, even weeks after his wife had disappeared. Nelson was obviously distraught. Perhaps the contrast between the men was why Jack was so convinced Eric had something to do with Julia's disappearance.

Holly smiled, but Mr. Nelson looked beyond her.

"Afternoon, Jack," he said.

She held in the disapproving sigh that threatened to escape her when Jack stepped onto the porch.

"Gary." Jack stopped at Holly's side. "This is Holly Austin, the private investigator I talked to you about."

He nodded slightly in greeting. "Ms. Austin. Come on in. Ignore the barking. I've locked them away."

She greeted him with a handshake before accepting his invitation to enter his home. As she stepped inside, she glanced back at Jack, giving him an exaggerated scowl. He couldn't have missed her face, but his soft smile remained as if he hadn't noticed her irritation. Inside, the house was cluttered. Not dirty, but clearly Gary Nelson hadn't kept up appearances as Eric Fredrickson had. Of course, the Fredricksons had a maid. One that Jack had pointed out hadn't been in the home for almost a full week.

Julia's home was neat and tidy, as if all were right in the world. Penelope's home was a reflection of the chaos her husband was likely feeling. Mail had been piled on the coffee table next to an empty glass and half-eaten sandwich.

"Did we interrupt your lunch?" Holly asked, despite the time. Nearly three thirty in the afternoon.

Gary moved around them toward the leftover food. "No. I just hadn't..." He gathered the dirty dishes and shrugged slightly. "Penelope is always telling me to clean up after myself. She's not my mother. So she says." His quiet laugh was more sad than amused.

Holly watched him leave the room before turning to Jack. "What are you doing?" she asked under her breath.

"Questioning a witness," he whispered in return.

"Risking your job."

"He knows me."

The shuffling of Gary's feet drew her attention from Jack. She'd tried to protect the idiot. If he got in trouble for meddling in this case, that was on him. Idiot.

"Sit," Gary said. "Please."

Holly and Jack eased onto the sofa, but it was Holly who sat forward, commanding his attention. Taking control of the interview.

"Mr. Nelson, I am so sorry for what you and your family are going through."

"It's just me," he said. "We wanted kids, but the time never seemed right." He gestured toward the back of the house. "That's why she keeps getting those damn dogs. I told her she needs to stop volunteering at the shelter, but she won't listen. She brought home that damn pug right before she disappeared. He won't quit pissing on the carpet. Every time they told her a sad story about one of their dogs, she wanted to rescue it. And they told her a lot of sad stories."

She smiled at his attempt at humor, but her ears had perked. She didn't recall reading anything about Penelope being a shelter volunteer in Jack's notes. "How often did she volunteer?"

"A few times a week. She cleaned out kennels and"—he chuckled—"scooped the poop out of the play area. I told her there had to be better ways to help the world be a better place, but she said she didn't mind."

"When did she adopt the pug?"

He shrugged. "Two weeks ago. His name is Elvis because he curls his lip up."

"Well, I'm sure she found that hard to resist. How had Penelope been acting? Was she nervous about anything? Worried?"

Gary shook his head. "No. Nothing like that."

"Was she working any more or less than usual?"

"No."

"Had she had any problems with anyone?"

Gary glanced at Jack. "No."

Holly tilted her head slightly. "Have *you* had problems with anyone lately?"

He hesitated. "No."

Jack leaned forward, resting his elbows on his knees. "Gary?"

"Anything you say to us stays between us," Holly said. "We aren't here to judge. We just want to find your wife."

Gary glanced at Jack again, and Holly caught on to his hesitation.

She focused on the cop sitting beside her. "Didn't you say you were going to check in with your mom?"

Jack lifted a brow at her. "No."

"I really think you should check in with your mom," she stated. She widened her eyes for emphasis when he didn't stand.

Finally Jack rose. "Excuse me, Gary. I need to check in with my mom."

Gary didn't say anything as Jack left. Once the door was closed, however, he looked at his hands.

"Sometimes we don't want the neighbors to know our business," she said gently. "I get that, but if you know anything that could help us find Penelope, you have to tell me."

"And you'll tell Jack, and he'll tell his mother—"

"No. This isn't about gossip. Jack's a cop. A good one. He knows how to keep his mouth shut."

Gary eyed her. "But do you?"

Holly held his stare before nodding. "It would be in Penelope's best interest if Jack and I shared everything, but if you need confidence, then you have it. I won't tell Jack, but you have to tell me. Mr. Nelson. I can't solve the puzzle if I don't have all the pieces."

"Jack suggested I go through her e-mail. He said I might find something. Boy, did I ever," he said, his tone taking on a hard edge.

"What did you find?" She frowned when he simply shook his head. "Between us. Okay? I won't tell Jack."

"He's going to want to know why you sent him away."

"I'll tell him I couldn't get it out of you. Do you want me to find her?"

"Of course."

Holly all but begged him. "Then give me all the pieces of the puzzle."

"She'd been...seeing someone."

Holly wasn't surprised, but she was sympathetic. She'd seen far too many people realize they were being cheated on. "Do you know who?"

"I didn't recognize his name."

"Have you told the police this?"

He shook his head.

"You should, Mr. Nelson. They aren't going to judge you either. We all just want to bring her home. Can you show me the e-mails? I won't share them with anyone," she assured him when he looked as if he would refuse.

"Yeah. Okay." He shoved the stack of bills aside and revealed a tablet buried underneath.

As he booted it up, Holly did a quick scan of the bills, many of them stamped as being the final notice. Without giving it a second thought, she grabbed one of the envelopes and stared at the logo in the top left corner. Appleseed Landscaping. The same company the Fredricksons used.

"I don't know how we got on their mailing list," Gary said. "They're always sending coupons and discounts trying to get our business. I pay the guy next door to mow. He charges a quarter of the cost."

"You've never used them?"

"No." He held the tablet out to her. "That's all of them. I put them in a folder."

"May I forward these to my e-mail? I won't share them with anyone else, but I might need to review them more than once," she explained.

"Sure."

After forwarding the messages to herself, Holly handed the tablet back to Gary. "I'll find whoever this is and let you know what I learn."

"I've tried to think of any other reason that she would be meeting someone, but I can't. Can you?"

"I will find out. Is there anything else you can think of that I might need to know?"

Gary sighed. "No. Jack knows everything else."

As she stood, she pulled a business card from her pocket and held it out. "Will you please reach out if that changes?"

"Sure."

"I'm sorry for all you're going through," she said as he accepted the card.

"Ms. Austin? You'll keep this between us, right?"

She nodded. "I will. But you should tell the police. Also, Elvis is still adjusting. Give him a chance to figure out the potty thing."

A smile curved his lips. "I will. Thanks."

JACK LEANED AGAINST HOLLY'S CAR, GRINDING HIS teeth, as she left the Nelsons' house. Pissed as he was about her dismissal of him, he couldn't help but take in the commanding way she walked toward him. The woman was confident, maybe a bit too much so at times, but he liked that she wasn't afraid to take control. Even if she had just kicked him out of an interview.

"Well?" he demanded when she neared him.

"Nothing."

She walked around the front bumper as the car chirped to notify him she'd unlocked the doors. He climbed in and slammed his door, much like she'd done after their interview with Fredrickson.

"Bullshit," Jack stated.

She didn't look at him. Didn't argue. She started the ignition and pulled from the curb. "Do you have time to check the shelter with me?"

He glanced at his watch. He had other work to do. Real work. As in his job, but he wasn't about to let Holly take over this case. He suspected she'd be more than happy to if he didn't stand his ground. "I've got time."

"You sure? I don't want you to—"

"I'm a big boy, Austin. I can look out for myself." He realized what he'd said and glanced over in time to see her lip curve into half a smile.

"Just looking out for my partner," she said.

"Suck it," he muttered. Her laugh took the edge off his anger. "He told you something."

She was quiet for a moment before saying, "In confidence. I can't share it with you."

"Why?"

"Because you are his neighbor's son and he is protecting his pride."

Jack considered her answer for a few moments. "She was having an affair."

Holly didn't answer, but the way she jerked her face to him confirmed his suspicion.

"With whom?"

"I didn't say she was having an affair."

He blew out his breath. "We don't have time for games."

"And I can't risk losing the trust of a witness."

"What about my trust?"

Holly's movement was subtle, but she tightened her hold on the steering wheel and clenched her jaw as if forcing the words to stay inside her mouth.

"We are working on this case together, Austin. I took you to Gary."

"He spoke to me in confidence, Tarek. You know I can't break that."

"Yeah, you can. Who the hell am I going to tell?"

She tightened her jaw again and then exhaled loudly. "Penelope volunteered at the shelter."

Jack drew a breath. "Julia volunteered at the shelter on Tuesdays before going to the store."

"Bingo."

Jack shook his head. "Changing the subject is a pretty lame tactic, Austin."

"You're just mad that you missed that."

"Drive," he muttered.

Tense silence hung in the car as she drove them toward the dog shelter on the outskirts of the city. She'd barely parked in the gravel lot before he jumped out. He slammed his door and marched toward the shelter entrance.

The little blonde behind the desk plastered a smile on her face as she glanced between the two. "Hi, I'm Bailey. How can I help you?"

Jack wasn't there on official business, but he flashed his badge anyway. "Detective Jack Tarek. Who can I talk to about your volunteer program?"

Bailey blinked. "You...you want to volunteer?"

Holly snorted. "He's not so great with animals. They can sense his lack of trust."

Smirking, he faced her. "That's rich coming from you, Austin."

"Actually," Holly told the girl, "we're trying to help locate Penelope Nelson and Julia Fredrickson. Do you know them?"

Her face sagged. "I know Penelope. She is such a sweetheart. I hope nothing bad happened to her."

"But you don't know Julia?" Jack asked, refusing to let Holly dominate the interview.

Bailey shook her head. "I don't recognize the name."

"She volunteered here on Tuesday mornings," Holly interjected.

Confusion clouded Bailey's eyes. "No. If she did, I would know her. I organize the volunteer schedule. We don't have a Julia. Haven't ever had one that I know of."

Jack glanced at Holly. If she was surprised, she hid it well. "Who does volunteer Tuesday mornings?"

Bailey hesitated before she pulled out a notebook and flipped a few pages. "We have a few local businesses who rotate through. They give their employees paid time to volunteer."

"Can we get a list of those businesses?" Jack asked. Holly had become unusually quiet, and he didn't blame her. She was clearly trying to make sense of the hole that had been punched in her theory that Julia Fredrickson's life was perfect.

As Bailey lifted the lid off the big copier in the corner, Jack whispered to Holly, "Did Eric lie about Julia volunteering at the shelter, or did she lie to him?"

She scoffed as she turned to look around the shelter. Dogs had barked incessantly since they'd entered, but this was the first time he'd noticed her looking toward the area where there were cages. They couldn't see the dogs from where they stood in the lobby, but they couldn't be too far away.

"Here you go," Bailey said, drawing their attention back to her.

Jack accepted the list and tucked it in his pocket. "Ever notice anyone hanging around Penelope who she seemed uncomfortable with? Or anything like that? Anything ever make you wonder if she was okay?"

"No. She always happy to be here. She really loves the dogs. I hope you find her."

"Me too," Jack said.

Holly turned and headed for the door with Jack right behind her. He nodded his thanks at a man in a dark gray uniform when he stepped aside and held the door open for them. The embroidered tag on the shirt identified him as staff of the shelter. Jack muttered his thanks, but Holly ignored the man.

Holly headed for the driver's side, but before she could open the door, Jack put his hand against it. She turned slowly in the space between his puffed-out chest and the car. He hadn't considered how he'd be violating her personal space by confronting her like this, but the moment she tilted her chin and arched her brow in warning, he realized just how close they were.

If he weren't so damned irritated with her, her tempting lips and piercing blue eyes might have lured him in. But right now, he just needed to get his point across. "We are working this investigation together."

"I'm aware."

"We have to be honest with each other."

She drew a breath before pressing her lips together.

"Any idea where Julia might have been going on Tuesday mornings if she wasn't walking dogs?"

"No."

He narrowed his eyes and leaned a bit closer. "You sure?"

A grin played across Holly's lips. "Are you trying to intimidate me, Tarek?"

"Of course not."

"Then stand down," she warned.

He didn't move, but he did ease his posture in an attempt to come across less threateningly. Not that she appeared to be threatened by him. In fact, she seemed amused that he was challenging her like this. Damn it. This woman was so damned infuriating. "I can't help if you don't tell me what you know."

"Detective Tarek," she said in a cool voice, "landing face first in the gravel will hurt a hell of a lot worse than on the floor of my conference room. Stand the fuck down."

He stared at her for another few seconds before lowering his hand from her car door and taking a step back.

Holly relaxed her posture as well. "I have no idea why Julia would lie to Eric about volunteering at the shelter. I'll go through her file again and see what I can find. As for Gary, I'm not trying to shut you out, but I have to respect his request. Let me look into this lead he gave me. If there is anything to it, I'll let you in. Right now it's just the speculation of a desperate man looking for answers where there might not be any. Okay?"

Jack licked his lips before biting them hard. "If the tables were turned, you'd be pissed too."

"Yeah, I would be. But I'd also know that my hurt feelings were secondary to earning and keeping the trust of a witness."

He jerked back with disbelief. "Hurt feelings?"

"Isn't that what's going on here? You're upset because he talked to me instead of you."

"No. I'm upset because you don't trust me."

She didn't deny his accusation. Instead she took a breath and looked toward the shelter. "Trusting you isn't my priority, Jack. My priority is finding Julia and Penelope. I'm not going to burn Gary Nelson the first time he trusts me. If this turns out to be something of importance, you'll be the first to know. Until then, it's something I was told in confidence and will keep in confidence. You don't have to like it, but you have to accept it."

Jack scoffed before walking around the car and climbing into the passenger side. She wasn't going to budge. She wasn't going to tell him a damn thing. He'd just have to find out what she'd learned another way.

5

THE NEXT MORNING, Holly scanned the coffee shop until she spotted a man hunched over a table with a mug cradled between his palms. Heading right for the table, she stood over him. "Dallas Kirby?"

He looked up and gave her a weak smile. "Ms. Austin. Have a seat."

She did, pulling her notebook from her pocket as she sat. "Thanks for meeting me."

"Any news on Penelope?"

"Not yet. No."

His frown deepened as he sat back. "I'm worried about her."

"How do you know her?"

Tapping his fingers on the table, he seemed to be putting his thoughts together before he sat forward again. This time, he pushed his mug aside and crossed his forearms in front of him. "We go to the same church. She taught Sunday school to my daughter. A long time ago."

Holly pulled a page from Rene's book and simply sat, waiting for him to continue. Clearly there was more to it than that. The e-mails they had shared made it clear that Mr. Kirby wanted to see Penelope and she was worried about her husband catching on.

Her tactic worked. Kirby started rambling to fill the silence. "I ran into Penny a few weeks ago. She'd come to the church office to talk to our pastor, but he wasn't in. She was upset, so I sat with her. She's had problems with depression in the past, and she was worried she was starting to have another episode, but she didn't want to get on medication. I guess it made her gain weight the last time she was on a prescription. Gary is a nice guy," Kirby said. "I'm not disrespecting him, but he is very concerned with outside appearances."

Holly recalled how the outside of his house was pristine but the inside, the part few people would see, was a mess. She nodded to encourage him to continue.

"My daughter, the one Penny taught at Sunday school, has battled depression too. I sat with her for a while, and we talked about her symptoms and what she was going through until she felt better. She didn't want Gary to know she was struggling again. He...he wasn't the most understanding about her condition. So many people think depression is just something you can get over, you know?"

"I know."

"It's not like she can turn it off."

"I get it."

"I was trying to convince her to get counseling. I think I almost had her convinced." He looked at his mug. "But then she disappeared."

Holly leaned forward. "Mr. Kirby, had Penelope ever talked about hurting herself?"

He jerked his eyes to hers. "She didn't kill herself, if that's what you're thinking. She would never do that."

Instead of pointing out that no one could ever know what another person would do, she redirected. "Would she run away? Try to hide from her problems?"

"No. She wanted help, Ms. Austin. She just hadn't figured out what help she needed yet."

"Did she ever talk to your pastor?"

He shook his head. "No. We started meeting a few times a week. Sometimes here, sometimes at the church, sometimes at a park."

"But always in the open?"

He eyed her, obviously picking apart the secret meaning of her question. "Yes. We weren't doing anything that we'd have to hide. I was supporting a friend. My sister in Christ, Ms. Austin. She was struggling, and I did what any good man would do. I reached out to help her."

"I'm not accusing you of anything, Mr. Kirby. I simply need to clarify some things to help me find your friend. The last e-mail you sent to Penelope was a thinly veiled threat to tell her husband that she'd been seeing you. Why did you feel the need to threaten her?"

"It wasn't a threat. I... My concern for her was growing.

She'd started getting paranoid. I saw that happen to my daughter before..." Kirby sat back. "My daughter did attempt to hurt herself. I saw the signs and I ignored them. I wasn't going to do the same with Penny. When she started displaying symptoms of paranoia, I knew I needed to force her hand before something bad happened."

"What symptoms had you so concerned?"

"She thought she was being followed."

Holly's heart dropped to her stomach. Penelope was being followed. Just like Julia. Penelope had had a previous bout of depression. Just like Julia.

The similarities between the women just kept growing.

"Did you ever notice anyone following her?" Holly asked.

Kirby shook his head. "No. But I didn't take her seriously."

Another box to check. Both women knew something was wrong, but nobody would listen.

"Is there security surveillance at the church? Videos I could look at?"

"Not that I know of."

"You said you met her here sometimes?"

He nodded.

"Do you know the dates? Times?"

He narrowed his eyes. "You think she was being followed?"

"There is another missing woman I'm looking into. She and Penelope are eerily similar. She also felt like she was being followed before disappearing. Do you know Julia Fredrickson?"

"I've heard her name on the news, but no. I never met her."

"Do you know if Penelope reached out to anyone else? A crisis line or group counseling? Anywhere that she might have met others having the same problems."

Anywhere that she might have met someone who targeted her was Holly's real question.

"Not that I know of. She was just starting to accept that this wasn't something to be ashamed of."

"And you are confident she didn't do anything rash."

"She didn't hurt herself. She was seeking help. She was trying to figure out where to turn."

Holly smiled. "Well, I'm glad she was able to turn to you."

"I should have told someone sooner. She begged me not to."

"It's impossible to fully understand how deeply someone else is struggling, Mr. Kirby. You were there for her. That's what matters. Can you think of anything else that I should know? Anything that gave you pause."

"No."

"If you do, will you call me?"

He nodded. "Of course. Please, call me if you need anything else. I'm really worried about her."

"I can see that. Thank you." Holly tucked her notebook away as she stood. When she turned, her eye caught briefly on a man tucked away in the corner of the café. He quickly moved his head down, hiding behind his ball cap. She pretended she didn't notice as she walked out but did casually glance over her shoulder to make sure she wasn't being followed.

JACK FOLLOWED THE MAN WHO HAD MET WITH HOLLY from the café, keeping enough distance between them to not be obvious in his actions. As soon as the man climbed into a dark blue sedan, Jack subtly snapped a photo of the license plate so he could run a search on his identity.

Tucking his phone into his pocket, he headed across the street toward where he'd parked his car. He had just reached for the door handle when a thin arm moved around him and a hand pressed the door shut. He knew who it was without turning around, but even so, he slowly spun.

"Fancy meeting you here," Holly said, trapping him between her body and the car, much as he'd done to her at the dog shelter.

He took a sharp breath and got a whiff of the subtle scent that had surrounded him the day she'd pinned him to the floor. She didn't wear perfume, but there was a distinct sweetness that drifted from her skin. Or maybe it was her hair. He smiled at the idea that he'd have to get even closer to her to determine which. "What's up, Austin?"

"Just a little coffee break."

"With Penelope Nelson's lover?"

She jerked the ball cap off his head and shoved it into his chest. "Maybe he's my lover."

"Maybe I'd believe that if you weren't so easy to read."

She lifted a brow at him. "Am I?"

"Your stiff posture, sympathetic smiles, encouraging nods. You only use those when interviewing witnesses."

She was clearly processing his observation. She'd likely be more aware of her actions in the future so someone else couldn't see through her so easily. "You're following me," she chastised.

He didn't even attempt to look ashamed of his actions. He wasn't. "If you don't want to share your intel, you leave me no choice but to gather it on my own."

"I told you I would share if it was important."

"You could have missed something."

Her jaw tensed and she lowered her hand, but Jack grabbed her left hip before she could step back. He pulled her closer. She didn't resist, but she did lift her brow ever so slightly, as if silently warning him against his blatant trespass into her space.

"I don't mean that as a slight," he said. "We all miss clues sometimes."

"Thanks for the pep talk, Detective. But I'm quite confident in my assessment."

"What assessment is that?"

She whispered, "That I was right not to trust you."

Her words were an unexpected punch to his gut. Though he'd suspected as much, having her admit to not trusting him caused his stomach to knot. "You're the one keeping secrets," he reminded her.

Anger flared in her eyes. "I'm doing whatever it takes to find these women before they both end up dead. Maybe you should set your ego aside and do the same."

Jack hadn't intended to pull her closer, but suddenly he was holding her body against his, digging his fingers into her hip. His chest tightened with two realizations: his anger at her not sharing Gary's secret had nothing to do with this case, and if he didn't put space between them—*now*—he was going to kiss her.

He pushed her back a step and released his hold on her. "How am I supposed to do whatever it takes when I don't know everything?"

Holly forced a breath between her lips before licking them. For a moment Jack thought maybe she was disappointed he'd let her go, but then she straightened her shoulders and pinned him with her hard stare.

"His name is Dallas Kirby. They know each other through church. She wasn't having an affair with him," she said. "She was seeking help for depression."

"Depression?"

"He said she was spiraling into paranoia because, get this, she thought she was being followed."

Jack's breath hitched. "How long?"

"Not long. He was trying to convince her to seek a

professional, but apparently Gary isn't keen on the weight gain caused by her previous use of antidepressants."

Jack frowned. He wasn't surprised by that. "He does seem to be about outward appearances, doesn't he?"

"Are you talking about his house?"

"Yeah."

"Did you ever know them to fight when you lived next to them?"

Jack thought of how happy Penelope always seemed to be. "No. But do we ever really know anyone?"

"Not really," Holly said. She took another step back. "I'm headed back to the office. In case you planned on following me."

He grinned. "I have to get back to my real job, but I'll catch up with you later. I'd like to hear more about your coffee date."

"I bet you would," she muttered before turning.

Jack continued leaning against his car, watching her leave. He had to chuckle at himself. He'd never been the type to fall under the spell of a woman, but he could literally feel himself becoming entranced with Holly Austin. The authority with which she walked away was like a siren song calling out to him. He wanted to follow her again, but this time just to watch her movements.

Jack turned and rested his palms against his car. The wind blew her hair, lifting the golden strands away from her face as she glanced to verify there were no cars headed toward her. He wished she'd take another look his way, but she crossed the street in several long strides and used her fob to unlock her car doors.

Opening the driver's door without so much as a glance his way, she climbed in. He couldn't see her because of the reflections mirrored on her windshield, but he suspected she was slipping the key into the ignition. Sure enough, her car came to life, but she didn't pull away from the curb because, he guessed, she was pulling her sunglasses from the compartment.

When she did leave her parking spot, Jack had to chuckle. She drove by him, sliding her dark glasses into place, as if to remind him how little concern she had for him. Too bad he saw through how hard she was trying to be dismissive.

Tapping his fingers on his car roof, Jack debated pointing out that denying the spark between them only made it more tempting to him. He stood upright and dug into his pocket and then paused in his movements as he noticed a man emerging from the café where, just a few minutes prior, Jack had sat watching Holly. The café was casual, but for some reason the man's dark uniform stood out; it didn't quite fit with the rest of the people in business dress who bustled along the street at this time of day.

Jack's intuition kicked into high gear, telling him that something about what he was seeing was significant, but he couldn't pinpoint why. The man seemed familiar, but not so much so that Jack instantly recognized him. As he stood watching, the man disappeared into the crowd moving along the sidewalk. He debated trotting across the street to see if he could get a better look, but a line of cars blocked his way as the light at the intersection changed.

Dismissing the feeling, he climbed into his car and headed back to the station before anyone could start to question where he'd gotten off to.

6

HOLLY STOPPED REVIEWING her notes on the Fredrickson case when Rene sat on the edge of her desk. Everyone said she was a workaholic, but maybe this was the real reason she always ended up working late—she was constantly being interrupted. Getting anything productive done took three times longer sitting behind her desk than when she was sitting on her sofa. She really needed to consider working from home more often. Especially now that Jack Tarek had wormed his way into her case and the women of HEARTS suddenly seemed even more intrusive on Holly's time.

Rene stared at her, silently demanding answers to unspoken questions. That was Rene's trick, her super-power. She could make grown men spill their guts with nothing but unyielding eye contact. That didn't work on Holly, though. She just leaned back in her chair, met her gaze, and waited Rene out.

"You partnering up with Tarek?" Rene finally asked.

Holly suspected she was hinting at something else. Rene was direct and candid, but she also worked her way to the big questions. She never started exactly where she wanted to be. She liked to work suspects down to that point. "Maybe."

"He's cute in a Rami Malek kinda way, don't you think?"

"In a what kind of way?"

Rene tilted her head and lifted her arched brows, looking like she didn't quite believe what Holly had asked. "Rami Malek. The actor. Jesus, Hol, crawl out from under your rock once in a while."

Holly smirked. She wasn't as out of touch as she let her co-workers believe. Yes, she had noticed how his close-trimmed facial hair and intentionally messed hair made him look more like a movie star than a police detective. She'd chosen not to admit that to anyone but herself for the sake of her sanity. If any one of these women even suspected Holly had noticed Jack was handsome as hell, they'd harass her more than they were already. She'd never get a moment of peace.

He hadn't been very subtle in pointing out that he, too, had noticed the natural pull between them, but his teasing didn't irritate her as much as she suspected it would if any of her team started taking part in that. Jack hadn't come right out and said he was attracted to her, but she'd noticed him staring at her more than once. And not just to point out how much she looked like the missing women.

He obviously felt the same strange attraction she did. Although he seemed more at ease with it. Tarek was probably the type of man who had no hesitation seducing or being seduced and moving on when the passion died. Holly wasn't much into relationships and didn't mind an occasional short-term fling. He would probably be good with that after this case was solved. But the key to that was *after* the case was solved. She wasn't going to let herself get distracted from the goal—bringing Julia home as soon as possible. She wouldn't investigate whatever was happening between Jack and her until after that.

A celebratory night in his bed definitely wouldn't be a bad thing. Until then, she needed to keep his subtle flirting and her desire to pin him under her once more in check.

"The point is," Rene continued, "you were cold as ice to him at the front desk. Only one thing makes a woman that cold."

"The fact that you keep jacking up the air conditioning and making the bill twice as high as it should be?"

Rene ignored the jab. She was the one always complaining about it being too hot in the office and was the most likely A/C culprit, but Holly didn't have proof. She did find Rene's lack of denial interesting, though.

"You don't want us to realize that you're hot for him," Rene continued.

Holly scoffed. "You saw me with him for all of two minutes."

"And it was enough."

"Enough to *what*?" Holly held up her hand. "No. I don't want to hear it. Did Sam put you up to this?"

"No."

The next on her list? "Alexa?"

"I don't need Sam or Alexa to point out the obvious. There's a sizzle between you and this detective."

"A sizzle?"

Rene made a hissing sound as she winked.

Holly let out a wry laugh. "My God. You guys are impossible. I don't even know him."

"You've never been physically attracted to someone without knowing them? Bullshit, Hol. That's human nature."

"Lucky for me, I can control my impulses and not pounce on every man I find attractive."

Rene cocked her head again. "Maybe you should. How long has it been?"

She snorted at the boldness of Rene's question. "Excuse me?"

Rene, as always, was unfazed by Holly's curt tone and continued to push. "I've known you almost a year now. I have *never* seen you give anything of yourself to anyone outside of this office and our clients. Maybe it's time you found a man to distract you."

"Maybe I'm gay and just don't want you to know."

"Oh, please." Rene rolled her eyes dramatically to emphasize her disbelief. "You've surrounded yourself with strong, independent, and—dare I say—*sexy* women. If you were gay, you'd have tried to sleep with one of us by now."

"Maybe I am sleeping with one of you, and she just knows how to keep her mouth shut."

"That would never happen in this office. I can't even burp without one of you bitches sending out a memo."

Holly chuckled not only because it was true but because that had actually happened. One of Rene's clients owned an Indian restaurant and had insisted on treating her to lunch after she'd caught their employees stealing from the cash register. Rene was too polite to turn down the pork vindaloo, which she knew wouldn't sit well in her stomach. She'd come back with horrible indigestion and, after taking a handful of antacids, spent the afternoon belching so loud, Sam concocted an official notice and e-mailed it out to the rest of HEARTS, warning them not to feed Rene Indian food. Ever.

Yeah, her team drove her nuts, but she adored them and their crazy antics. She wouldn't trade them for anything.

"Besides that," Rene said, "if you were seeing someone, male *or* female, you wouldn't be so hot for the good detective."

Holly opened her mouth, another smart retort on the tip of her tongue, but her phone rang. She cleared her throat when she noticed Jack's name on the screen. She made it a point to sound official as Rene stared at her. "Holly Austin."

"Hey, it's Jack," he said.

Damn it. Just those three simple words spoken in his smooth baritone made her core vibrate. She wanted to spin her chair to turn her back on Rene's scrutiny, but that would just make her more suspicious.

"I thought if you had some time, we could go over a few things," he continued in her ear.

She swallowed, shifted slightly, and answered, as casually as possible, "Sure. When?"

"You available now?"

"Yeah."

"Good. Have you eaten?"

She stuttered, not sure what to say and why she couldn't say anything. It wasn't as if he'd asked her to strip naked and climb into his lap. Which she probably would have figured out how to respond to more quickly than his simple question of whether she had or hadn't put food in her stomach recently.

Speak, she screamed in her mind.

"Sustenance, Princess. Have you had any lately?"

She wanted to call him out on using that vile nickname again, but she wasn't about to banter with him under Rene's watchful eye. She was already stuttering and warming from the inside out at the sound of his voice. "Uh. No."

"Good, I'll swing by and pick you up. I can be there in ten."

"Okay." She pulled the phone from her ear and focused much more than necessary on ending the call.

Rene slid off the desk. "You're blushing."

Holly exhaled loudly. She couldn't deny it. The heat in her cheeks was so excessive she was about to break her own rule and turn the office temperature down even more to stop the nervous sweat from starting. "He wants to pick me up to go over some things."

"You can't do that here?"

"He's, uh...hungry, apparently."

Rene tilted her head and grinned. "Ah. A dinner date."

"*No,*" Holly said, much too quickly and her tone far too firm. "No. Nothing like that. Just food while we talk about this case. Like...like a dinner *meeting.*" She nodded confidently. "It's just a dinner meeting."

"You should brush your hair and touch up your makeup before your dinner *meeting.* You look like a mess. Most men only appreciate that disheveled look *after* sex."

Holly frowned. She did *not* need post-coital images of Jack Tarek slinking around her brain. "Screw you, Schwartz."

"You should be so lucky," she sang as she headed for the door. Stopping, she turned and offered Holly a soft smile. "Take your damn tracker. We didn't buy that so we'd know where your desk is. If something happens, we need to be able to find each other. And Holly? A little social interaction would do you good. Getting laid would do you even better."

Holly opened her mouth to chastise Rene, but her co-worker disappeared. "My God," she whispered. "Not an ounce of professionalism among them."

But then Jack's smile flashed through her mind, and she jerked her desk drawer open. After dragging a brush through her hair, she opened a compact and swiped foundation over her blotchy skin. Tapping at the bags under her eyes, she frowned. There wasn't anything she could do about that. She needed some sleep. Real sleep. But she hadn't gotten a solid night of rest since Eric Fredrickson had hired HEARTS to find his wife.

She didn't have time to sleep. Not when there was a missing woman out there who could still possibly be alive.

The front door opened and closed as Holly tossed the makeup back into the drawer. She dropped her keys in her pocket as she stood, touched the gun on her hip just to verify it was there, and headed for the lobby. She stopped as she remembered this was *not* a dinner date and grabbed the Fredrickson file off her desk. She froze midstep once more and then dug in her drawer for the one-inch-by-one-inch GPS tracker.

The small black squares had been Rene's idea. If she'd known where her agent had been, she might have been able to intervene before losing a team member. She wasn't about to let that happen again. Not that this little bit of plastic could protect them from everything, but it made Rene feel better, so they'd all agreed to carry them. When they could remember. Holly was the biggest offender of that particular company rule.

With her tracker tucked in her pocket, she headed to the lobby, where she absolutely refused to acknowledge the twitch low in her gut when she spotted Jack casually leaning against the desk where Sam usually sat. He was admiring a framed photo of the six women of HEARTS celebrating Alexa's birthday. Rare evidence that they could all look happy simultaneously.

He looked at Holly, and she didn't miss the way his gaze skimmed over her. She did dismiss it, however. Despite the obvious attraction they shared and the pushiness of her co-workers, she wasn't looking for a man. And if she were, she sure as shit wouldn't get involved with one while working a case. That was the kind of trouble she left for Rene and Alexa to get into. But she couldn't deny the temptation was there.

"I'll drive," she said as she passed him and headed for the door without casting him another glance.

"My car's right outside."

"So is mine." She didn't look back, denying him a chance to argue. She unlocked her car, slid into the front seat, and then dropped the file in his lap as he sat next to her. "Burgers?"

"Sounds good."

She barely looked at him but noticed the smirk on his face. He probably thought he was appeasing her by letting her drive. He'd figure it out if they worked together long enough. Holly drove. That wasn't a question. And that wasn't up for debate. And it wasn't an ego thing, either. She'd learned long ago that being in control meant she was responsible for the outcome of what happened in her life, and she wasn't about to let someone else be in control of what happened to her—even while grabbing a burger.

So Holly drove.

Always.

And if Jack Tarek thought he was kowtowing to her, that was fine. He could sneer and feel superior all he wanted. She didn't care. But then she frowned because part of her did care. She didn't want him to think she was full of herself or didn't trust him or...whatever he was thinking.

As she fondled the pendant hanging around her neck, she debated explaining to him, but she didn't because the reality was, she couldn't. Driving was a false sense of security, and she knew it. Accidents happened all the time, no matter who was driving, and there was no guarantee she could make better snap decisions than Jack or anyone else. Holly had just convinced herself of that.

"You okay?" he asked, pulling her from her thoughts.

"Yeah."

"You're sighing."

"Sighing?"

"Yeah. I've counted three in as many blocks. And you're playing with your necklace. Both indicate increased stress. Wanna tell me why?"

She released the heart around her neck and tightened her hold on the steering wheel.

"Look," he said after a moment. "If this is about keeping Gary's concerns under wraps, I get it. I don't like it, but I get it."

"It's not that."

He glanced her way. "No? Then what is it?"

Holly forced her attention on the road so she didn't have to see his reaction. "After my mother died, my father started drinking. A lot. He got into accidents. *A lot.* More than once I was in the car. We are both very lucky we survived his stupidity."

"Wow. I'm sorry."

She dismissed his sympathy. "I started driving him around long before I had a license. For both our sakes. So. I prefer to drive."

Thankfully, he didn't say anything else on the matter. Only, her appreciation for the silence didn't last. After a few heartbeats, the quiet started to feel tense, and for reasons she couldn't explain, the tension was uncomfortable.

She didn't like anyone to feel sorry for her, but when he put his hand on her forearm and gently squeezed, part of her nearly cried out with relief. She was aware that she'd ignored the pain of her past for far too long—Rene and Alexa reminded her of that on a regular basis—but acknowledging how broken she still felt hurt too much. He pulled his hand away, and she nearly reached for his hand to pull it back to her. Just so she felt connected to someone, even if just for a moment.

"We weren't close," she said. "I didn't want to be responsible for him, so I joined the Army right out of high school. I thought about re-enlisting after my second tour, but..."

"You'd seen enough?"

She nodded. "More than enough."

"And the necklace?"

Holly swallowed. "It was my mother's."

He was silent just long enough for Holly to mentally kick herself for saying too much. Then he overshared, too.

"My dad split when Mom was pregnant with me. I'm sure you can imagine how difficult being a single pregnant woman in Egypt was back then. Her parents disowned her. She didn't have a chance at making a decent life for us, so she moved to America before I was born. She had a cousin here who was more open-minded about her situation."

"She likes being here? The Midwest is about as different from Egypt as a person can get."

"She hates the winters, but not enough to leave."

Holly smiled. "I hate the winters, too. Has she ever considered going back?"

"Nah, this is home now. She's made a life for herself."

"Good for her." Holly pulled up to her favorite pub and parked near the door. Flicking her gaze toward his face as she reached to release her seat belt, she wondered why the hell she felt the need to make small talk with him. No, that hadn't been small talk. She'd told him things about herself that some of her teammates didn't even know.

They knew about her mom, but they didn't know she'd enlisted in the Army to get away so she didn't have to watch her father drink himself to death or that she'd left the Army because she couldn't see one more person die on her watch. Or that she hated the winter.

"You sighed again." Jack reached for the door handle.

Instead of responding, she climbed out of her car and led them into the dimly lit pub. The scents of grease and beer mixed in the air. Some people might find the smell offensive, but it soothed her in some way she couldn't define as she led them to a corner table in the back. The booth was curved, made for a larger party than two, but allowed both of them to sit with their backs to a wall without sitting so close she could feel his heat sinking into her.

The waitress was on them before Holly even settled into the booth.

She ordered a soda and a double cheeseburger basket without even looking at the menu. Jack ordered the same, probably because she hadn't given him a chance to see his options. Damn it, she really needed to learn to be more accommodating to other people. Her manners were atrocious, and she knew that, but she never actually remembered that until it was too late. "They have other stuff if you want more time to look at a menu—"

"I'm good." He rested his forearms on the table. "Relax."

She did. Or as much as she could. She scanned the bar, evaluating the environment, seeking out any signs of trouble before finally letting her full attention fall on Jack. He was doing the same, scanning the bar, taking assessment of the area before letting his eyes meet hers. She wasn't one to swoon or gush, but his dark eyes had a mesmerizing quality she couldn't deny. Staring into his dark irises was like getting caught in the crosshairs. Her heart tripped over itself, and a crazy mixture of fear, anticipation, and excitement rushed through her as she waited to see what was going to happen.

Frowning, Holly broke the eye contact and glanced around the dark room again. Who the fuck compared sexual attraction to getting shot? Holly Austin, that's who. Christ, no wonder she couldn't ever see herself settling down.

"Anything more you want to tell me about your coffee date today?" Jack asked.

She ignored her internal chastising and turned her focus on the reason they were sitting there in the first place. "Dallas Kirby attends the same church as Gary and Penelope. She started struggling with depression, and he was trying to help her through it. He said it was bad enough he wanted her to get professional help, but she was hesitant."

"Do you think—"

"She hurt herself or ran off? I don't know. Kirby said it wasn't that bad. I reached out to Gary, but he hasn't returned my call. How well do you know the Nelsons?"

"Not that well. Like I said, I was a teenager when Mom bought that house. Teenagers don't really hang out with the neighbors. Anything new on the Fredrickson case today? Did you find out where Julia was going Tuesday mornings before the grocery store?"

"Uh, no. Eric hasn't called me back." She opened the file and spread her notes on the scratched tabletop, covering a set of initials carved in the wood. "I compared Julia's and Penelope's schedules, their shopping places, their exercise habits—everything I could find. If Julia wasn't volunteering at the shelter, I don't see any other place where their paths could have crossed the same man.

Maybe this is a guy looking for a woman, *any woman*, who fits his criteria. These two just happened to."

It was his turn to sigh. "I hope you're wrong. If this was opportunistic, the odds of finding this guy become infinitely slimmer."

She nodded. "I know, but if there's a connection, I'm not finding it."

He flipped through the pages. "Maybe we need to go back further. Did their kids go to the same schools? Husbands ever work at the same firm? Did they ever use the same electrician or Internet service?"

Holly grimaced as she thought how long it would take to make those comparisons. "It could take months to dig that deep. I really doubt these women have months for us to find them."

"You have a better idea?"

She leaned back as a basket of food and a soda were set in front of her. Jack's dinner hadn't even been put on the table when she finally grasped how famished she was. The burger wasn't just calling out to her; the damn thing was screaming, demanding to be eaten *now*. She picked up the overstuffed sandwich and shoved the bun, melted-cheese-covered patties, onions, tomatoes, pickles, and oozing condiments into her mouth, taking the biggest bite she could.

She moaned as the combination of flavors exploded on her tongue. Damn, she loved a good cheeseburger. After she chewed and swallowed, she licked a glob of mustard from the side of her hand before stuffing a fry into her mouth. She was about to take another bite when she caught Jack watching her.

His lips were curved up in that annoying smirk of his.

"What?" she asked.

He chuckled and returned his focus to his sandwich. "Nothing."

"Am I not dainty enough for you?"

He stopped before sinking his slightly crooked teeth into his dinner. "Actually, I like my women a little butch, Austin."

She tried to glare at him, but she couldn't stop the grin spreading across her lips. "Really? You seem like the type who would be intimidated by a strong woman."

While she took another huge bite, he set down his sandwich and sat forward, obviously challenging her assessment. She held his gaze as she chewed. He was waiting for her to look away as women tended to do when stared at for too long. She didn't even blink. She was going to wait him out, stare him down, and win.

Finally he smirked and shook his head as he lost the contest. "So when you aren't chasing your tail on a case, what are you doing?"

She dropped her sandwich and yanked a few napkins from the dispenser. "Turning around to chase my tail the other way."

He nodded, clearly understanding. "This line of work can consume you, huh?"

She wiped her hands and tossed her trash on the table in front of her. "I was determined not to let it, but this case…" She squeezed the bottle of ketchup over her basket, coating her fries.

Jack widened his eyes as he watched. "What are you *doing*?"

She looked up at him, down at her food, and then to him again. "Putting ketchup on my fries."

"That…" He exhaled heavily. "That is sacrilegious, Austin."

"You don't like ketchup?"

"You don't *coat* the fries. You *dip* the fries." He took the bottle from her and squirted a glob in the corner of his basket. "Like so." He immersed a greasy, golden-fried potato into the condiment to show her how it was done.

She watched his display intently. Mostly because she was really enjoying looking at his lips. "I'd heard there were ketchup elitists in the world, but this is the first time I've actually met one. You should write an essay on this. I'm sure the culinary world has been dying to be enlightened on the coat versus dip element of french-fry consumption."

The way he gestured toward her basket implied he was unaffected by her sarcasm. "If you squirt the fries, they get soggy. You have to dip the fries so they stay crisp."

"Maybe I like my fries soggy, Tarek."

He closed his eyes and dropped his face. "Man. You're trying to kill me, aren't you?"

She chuckled at his theatrics. "If how I eat my fries is enough to do you in, you'd never last anyway."

He lifted his gaze to her and quirked his brows. "I don't

mind the challenge. I'll turn you into a dipper before this case is over."

Reality stole the smile from her face. "I hope we're not working this case long enough for anyone to change bad habits. For their sakes." She nodded toward the files, and his smile faded as well.

A cloud—something like guilt—moved over the table. Holly had no right doing whatever it was she was doing with this man when two women were missing. She wasn't exactly flirting—she'd never been good at that—but she was enjoying his company more than she should have, given the circumstances.

Dropping her ketchup-coated fry back into her basket, she pushed her dinner away and wiped her hands, her appetite gone. "I'll drop in on Fredrickson in the morning. I suspect he's avoiding my calls after our last visit. I want to know if he knew Julia wasn't at the dog shelter. I'll also ask what services they've used in the last six months."

"I'll do the same with Nelson's husband. Let's plan to cross references tomorrow afternoon. I'll swing by your office when I get a chance."

She met his gaze, and that same mix of emotions rushed through her, settling low in her stomach. Their comparisons could be done over the phone or through e-mail. They didn't have to meet up for that, and she was tempted to point that out to him. However, she didn't doubt he knew that as well as she did. He had an ulterior motive to want to see her. She suspected she knew exactly what that was and just how dangerous this little game of temptation was going to get before this case came to a close.

"Yeah," she said, "let's do that."

She wasn't going to go out of her way to find reasons to see Jack. But she wasn't going to turn away from an opportunity, either.

THE FIRST THING JACK HAD DONE WITH THE LIST OF shelter volunteers was to verify that none of the women listed—other than Penelope—had gone missing. The second thing was to check the police records of all the men who had been named. None had records that made him think they would be capable of kidnapping two women.

The list for Tuesdays, however, only had the names of businesses that offered employees to volunteer. There were no individuals for him to look into. That left him feeling uneasy.

He glanced at his watch. The time was closing in on eleven thirty, but he would bet his badge that Holly was still awake and doing the exact same thing he was. Instead of calling her, he texted, asking if she was still up. His phone rang within seconds of sending.

"Did you find something?" Holly asked.

"No, but one of the businesses listed on the volunteer rotation stuck out to me and I can't figure out why. Bailey just has it listed as *Appleseed*."

"That's the landscaping company Eric and Julia use."

The lightbulb went off in Jack's head. "Right. We should look into—"

"Gary uses a neighbor for his landscaping. I already asked."

Jack smirked. He should have known.

She continued. "He had junk mail from Appleseed sitting on his table. I recognized the name."

"Gotcha," Jack said thoughtfully. "So there's nothing to that. Any word on where Julia really was spending her Tuesday mornings?"

"Not yet. I'm meeting with Eric tomorrow."

"Alone?" Jack asked before he could censor himself. He still didn't trust Eric Fredrickson.

Holly laughed softly in his ear. "I'm really glad you came along, Tarek. It's been a while since someone has been so insecure about my ability to take care of myself."

"That's not what I meant."

"Of course not."

"Holly," he called, fearing she'd hang up.

"Hmm?"

The low hum of her response sent a shot to his groin. "I'm this close to making an arrest in this other case I've been working on. If you can wait to see Fredrickson until tomorrow afternoon—"

"I don't need a babysitter, Tarek."

"I know that."

"Do you?"

"I can't explain it," he said. "But you know that feeling.

I know you do. My gut is telling me something is off with that man. Don't be too trusting of him."

She was quiet for a moment. He guessed she was processing his warning. "I do know that feeling. I'll keep my guard up."

"Thank you."

"Anything else?" she asked when he heaved out a breath.

"No. I guess not. I'll see you at your office tomorrow."

"Jack," she said in the soft, soothing tone she used while interviewing witnesses. Hearing his name in that low voice made his heart skip a beat. "I know I don't show it well, but I appreciate you looking out for me."

"I'll always look out for you," he said in a gentle voice that matched hers. Closing his eyes tightly, he mentally kicked himself in the ass. That wasn't what he'd meant to say or the voice he should have used to say it. "I just mean..."

Opening his eyes, he focused on the silence on the line. Pulling the phone from his ear, he breathed a sigh of relief when the screen showed that the call had ended. If he was lucky, she hadn't heard that last little bit of their conversation. Something told him she'd never let him live that moment of sentimentality down if she had.

7

HOLLY TRUSTED HER INSTINCT, but damned if Jack's constant worrying about Eric Fredrickson hadn't taken root in her mind. She knocked on the door and stepped to the side. Not out of view if he opened the door, but if he had malicious intent, he'd have to step onto the porch to grab her. That was a safety measure she hadn't consciously taken with Fredrickson in weeks.

This morning, her adrenaline pumped a bit higher as she waited for him to answer. When he did, she skimmed over him, looking for signs that he was on edge. She found none.

"Ms. Austin," he said, gesturing for her to enter.

She kept her right hand close to her hip, ready to draw her gun if needed. He took his usual seat on the other side of the coffee table, but instead of sitting, she stood behind the couch. "I just need a minute of your time," she said to justify not sitting on the couch. "First, I wanted to apologize again about how things went with Detective Tarek yesterday. He's a bit rough around the edges."

"Fucking cops," he muttered. "They don't care. They just want to pin this on her having an affair so they can be done with it."

"We did look into the county animal shelter, Mr. Fredrickson. After leaving here, we went to the shelter, and...Julia isn't listed as a volunteer."

He sat taller, narrowing his eyes a bit. Not angrily but with obvious confusion. "What does that mean?"

"We spoke with the woman who organizes volunteers. She didn't know Julia. Is it possible Julia was going to a different shelter? One outside of the city?"

"No. They gave her a sticker when she started a few months ago. I was pissed when I saw it on her bumper. I didn't want her ruining the paint."

Holly bit her lip, trying to make sense of the two conflicting stories. Eric jumped to his feet, startling her, and as she'd done the day before, Holly lifted her left hand as she moved her right closer to her gun. Eric didn't notice; he was looking at his phone.

"Look," he said, coming closer. "Every week she sent me these damn pictures of the dogs she was walking. *Can we adopt one?* She asked the same thing every damn week. *Can we adopt one?* I always said no. We have a grandbaby on the way. The last thing we need is a dog."

Holly watched as he scrolled through photos that Julia had sent to him. Every image was of her cuddling a different dog. The thing that struck Holly, though, was that Julia was *in* the photo.

"Do you know who took these pictures?" she asked.

Eric looked at his phone and shrugged. "No. I never asked."

Damn it. This just wasn't adding up.

"Could you send me a list of all the services you've had in the last six months? Any electrician or plumber or cable repair. Anything like that."

Eric lowered his phone. "You're getting desperate."

"We're checking into every possible lead."

He ran his fingers through his hair and exhaled loudly. "I'll see what I can find for you."

"That would be helpful." As she headed toward the door, Holly glanced around the room. Jack was right. The house was too neat. Too tidy.

Too perfect.

As soon as she was in her car, she pulled her phone from her pocket and called Jack. She knew he had other cases to tend to, but she still sighed with frustration when her call went to his voice mail. "Fredrickson had photos of his wife with the dogs she walked. She sent them to him every Tuesday. She might have been sending him those to cover her tracks, but she had that volunteer sticker on her car. She had to get that somewhere. I'm headed back to the shelter. Let me know if you have other ideas."

She ended the call and dropped her phone into the passenger seat. She alternated between tapping her fingers on the steering wheel and squeezing the damn thing so hard her knuckles turned white. There had to be a connection between Julia and Penelope. What was it?

After parking in the same spot she had the day before, Holly headed right for Bailey.

"Hey," the girl said with the same bright smile. She tilted her head. "Where's your partner?"

"With his wife," Holly said. She had no idea why, but she didn't like the way the bubbly woman immediately focused on Jack's absence. Jack wasn't married, but stating so would put an end to any notion she had of hooking up with a cop. "You said yesterday that Julia Fredrickson doesn't volunteer at this shelter."

"No, ma'am," Bailey said.

"She had a volunteer sticker from this shelter. Do you know where she would have gotten that?"

Bailey shrugged. "We stopped giving those stickers out a long time ago. We have T-shirts for our volunteers now."

"Do you know when you stopped handing out stickers?"

"About six months ago."

"What happened to the leftover stickers?"

She gestured over her shoulder with her thumb. "They're in a box in the storage room."

"Who has access to that room?"

Bailey shrugged. "Pretty much everyone. If I have to run errands or help with intake on a new dog, a volunteer runs the desk."

Holly tilted her head. "So is it possible Julia came in to volunteer and you weren't the one here to help her?"

Confusion filled her eyes. "I...guess. But why would someone... I mean, there are forms to fill out, and I'd have to put her on the schedule. So... I don't know why someone would tell her to volunteer without running it by me."

Because she was immediately targeted, Holly realized. "Great," she muttered. "Thanks, Bailey."

Back in her car, Holly tried to call Jack again. Voice mail.

She didn't know why she was so damned irritated about that. She understood he had other obligations, but for some reason him not answering her call irritated the hell out of her. Actually, there were a dozen reasons why. The main one being that she felt like she was beginning to flounder in this case. Julia and Penelope were counting on her, and Holly couldn't seem to make two and two add up to four.

She'd never been on the losing side of a case before, but she certainly felt she was there now. Eric had accused her of becoming desperate. She hated to admit it, but he was right. Holly was grasping at straws, and they all seemed to be slipping through her hands. And that pissed her the hell off.

"Jack," she said after the tone, "it's Holly. I think we need to dig deeper into the shelter volunteers." She started to ask him to drop whatever he was doing and come to her office now rather than later, but that sounded desperate. And not just to solve the case.

Instead of adding the last bit, she ended the call and

tossed her phone aside. Cursing herself, Jack, and the questions in this case that she couldn't seem to answer.

"WHAT AM I DOING?" JACK MUMBLED AS HE PARKED next to Holly's car. "What the hell am I doing?" He tapped his fingers on the steering wheel and then looked at the dish containing the faatah his mother had sent with him. He didn't even know if Holly liked Middle Eastern food. What if she thought eating lamb was revolting? Lots of people did. Just because she ate beef didn't mean she wanted a cute little baby sheep chopped up and served for dinner.

And what if she got the wrong impression? And what, exactly, was the *right* impression?

Just as he had suspected, he'd barely walked into his mother's house before she'd started peppering Jack with questions about the PI he'd mentioned. And as he knew would happen, he'd said way more than he should about how intuitive and hardworking Holly was and how she wasn't going to stop until she solved this case. His mother would've had to be deaf, dumb, and dead to miss the admiration in Jack's voice. Even he'd heard it; he just hadn't been able to stop gushing.

So here he was, showing up with his mother's favorite dish—at her insistence that no woman could resist a man who served her a home-cooked meal.

"I'll bring dinner," Jack muttered, mimicking his pathetic call to Holly. "Mom threw something together."

Actually, Mom had spent all afternoon obsessing over the food, texting him questions about Holly he couldn't answer, and reminding him how to be a gentleman.

"*I want grandchildren before I'm too old to enjoy them, babba,*" she'd said when he stopped by to pick up the dinner she insisted he take with him. "*Feed her. Maybe she'll like you, too. And you can finally find a nice woman to make you a home.*"

Jack laughed as he shook his head. He couldn't look at a woman without his mother reminding him how much she wanted to be a grandmother. Her only child was Jack, and he was in no hurry to settle down, which was a great stressor for the woman eager to join her friends in showing pictures of grandbabies. Holly was not the soft, sweet woman his mother probably had in mind. Then again, Holly had a pulse, and at this point, his mother was probably so desperate for him to get married that would be more than enough for her.

Climbing out of the car, he grabbed the dish and bag of disposable plates and cutlery. Holly probably wouldn't mind if he just tossed the casserole on the table and told her to dig in, but he'd brought paper plates and plastic utensils anyway.

He smiled as he recalled her stuffing that cheeseburger into her mouth. Adorable wasn't exactly the word to describe the way she'd attacked her meal, but he couldn't think of anything else. Most men might have been turned off, but her lack of interest in looking or being refined was just one more layer of Jack's attraction to her.

The other layers?

She was brilliant and brave and fearless. Her wit was dry, but he liked the subtlety of her humor. Her eyes were haunted but lit when she teased him. Her smile...her lips... her lithe body. Damn that body.

He opened the door to the agency. The desk where Sam usually met him with her bored expression was empty. The light in the conference room was on, though, so he headed straight there. He found Holly staring at the whiteboard with a list of what he assumed to be Fredrickson's six months' worth of services and the words *DOG SHELTER* in all caps, circled several times.

He had barely set the food down when she turned around, her eyes wide.

"What smells so good?" she demanded.

"Faatah. It's like a casserole made out of lamb and rice and—"

"I know." She put the dry-erase marker down and marched toward him. The look in her eye was that of a woman on the prowl, but sadly her attention was directed at the dish instead of him. "If you didn't bring enough to share, you're going home hungry. Is that homemade?"

"Yes. My mother sent it over. A thank-you for helping look for Penelope." Or his mother's idea of seducing Holly into marriage and children before she had to break down and start sharing pictures of Jack's cat in lieu of grandchildren. He uncovered the dish and thought he might have to wipe the drool from her chin. "You're hungry, then?"

"Somehow I never realize how hungry I am until you start waving food around."

He smiled as he scooped some casserole onto a plate. "You shouldn't neglect your stomach, Princess."

"Keep calling me that, jackass. See what happens." She accepted the food he'd just served and inhaled deeply. "Oh my God. I love your mother so much."

"I'll remind you of that someday."

She didn't respond. She was too focused on shoveling food in her mouth. And then she made that damned moaning sound that she'd made while eating her cheese-burger—a sound that had preoccupied him when he was trying to sleep the night before. The one that shot straight to his groin and made him want to strip her naked so he could bury himself as deep into her waiting heat as their bodies would allow.

"What is that smell?" came a soft, husky voice from behind them.

"Faatah," Holly said around a mouthful.

A redhead came walking in, completely ignoring Jack as she examined the dish. He offered her a plate, and she barely glanced at him before accepting the food. He had just filled another plate when Sam came strolling into the room with a young woman right behind her. He hadn't met her, but recognized her as Tika, the team's legal expert. She *looked* like the stereotype of a lawyer, with her black hair pulled back into a tight bun and slacks that looked as freshly pressed at this late hour as they likely were when she put them on. Her russet brown skin was smooth except for the crease between her eyes, as if she had spent too much time furrowing her brow. She flashed him a bright white smile but quickly turned her attention to the food on the table and rubbed her hands together as if she hadn't eaten in days.

Rene, the suspicious Mama Bear from the day before, poked her head in and yelled for Alexa to come to dinner. Then the room was somehow full of women scarfing down the dinner he'd brought for Holly.

Though his plan was to be locked in the conference room, eating a home-cooked meal with the woman who had been haunting his dreams since the moment she had thrown him to the ground, he didn't mind sharing his food or his time with her team. This was the most relaxed she'd looked since he had met her—which still wasn't very relaxed. She was smiling, though, and that made him smile, too.

"What's in this?" Sam asked, poking at the food on her plate.

"Beef," Holly lied, while Rene simultaneously said, "Lamb."

Sam looked horrified. Eva, the redhead, started singing a nursery rhyme about bags of wool, and Sam's lip trembled.

"Stop," Holly insisted.

Sam's lips quivered even harder as she gawked at Holly, clearly seeking a truth she didn't want to know.

"Yes, it's lamb, but it's delicious. Just try it."

"I did. That's why I asked what it was." Sam stuck her lip out in a pout and pushed the food aside.

"I'll have Mama make something for you without meat next time," Jack offered.

Sam gave him a sad smile. "Thanks."

Watching Holly take control of the dinner conversation showed Jack just how important her role in the office was. She had said she didn't want to be a leader, but that was exactly what she was to every woman in the room. She was in control, and while the other members of her team were clearly strong in their own right, it was obvious to Jack each took her lead from Holly.

"She doesn't date," Alexa said, pulling Jack from his thoughts.

"Huh?"

She nodded her head toward Holly. "She doesn't date. Hasn't since I've known her."

Jack figured there was some correct response to her comment, but he didn't know what that could be. He was glad, however, to learn that Holly apparently was single. He hadn't realized until that moment that he hadn't even considered she might be seeing someone. He just knew he found her irresistible and hoped she felt the same.

"She's too focused on us," Alexa continued. "She feels responsible for us, even though she isn't. She's afraid to let her guard down."

He caught Holly's gaze. She looked...suspicious? Her attention drifted toward Alexa for a moment, but she blinked away whatever had flashed in her eyes and returned her focus to Eva.

"Maybe you can help her with that," Alexa whispered.

He looked at her, and she smiled, though the sparkle in her eyes looked a bit mischievous.

"I see how you look at her, Detective. And I see how she looks at you. She needs someone to distract her from all the misery we see day in and day out in this place. Why not you?"

He met Holly's eye again. She held his stare until Eva said something that drew her attention, giving Jack an opportunity to take in Holly's profile—to *really* look at her —without her tossing a sarcastic comeback his way.

He didn't know how it was possible for her to be more beautiful today than she'd been the day before, but he'd swear it was so. On the surface, she looked tired and over-worked and overstressed, but he was looking beyond the dark circles under her eyes to the soft curve of her jawline and the not-too-obvious bump in her nose that made him wonder if it'd been broken once before or if that was a natural imperfection simply adding to her appeal. Her smile was soft but genuine, and he could swear he felt the warmth of it spread through his entire body. She had one of the toughest exteriors he'd ever seen, but he knew in that moment she had built that shell to protect something incredibly vulnerable.

She glanced at him, catching him once again staring at her, but he didn't break away. Instead, he hoped Alexa was right, that Holly wanted him just as much as he wanted her. He definitely felt a spark between them.

He sat silently, debating Alexa's question—why not him?—while the women finished eating and running through their cases. As they filtered out of the room, he thanked them for their compliments and promised to have his mother cook for them again soon. Alexa nudged him as she stood, nodded her head toward Holly, and then eased the conference room door closed on her way out. That was man code for "go for it." He wasn't sure if that meant the same in woman code, but he was beginning to suspect these women didn't abide by what men had come to expect of them.

Holly tossed an empty plate in the trash can next to Jack's chair. "Hope you weren't wanting leftovers."

"Are you kidding? My mother would take offense."

"We don't get real food around here often. Eva used to bring in dinner about once a week, but since she and her boyfriend broke up a few months ago, she doesn't cook much."

"So," he said before she could step away, "you don't cook?"

"I'm single. It seems pointless. But I *can* cook, if that is what you are asking. At least well enough to get by. You?"

"I kick ass at ordering take-out."

She laughed, and he had to force air into his lungs. This woman could kill him without even trying. Brushing her hands together, as if ridding them of crumbs, she seemed oblivious to how every movement she made entranced him.

He had to fight the urge to take her hands in his and pull her to him.

She caught him staring yet again—he'd lost count how many times that'd happened during their impromptu dinner party. Each time he felt trapped in her gaze, incapable of breaking the contact. Her eyes captivated him in a way he didn't understand. He thought, for the first time in his life, something was a mystery to him that he wasn't determined to pick apart.

Moving away from him, she focused on the whiteboard, and he instantly missed her being so close. Logic tried to push into his mind—slow down, take a step back, wait for her to make a move. But he snuffed that voice as easily as he would blow out a candle. He stepped to her side, far closer than necessary.

Holly drew an audible breath and then exhaled slowly as she gestured toward the board. "I compared the list of services and utilities for the Nelsons that you e-mailed to the list I got from Fredrickson. One match." She pointed. "Both had cable providers in-home for services in June. I haven't been able to determine if it was the same serviceperson for both. Julia shopped online several times a month. I thought we should check into the delivery services. Maybe they are on the same route. He could have seen them while delivering their packages. I keep coming back to this dog-shelter sticker, though. There is something more to that." She glanced his way, as if to get his feedback, and caught him watching her. She tilted her head and cocked her brow. "You're staring at me. Why?"

A hundred lame excuses and denials ran through his mind, but none came out. She didn't seem to care for games any more than he did. She'd given him an opening, and he wanted to take it.

"You have to ask?"

She responded by lifting her other brow.

Jack couldn't resist. He lightly traced the arch with the tip of his forefinger. "I can't help it. You're beautiful, Holly."

Her eyes widened slightly and her perfect lips parted, but she didn't say anything.

"That's inappropriate. I know." His acknowledgement didn't stop him from running his finger along her jawline. "But the more I'm around you, the more I feel the need to memorize everything about you." With his fingers now under her chin, he brushed his thumb over her lips.

She gasped, as if she had just remembered to breathe. "There are two missing women—"

"I know." He cupped her cheek.

"We can't afford any distractions."

"I know." He slid his fingers into her hair to find the strands as soft as he'd imagined.

"Their families are counting on us."

"I know."

She didn't resist as he pulled her to him. He tugged her hair gently enough to tilt her head back so she was looking up at him. Her breath hit his face in short warm bursts. As she looked into his eyes, the shade of her irises shifted from light blue to a much darker color as her pupils dilated.

Her compliance was all the invitation he needed. He crushed his lips to hers, pushed his tongue into her mouth, and fisted her hair in one hand while the other jerked her body against his. She fit as perfectly as he'd known she would. She slid her hands up his chest and around his neck as she blessed him with that moaning sound that went straight to his crotch. His body came alive and begged for more. He dragged his palms down her sides, over her slender hips. Reaching around her, he cupped the perfect ass he'd been admiring all week. Lifting her against him, he took the two steps needed to press her back against the wall as he kissed her hard.

The best part was she kissed him just as desperately. She moved her mouth against his as she gripped his hair and pressed her body into his, confirming what he needed to know—he definitely wasn't alone in this insane attraction he had for her.

Pulling her arms from around his neck, he used one of his hands to press and hold both of hers above her head. She could break free if she wanted—hell, she'd have his nuts crushed and his arm broken in a split second if she wanted. But she didn't. She let him hold her there as his mouth assaulted hers. He used his other hand to brush her hair from her neck and push aside the collar of her blouse, clearing the way for his kisses to move there.

He licked her neck and then gently sank his teeth into her flesh, and she moaned. When he gripped her breast, she arched into him.

"I want to touch you all over," he whispered before nipping her earlobe. "I want to feel every part of you."

She responded by exhaling harshly. He took that as her acceptance of what was coming next and slid his hand down between her legs, cupping her hot center through her slacks. In the next instant, she kicked one of his legs from beneath him and shoved her body against his. He was falling, bound to land flat on his back, but she clutched his lapel and eased his descent. His landing wasn't exactly gentle, but he hit the floor with far less momentum than he would have had she not grabbed his jacket.

He wasn't sure why she'd thrown him to the ground—maybe he'd pushed her too far—but then she sat, straddling his hips and leaning down. *Holy. Shit.* He'd fantasized about this since the first day they'd met—her over him, hair hanging down, with raw lust in her eyes.

She kissed him then, exerting her control over the situation. Another thing he was more than okay with. Some men might be intimidated by her strength and determination, but he found her independence sexy as hell. She could throw him down anytime she wanted. He squeezed her thighs and pulled her even closer to him. She responded by grinding her hips, rolling over his hard-on as she bit his lip and tugged the plump flesh and then let it snap back into place.

Leaning up a few inches, she met his gaze. "What part of no distractions didn't you understand?"

"All of it."

She held his stare and rolled her hips again. Neither

could possibly miss how rigid he was against her. She was torturing him, and he had no doubt from the glimmer in her eyes that she was loving it.

"You should stop doing that, Princess," he whispered.

"Why, *Jackass?*"

He grinned as he exhaled and tightened his hold on her hips when she shifted again, causing a tightness deep in his groin. "It's been a while since... I don't want to..." He moaned when she moved again, and then a small laugh of embarrassment left him as the pressure started to build in his balls. "I'll finish in my pants if you don't stop."

That clearly was the wrong thing to say. Mischief lit in her eyes as her grin widened.

"Holly," he breathed, but he wasn't sure if he was warning her to stop or pleading for her not to.

She ground into him again as she put her lips to his ear. "You shouldn't have called me Princess."

He swallowed hard as his mind went blank and he gladly accepted his punishment. Only this was the furthest from punishment he could imagine. Feeling her body pressed against his, moving over him, was heaven. Yes, he wished they were skin-on-skin, but this was good enough. Gripping her ass, he held on as she slid over him, her body caressing his.

Lying against him, pressing her chest to his, she whispered in his ear, "Would you like me to come for you, Jack?"

Jesus, this woman was perfect. "Yes," he panted.

"Say please."

Pulling her to him, he kissed her deeply, dragging his tongue over hers, before putting his forehead to hers. "Please," he whispered, because no man in his position was above begging, no matter how tough he pretended to be.

She leaned back, putting more pressure on him, pressing herself against him in just the right way. Watching her cup her breasts, even though they were fully clothed, was about the sexiest damn thing he'd ever seen. She was a mess—her hair was in disarray, her clothes disheveled, and her face flushed—and he wanted her more than he'd ever wanted any other woman.

He tried to push her up, roll her beneath him, but she pressed back, keeping him pinned. Moving his hands to her thighs, he ran his palms over her muscles as they tensed and she moved herself over him again. He really needed to make her stop before he actually did fill his underwear with what had been building since the first moment he'd seen her.

As much as he wanted her to end this torture, he wanted her to continue. She moaned—that damned moan of hers—as he ground into her.

"You like that?" he asked breathlessly.

"Mmm. I think you like it, too."

"Jesus, I want to be inside you." More than that, he wanted to see what she looked like without the shield of her suit. Wanted to feel her skin against his.

She bucked again, and his body pulled tight. To hell with it. He grabbed her by the back of the neck and jerked her down. If he was going to go off like a hormonal teen, he wasn't going alone. So long as she came with him, he didn't care if he embarrassed himself.

He tugged her hair, forced her to look at him as he rolled her beneath him. His hand moved between her legs again, and while he didn't have the best access to her clitoris through her slacks, he knew the moment he found the little bundle of nerves by the way she jolted and took a sharp breath.

Oh, no, he was *not* going over the edge alone.

She lifted her head, catching his mouth with hers. One more grinding of his hips, and she stiffened as her breath caught. She was having an orgasm. For him. Right there on the conference room floor where she'd first body slammed him into submission. Now it was her turn to lie there at his mercy. And seeing her give in to him was fantastic.

She bit her lip and creased her brow as her entire body tensed. One long groan ripped from her, and he lost what was left of his control. Rubbing his body against hers, he let go just as she had. She lifted her hips against him, and he grunted and finished in his pants, just like a goddamn schoolboy.

Finally, she relaxed beneath him, and he let out one last deep groan. He laughed softy as he buried his face into her hair, taking a few moments to slow down his breathing.

"Holy shit," she whispered.

He leaned back and brushed her hair from her face. In response, she closed her eyes and shook her head.

"Why are *you* looking so embarrassed?" he panted. "I'm the one with a mess in his underwear."

She laughed quietly as her cheeks turned an even darker shade of red. "Did we just do that?"

"Act like two horny teens on their parents' sofa? Yes, we did."

She turned her face away as she untangled her legs from his. "I can't believe we let that happen."

He used his fingers to turn her chin back to him. "Believe it." He kissed her. "And believe it *will* happen again. Hopefully with less clothing and in a much more appropriate location."

She stared at him for a moment. "There's a bathroom at the back of the room. You go first."

"Such a gentlewoman." He pressed his lips lightly to hers before grabbing her hands and pulling her up with him, much the way she'd done when she helped him to his feet. Before stepping away, he ran his hand over her hair. "That was amazing."

She diverted her gaze. "We just dry-humped each other."

"And it was *amazing*. Sleeping with you is going to be incredible." He kissed her lightly before heading to the bathroom.

8

HOLLY DIDN'T LOOK up when someone walked into her office. She was finding it incredibly difficult to look at her teammates without feeling ashamed of her behavior.

Alexa set a cup of coffee and a bagel on her desk. "You've been distant today."

Holly exhaled as she forced the image of Jack hovering over her from her mind. She'd replayed those few minutes over and over in her mind. So much so that she'd been tempted to call him in the middle of the night and beg him to come to her place to finish what they'd playacted.

She cleared her throat and gestured to the papers in front of her. "I'm trying to get a list of employees together for the company that crossed the Nelson and Fredrickson homes. If the same man happened to be in both homes, I'll run the background check, and hopefully we'll find this bastard. Jack said he'd take the evidence to the detective working the case."

"Where is *your* handsome detective today?"

Holly started to argue, but the barely visible grin on Alexa's face made her realize the reference to Jack belonging to her was a trap. "Detective Tarek has active cases he's working on for the department. I'm taking the lead on this. He'll be by later."

Alexa sat in the chair across from Holly and stared at her in the way that Rene did when silently demanding information. Alexa wasn't nearly as good at breaking people as Rene, though. Alexa's talents were better used playing big sister, but that didn't work on a loner like Holly, either. She didn't have that unrelenting need to please a disapproving sibling.

"You like him," Alexa finally accused.

Holly tilted her head and cocked her brow—her go-to move that usually convinced people to spill their guts or back off a subject she didn't want to delve into. However, just as Holly was immune to Alexa's special power, Alexa was immune to hers.

Holly sighed and gave a nonchalant shrug. "I barely know him."

"And yet, he's getting to you."

"What makes you say that?"

"The way you stare at him."

She couldn't stop the way her brow creased as she denied the accusation. "I don't stare—"

"Bullshit. I watched you during dinner last night. You could barely take your eyes off him, and I don't blame you. He's as adorable as my abuela's chow chow. Not quite as hairy, though. At least I hope." She scrunched up her nose and shivered. "Hairy men creep me out."

Holly smiled but fell short of laughing. "I didn't realize you had standards for men."

Alexa dropped her mouth open at the jab. "And I brought you coffee."

"You did. Thank you."

"He seems like a nice guy."

"He does."

Alexa gave Holly an exaggerated frown. "You really need to work on your girl talk. I'm trying to dish about this hottie who is clearly into you, and you're not giving me an ounce of dirt."

Holly took a breath, very nearly confessing to her own attraction, but then snapped her jaw shut. The last thing she wanted was for her co-workers to be any more distracted by Jack than they already appeared to be.

Alexa didn't miss the sudden change of Holly's mind and sat forward, her eyes and her smile widening. "Nope. Uh-uh. Spit it out."

"What?"

"Damn it, Holly. Don't think I won't resort to torture to get this out of you. I will make you listen to Sam munch on those damned mints until you crack."

Holly should have laughed at the threat, but instead she frowned. She tapped her pen on the desk a few times before dropping it and looking at Alexa. "I'm not like you and Sam."

"You're not a slut?"

Holly's eyes widened. "What? No. That's not—"

"I'm kidding." Alexa grinned wickedly. "*I'm* not a slut."

Holly didn't take the opportunity to comment on Sam's always-active social life. "I meant I'm not good at...you know..."

"Sex?"

"*No.* Sex is the only part of being with a man that does come easy for me." She laughed softly, and her skin warmed as a flash of memory struck her—Jack pressing himself against her as they both groaned with release. "No pun intended."

Alexa simply lifted her dark brows suggestively.

"I've never been good at relating to people. Even when I was younger, before..."

"You relate to us just fine."

"That's different. You're my team. We have to know how to read each other. We have to trust each other. But I've always been on guard. I don't know how to relax and just...*be.* Jack... He makes me feel like I can let go a little, and that's nice."

"But it's also frightening," Alexa said gently.

Holly nodded. "Incredibly."

"I was a kid when my sister disappeared, but I remember the fear I felt. I remember the horror of never knowing what happened to her and wondering if whoever took her could still be out there just waiting for a chance to get me, too."

Holly closed her eyes and shook her head. "That's not what I mean. I'm not on guard for my physical safety, Lex. I just don't know how to let people in. Emotionally. Does that make sense?"

Understanding softened her eyes as she nodded. "Perfect sense. But you can't shut everyone out forever, Hol. At some point, you have to try to connect with someone. He likes you."

"He doesn't know me."

Alexa shrugged. "Sometimes you don't have to know someone to know you click. The way you two look at each other—the tension in the air when you are close—you click. And trust me, Rene looked into every dark corner of that man's life she could find. He's a good guy."

Holly wasn't surprised by the revelation that her co-workers had done a background check on Jack without her knowledge. As paranoid as she could be, Rene was tenfold.

"He's the kind of guy who still looks out for his mom and helps old ladies cross the street. A real Boy Scout kind of guy."

Holly bit her lip, debating whether she should tell Alexa she and Jack had kissed. She wasn't about to tell her the rest, but maybe Lex could help her sort out this mess of emotions going on inside if she knew half of the truth.

Alexa gasped and leaned so far forward in the chair, Holly was certain she could fall off the seat and land on her ass at any moment. "You slept with him."

"No," Holly snapped.

"Yes, you did! I can see the guilt on your face."

"No. We just... We kissed. A few times."

Alexa narrowed her eyes, and for the first time ever, that demanding sisterly look hit the mark with Holly.

She swallowed but couldn't stop herself from confessing. "Okay, it was more like severe heavy petting."

Alexa clapped and laughed. "Yes! How severe?"

"That's all you need to know."

"Clothes on or off?"

Holly widened her eyes. "On."

"Did he get his hand inside your shirt?"

"No."

"Your pants?"

"*No.*"

Some of Alexa's glee abated into clear disappointment. "So how was this junior-high-school-level heavy-petting session?"

Holly's cheeks started to burn. "Very good." She let a laugh leave her, something reminiscent of a giggle, if she were honest. "Very, *very* good. And it was more like... sophomore-year-level petting. I mean, it was a little adultish."

Excitement lit Alexa's eyes again. "Who started it?"

She drew a breath. She didn't want to share. She was a private person and never partook in the kiss-and-tell mentality of her friends, but then she said, "He did. In the conference room last night."

Alexa did that head-throwing, hand-clapping laugh thing again. "*Oh. Em. Gee*, Holly. That is awesome."

"No. It isn't awesome, Alexa." She lowered her voice to just above a whisper. "I practically screwed him in the conference room while you guys were in your offices working."

"Oh, honey, we weren't in our offices working. We were in the lobby eating Sam's candy and wondering how long before you two got down to business. You *are* going to screw him, aren't you?"

"God, I hope so," she muttered, surprising even herself. She closed her eyes as another round of Alexa's whooping laugh filled her office. "It's just..." Holly's amusement faded, and she shook her head slightly. Lifting her gaze to her friend, she sighed. "I sense that he's looking for more than a few rounds of inappropriate sex. I don't get the impression he's the fuck-buddy type. He's too...honorable for that. I'm actually surprised he made a move last night. That seems a bit soon for a guy like him."

"Oh, come on, Holly. First, the guy has a penis. No move toward sex is too soon as far as a penis is concerned. Second, don't act as if you don't want more. Everyone does, at least on some level. You aren't twenty anymore, honey. Even if you don't want the whole two-point-five kids locked behind a white picket fence thing, you have to want more in your life besides this team of crazy-assed women who try your patience for the fun of it. Wouldn't it be nice to have someone to go home to who could take your mind off all the shit we see here?"

She swallowed before confessing something she'd been denying. With a single nod of her head, she let Alexa in on her deepest secret. She did want more. She was tired of being on her own with no one to turn to. She was tired of feeling as if the weight of the world was hers alone to carry.

That simple move, that unspoken confession, struck a nerve, and the unfamiliar sensation of tears stinging her eyes surprised her. Blinking several times, she cleared her throat and looked at the papers scattered in front of her. "I've been digging into these women's lives, learning everything I can about them. They had everything, Lex. Husbands who loved them. Children they adored. Beautiful houses to call home." She lifted a photo of Penelope surrounded by smiling faces. "Friends they spent time with." She creased her brow as a light went off. "Wait a second." Sitting up, she started sorting through Julia's file.

Alexa leaned forward. "What?"

Instead of answering, Holly pulled out a photo and looked between the images for a moment, comparing the backgrounds behind each group of women—one that included Julia and the other that included Penelope—and then showed the photos to Alexa. "Does this look like the same place to you?"

Alexa took the pictures and did the same, looking from one to the other and back again several times. "Not only the same place but the same bartender."

Holly took the photos back. Lex was right. The same young, Caucasian, well-built man was serving drinks in the background.

"These women were taken in broad daylight. It didn't make sense before, but bartenders work nights, right? He'd have the time in the middle of the day *and* he's seen both women." She tapped the photos together and then smirked. "That's him. It has to be."

PATIENCE WASN'T AT THE TOP OF JACK'S LIST OF assets. As soon as Holly had e-mailed him copies of the photos, he'd taken them to the detective leading Penelope Nelson's case. That was enough to get the bartender on the radar. The lead detective, Jason Meyer, made some calls to the women's friends and located the bar. By six p.m., the bartender was brought in for questioning.

"It's gotta be him," Jack said for what was likely the tenth time since the detective had taken the man to interrogation. He looked at Holly, sipping yet another cup of terrible coffee from the carafe of the old-style coffee pot, and smiled—pleased they were going to be able to wrap up this case any time now. "Where do you want to go for dinner?"

She stopped drinking and lifted her brows at him over the paper cup.

"You did it. You found him. I owe you dinner." He smiled. "And more."

She hesitated before lowering her cup. There was a smirk on her lips, but she pushed it away. "We don't know that it's him."

"It's him."

"We don't *know* that. We haven't compared all the employees on their matching services. It could be—"

He ran his hand over her hair until he cupped the back of her head. She gasped and he smirked, pleased his bold move had surprised her. He liked getting those little reactions from her. He guessed very few people could conjure up those moments of shock before she quickly buried them behind her cool exterior. "It's him. He's going to tell us where to find them. Thanks to you." He started to pull her closer, forgetting where they were, forgetting the need for professionalism. He forgot everything except the need to feel her against him.

"Miss Austin?"

She jerked back from Jack's hold and faced the man who'd called out to her. "Mr. Fredrickson, what are you doing here?"

The way his face tensed as he looked between Holly and Jack was unmistakable. He was angry, and Jack suspected, from the glare on his face, Fredrickson didn't approve of the way Jack had been leaning in to kiss Holly.

"Is it true? Did you find the man who took Julia?"

Holly creased her brow. "We have a suspect. The police are questioning him now. How did you—"

"When you didn't answer your phone, I called the office. Whoever answered told me you were here."

Holly frowned. "Well, she shouldn't have done that. We don't know if this is the man who took your wife. We just noticed that he appeared in photos that both Mrs. Fredrickson and Mrs. Nelson had taken while at a bar with friends. It could just be a coincidence."

He looked at Jack again. "That's not what your boyfriend said."

The clip in his tone confirmed in Jack's mind that his annoyance was that he'd caught an intimate moment—even if it was just a touch—between the woman investigating his wife's disappearance and the detective helping her. Jack hadn't intended to cross the line of professionalism. It was just a moment, just a brief lapse in judgment. Guilt clouded over him as Fredrickson clenched his jaw, making the muscles in his face bulge.

"We don't know anything for certain yet," she said softly.

"I'm just trying to be positive," Jack said.

Fredrickson looked beyond Holly's head, and she and Jack turned to see what had distracted him. Their suspect was being led down a hallway toward them without any sign that he was still in custody. No handcuffs, no defensive cop, and no attorney. Jack exhaled as he glanced to Holly, checking to see if she was thinking the same thing. She clearly was by the way she looked at him with disappointment in her eyes.

This wasn't their guy.

"Is that him?" Fredrickson asked. Before either could confirm, he started toward the man. "Where's my wife, you son of a bitch?"

"Mr. Fredrickson." Holly blocked his way and put her hand to his chest. She gave him a sorrowful look, her eyes soft and her mouth dipped into a slight frown. "It's not him. I'm sorry."

Meyer walked by, narrowing his eyes at Holly and Jack. "He's got a rock-solid alibi for both kidnappings. This was a waste of our time."

Fredrickson let out a breath so hard his nostrils flared. Holly opened her mouth, but the man pointed a finger in her face. "I hired you to find my wife. You've had over two weeks now."

Jack wanted to again tell the man that she was doing all she could, but he opted to heed her previous warning that he not defend her honor. She could handle herself and anything Fredrickson threw her way.

"Yes, sir," she said softly.

"So stop drooling over this guy and do your goddamned job." He stormed out of the police station as Holly watched, hands on hips, before turning to face the other angry party waiting to lecture her on her mistake.

Meyer crossed his arms over his chest, looking at Jack just as hard as Fredrickson had looked at Holly. He didn't even try to hide his irritation, not that he ever did. This was one moody son of a bitch, and Jack had just tripped his trigger. "I need to see you, Tarek. Now."

"Detective," Holly started, "this is my fault." Her attempt at taking the blame went unanswered.

"Now, Tarek." Meyer stalked off.

"I'm so sorry," Holly whispered.

Jack pressed his lips together as he tilted his head, eyeing her curiously. "Were you just trying to protect me, Austin?"

She opened her mouth and then closed it.

He smirked, despite the shitstorm they'd just found themselves in. "So it's okay for you to jump to my defense, but I can't jump to yours?"

"But this *is* my fault. I brought the bartender to you, and you stuck your neck out by bringing him to the lead detective."

He shrugged, dismissing her justification for doing exactly what she'd warned him against. "I reviewed the evidence you brought to me and took said evidence to the lead detective because I agreed. I didn't do that for *you*. I did it for those two missing women."

Meyer cleared his throat from across the room.

Jack fought the urge to roll his eyes. "Time to face the music."

"Will you come see me when you're done?"

He smiled and winked. "Was planning to. Hey," he called when she started to leave. "This was the right call, Holly. Don't beat yourself up that it didn't pan out."

He watched her leave, taking a moment to appreciate her slender body before going to get his ass ripped for sticking his nose in where he had already been told it didn't belong.

9

HOLLY STARED at the files she had on Julia and Penelope. Nothing stood out. Nothing hinted at who had done this to them. She had *nothing*. The one lead she'd been convinced she'd found had ended up being a dead end that got Jack in trouble.

Standing in front of the whiteboard, she looked at the evidence she had collected. She needed to focus on the company she'd discovered that serviced both the Fredricksons and the Nelsons. She'd been so convinced that the bartender was the guy, she hadn't even followed up on the other leads. Now they'd have to wait until the next day to talk to the cable provider. One more day that Julia and Penelope might not have.

Damn it. Why hadn't she just let Jack handle the bartender while she took care of the other possibility? Why had she let herself get so damned confident that she'd found the man who'd done this? She should have known better than to put all her money on one bet. She shouldn't have gotten so cocky. She knew better than that.

"Beating yourself up?"

She looked over her shoulder at Jack. He looked more concerned about her wellbeing than his own. Frowning, not wanting to see the sympathy in his dark eyes, she scanned the board again. "Yeah. A little bit."

"Why?"

"You mean besides following the wrong lead and wasting even more precious time these women don't have while I simultaneously got Fredrickson's hopes up for no reason and your ass ripped for stepping all over another detective's investigation?" She finally worked up the courage to fully face him. "You okay?"

"Meyer doesn't intimidate me."

"Jack?"

Pushing himself from the doorframe, he stuck his hands in his pockets and strolled to her. "He gave me two options: I can stay out of his case or he'll file a complaint."

"So you're going to stay out of it."

He shook his head. "I promised my mother I'd help her friend."

"You did. You brought her case to me. Let me take it from here."

"No."

She held up her hand. "I won't screw up again."

Grabbing her hand, he pulled her the last step to close the distance between them. "You didn't screw up. You caught something that had slipped by all of us. It was a solid lead. It just didn't pan out."

"Which made it a bad lead and one that landed you in trouble."

"Stop." He gripped her sides, and somehow the suffocating guilt she'd been struggling with seemed a bit lighter. "You aren't responsible for every single thing that happens around you, Holly. My choice to take this to Meyer isn't on you. The fact that it was a dead end isn't on you. Whatever has happened to those women *isn't on you*. You can't control everything."

She tried to step back, but he dug his fingers just a bit deeper into her ribs, holding her still.

He bored his eyes into hers until she couldn't look away. "It's been a week now since Penelope went missing. We both know the likelihood of her coming home safe decreases every day. The fact that Julia has been missing for so long all but ensures that she's not coming home alive, Holly. You know that as well as I do, don't you?"

She closed her eyes. She didn't need to be reminded of the reality that was always lurking in the back of her mind. "Yes," she whispered. "I know."

"But do you know that isn't your fault? Look at me," he insisted when she kept her eyes closed.

She slowly lifted her lids, and the intensity in his near-black eyes deepened.

"Do you know that isn't your fault?" he repeated.

She drew a slow breath, hating that he was so good at reading her. Pushing his hands away, she moved to the whiteboard. "I'm going to call the cable provider and gardener first thing tomorrow. It has to be one of their guys. Because..." She turned and faced him. "If these were random kidnappings, we're screwed, Jack. We'll never find them now."

"Holly."

She shook her head and stepped around him to the table, where she had the files spread out. Planting her palms on the cool surface, she scanned over the papers and photos she'd reviewed a thousand times. "He chose them, right? There are too many similarities for him not to have chosen them. They represent someone. His wife or his mother. A sister. Someone who rejected him. Someone who hurt him. Maybe we should look for older cases. Maybe if we find the first victim—"

"That's a lot of digging, Holly."

"Well, we have to start thinking outside the box now, Jack. We have to start looking for a bigger picture."

"Not tonight. Not right now." He stepped beside her and rested his hand on the small of her back. "Right now, we need to get some rest and wait until morning, when we can follow these other leads. Right now, we need to clear our heads so we can think more clearly tomorrow."

She exhaled harshly as that fist of guilt gripped her again. "I wasted too much time today. I was so certain I had him that I didn't even follow up on anything else. I could have sent other members of my team to follow up on the other leads. But I didn't. I was so sure this was him. I cost them time. Time that could mean life or death. I could have killed them, Jack."

"Don't do that."

"You know I'm right."

He scoffed as he creased his brow and gave his head a hard shake. "Jesus, Holly, you can't save everyone. This man, whoever took them, you can't control him and what he does any more than you could control..." He gestured his arm wildly. "Any more than you could control whatever happened in the Army that made you leave."

His words hit a mark she hadn't even realized was vulnerable to him. She leaned back a bit and narrowed her eyes. "What?"

"You couldn't save everyone in your battalion—"

"This has nothing to do with—"

"And you can't save every missing person who comes across your desk. You aren't responsible for every single thing—"

"Enough!"

His words took her breath away and made her want to vomit until the unexpected waves of pain eased. Until the faces of every person she'd ever lost stopped rolling through her mind.

"You don't know me," she said with a quiet calm that sent a chill down her own spine. "You don't know anything about me."

She jerked away from him and paced as she tried to control the tornado of emotions whirling inside her. Who the hell did this guy think he was? Who the hell was he to stand there analyzing her, to tell her what she was and wasn't capable of? With her back to him, she put her hands low on her hips and drew a slow breath to calm herself. One-two-three. Exhale. One-two-three. Inhale.

Jack moved to her side and dipped his head down to look at her. "I know enough to see that you are blaming yourself for things you can't possibly control," he said gently. "And I know that kind of approach isn't healthy. Having an unyielding sense of responsibility for the world around us doesn't end well for people in our line of work."

She closed her eyes and shook her head. "Save your pep talk for the rookies, Tarek."

"Rookies aren't the only ones who need to be reminded they can't save everyone."

No. She couldn't save everyone. But she could have saved her mom. If she'd been brave enough, strong enough. She could have saved her mom if she hadn't been so scared.

As far as the members of her battalion... She was their leader. Their lives were her responsibility. Their deaths were on her hands. Her burden to carry.

The missing women... Someone had to be responsible for them. Someone had to shoulder the blame.

She swallowed as she tried to find the right words to tell him all that she was thinking. But there were none. Taking another deep breath, she ground her teeth together to stop the swell of emotion from filling her chest.

Jack put his hands on her shoulders and whispered her name.

The tenderness of his action sent another lightning bolt

of pain through her. She jerked around and shoved him as she felt hot tears drip from her eyes. "Leave."

"No."

She ground her teeth as every muscle in her body tensed. Pushing her breath out with a huff, she pointed to the door. "Leave!"

"*No.*"

He gripped her upper arms, gently holding her. Before he could say whatever Pollyanna bullshit was on his mind, she knocked his arms away and shoved him back several steps. She didn't verbalize her warning, but she silently dared him to touch her again. He either missed her warning or chose to ignore it. He reached out, aiming for her hips this time. She grabbed his wrist, twisted his arm, and had him turned and grunting—not in pain, but she had no doubt there was definite discomfort shooting through his muscles. She was expecting him to fight her, to get pissed off enough to try to get out of her hold. To push back so she could push even harder to release some of her pent-up frustrations.

He didn't. But he didn't give up, either.

"Tell me you don't blame yourself for every shit thing that has happened in your life," he said. "Tell me I'm wrong."

She leaned in close, bending his arm just a touch farther. "Are you done trying to touch me?"

"No." He proved he had his own set of defensive moves by turning and reaching for her with his free arm. Pulling her against him, he brushed his nose against hers. "I'm just getting started, Princess."

She jerked her arms, slamming her forearms against his, knocking him away, but he responded just as quickly. By the time she prepared to shove him away, he'd wrapped his fingers around her wrists and held her firmly to him, even when she twisted to get away.

Breathless, she stopped struggling before they both ended up bruised. "You don't know me, Tarek."

"I know you better than you think, *Austin*."

"No. You don't. Those women—"

"Are probably dead already. And that isn't on you, either."

His declaration took what was left of her breath away. She could no longer try to deny there was little to no hope in her heart that Julia Fredrickson was alive. She'd lost that hope the moment he'd walked into the conference room and shown her a picture of Penelope Nelson.

Julia was dead. Wherever she was. Wherever that man had taken her. She was gone now. Holly was convinced, and the guilt and shame she felt for not saving her was enough to make her knees go weak.

Sagging against Jack, she exhaled slowly. She didn't have any fight left in her after his reminder of what she already knew. She wanted to be comforted by his assurances that she wasn't to blame, but his words couldn't seem to breach the years of culpability she'd carried.

He stroked her hair. Kissed her head. Then whispered, "What happened to your mom, Holly?"

She slumped against him and closed her eyes, trying to stop the images that were coming at her like flaming arrows from the past. "She...she was murdered when I was eight. My dad was working third shift. We were watching TV before I went to bed, and someone kicked the back door in. Mom hid me behind the couch and told me not to come out. So I didn't. I could hear her screaming and him telling her to be quiet. Then I could see their feet in the space between the bottom of the couch and the floor as she tried to get away from him. He picked her up and threw her down and...climbed on top of her." She bit her lips, choking down the sob filling her. "I didn't understand what I'd witnessed until I got older."

"Jesus, Holly," he whispered.

The knot in the throat nearly choked her, but she managed to get the words out anyway, even though they sounded strained. "She kept screaming 'Help me! Please help me!' The entire time. When he was done, he stabbed her fourteen times. She stopped screaming after the third one." Clenching her jaw tight, she forced herself to swallow. "I didn't come out until my dad got home after he got off work. He found her and started yelling for me. When he pulled me from behind the couch, he tried to shield my eyes, but I saw her lying there covered in blood. She was staring at the ceiling, but...her eyes were empty. Dad had blood all over him, too, from trying to help her. It ended up on my nightgown and in my hair. I remember it was so sticky. I don't know how many hours went by, but...her blood was sticky. And the smell— The smell of blood still makes me sick."

"Holly."

She jolted when he touched her, pulling her from the image in her mind. "I was there, Jack. She was murdered right in front of me, and I didn't help her."

"You were a kid."

"Even so, I could have run. I could have opened the window and screamed."

"And he would have killed you, too."

She drew a breath. "I didn't even try. And when he left, I didn't go to her. I didn't get help."

"You were in shock."

"I failed her."

"No," he breathed. "You were *just* a kid."

Pulling from his hold on her, she turned and looked at the whiteboard but didn't see the notes she'd made there. "My dad blamed me. He never said so, but I could tell. He started drinking. Stopped talking to me. By the time I was thirteen, I was basically on my own. I took care of him the best I could, but I could feel his resentment. I still do."

"No, Holly—"

"*Yes, Jack.* I was young, but I was never stupid. I know what I saw in his eyes. That's why I left. Why I joined the Army. I didn't have any other way out, and I couldn't stay. The first time we came under attack in Fallujah, a boy—not much older than I was when my mother died—was kicking a ball down the street. I noticed him because the scene was so normal. Seeing him reminded me of home. The next thing I knew, all hell broke loose. I ran after the kid. How could I not try to save him? Before I could reach him, he was flat on his back with his chest full of shrapnel. He was gasping for air, but blood was coming from his mouth. And you know what he said? 'Help me. Please help me.' And I didn't."

"You *couldn't*. There is a difference."

She faced him. "No. There isn't."

"Your mom was murdered. Your dad *chose* to drink rather than deal with reality. That boy lived in a warzone. Julia Fredrickson disappeared weeks before her husband asked for your help. *Weeks*, Holly."

"Her husband came to me. He stood in this room, right here, and he said, 'Help me.' And I promised him—I *promised* him I would."

Cupping her face, Jack looked in her eyes. "You have tried. *We* have tried. And we aren't giving up. We are going to find them—dead or alive, we'll find them. But you aren't to blame. Do you understand me?"

"Jack—"

"You didn't kill your mother or that kid, and you didn't kidnap Julia."

She closed her eyes and lowered her face. She heard his words. Understood them. Even acknowledged their logic. But she didn't believe them. Something in her couldn't. "I didn't save them, either."

He put his finger under her chin and lifted until she looked at him. "You can blame yourself all you want. I can't stop you. But at some point, Holly, you have to accept that you can't save everyone." Brushing his hand over her hair, he started to lean in and then stopped. "Are you going to hurt me if I kiss you?"

Despite the dark cloud hanging over her soul, her lip twitched with the urge to grin. "That's a risk you're going to have to take."

"It's worth it." He put his mouth to hers, but unlike the day before, he kissed her sweetly, letting the tenderness linger. He kissed the corners of her mouth and then her forehead before hugging her to him.

She hugged him back. "Did I hurt you?"

"No."

"Hmm. I'll try harder next time." Laughing softly, she leaned back. "Just kidding. I'm sorry. I'm not good at this intimacy thing."

"Don't be sorry. Just remember that I get to pin you down next time." He smiled. "Let's get out of here so we can stop butting our heads against this particular wall. Just for a bit."

She couldn't do anything else to help Julia until she talked to the businesses that could lead to whoever had taken her. Nodding, she pulled away from him and then stopped at the conference room door and looked up at him. "I don't talk about my parents often. It hurts too much. Thank you for listening."

Dipping his head, he gently kissed her. "You can talk to me anytime. About anything." He hugged her to him for a few moments before guiding her out of the office.

"BRINGING ME TO YOUR APARTMENT WITH TAKEOUT isn't even subtle," Holly said as Jack unlocked his front door.

He grinned and lifted his brows as he pushed the door open and gestured for her to enter. She'd been quiet when they left her office, but the tension had started to ease out of her muscles as they sat at the pizza joint waiting for their order. He'd followed her there, but she had followed him to his apartment.

With the pizza in one hand and a six-pack of beer in the other, she stepped inside and blatantly looked around. "Nice place."

"I'd love to take credit, but my mom did everything. She even comes over to clean once a week. I won't deny that."

Holly smiled as she slid their dinner onto the table. "That's actually really sweet."

"You don't think it makes me a mama's boy."

"It definitely makes you a mama's boy, but coming from someone with no family, that's not a bad thing." Shrugging out of her black blazer, she turned and faced him as she draped the material over a chair. "You're close with her, then?"

He did the same and then put his badge and gun on the table. "I am. And I've told her to stop cleaning my house and cooking for me, but she feels it is her responsibility until I'm married."

"And then it's your wife's responsibility?" she asked with that defiant tilt to her brow as she cracked open a beer.

"As modern as my mother is, she still grew up in Egypt. There are different expectations of women in our culture. I don't share them," he said before kissing her. "First, I don't cling to religious tradition, much to my mother's dismay. Second, I like my women a little butch, remember?"

She laughed. "How does your mother feel about that?"

"I adore my mother, but it's not her decision who I get involved with."

She swallowed another gulp of beer. "Glad to know there's a line in that mother–son relationship. There's being a mama's boy, and then there's being a *mama's boy*. The first is sweet. The second is a giant red flag being waved as flares explode."

Laughing, he carried the pizza to the couch and dropped it on the coffee table before plopping onto the plush cushions. As she sat next to him, setting a bottle of beer in front of him, he flipped the top off the box and grabbed a slice. "I'm assuming you don't need a plate?"

"Real women eat with their hands."

He nodded his agreement before stuffing his mouth full. "Just one more thing I respect about you."

"You know all about me now," she said, sounding a bit uncertain as she skimmed over the pizza before reaching for the slice with the most pepperoni. "Tell me more about your mom."

"You remind me of her. In good ways," he quickly clarified. He took a long pull of his beer before continuing.

"She's the strongest woman I know. Well, one of them anyway." He winked at Holly.

She shook her head before saying around her food, "You give me too much credit."

"I don't."

Swallowing hard, she grabbed her beer. "You do. But we're talking about your mother. What makes her so strong?"

"My father didn't stick around after she got pregnant, and her family was ashamed of her for not being able to keep him happy."

"She was shunned."

"You know how some religious traditions can be. I don't just mean Islam—any religion can show antiquated thoughts—but in a place like Egypt, those views can run deep. She didn't have anyone to defend her. She came here to live with her cousin. I'm sure her family thought it was a great punishment, but America was much more accepting of single mothers." He stuffed what was left of his crust into his mouth.

"She is a strong woman."

He picked up a second slice. "Yeah, but her cousin was great. She got Mom a job at a bakery. She's been there all these years. She works long hours, but her boss respects her and treats her well. She's been his business manager for a long time."

Holly smiled. "That is nice." She wiped her hands on a napkin. "So how'd you grow up to be a cop?"

He frowned as he dropped his pizza back into the box.

"I got in trouble when I was a teenager. Some asshole at school started talking shit about Muslims and saying some pretty terrible things about my mom and her cousin after they came to a basketball game wearing hijabs. I beat the living shit outta that kid. Then it happened again. And a third time." He laughed, but the sound held tones of regret. "I was on the verge of being expelled, but this counselor stood up for me. Said it was wrong that I got in a fight but it was more wrong that the school wasn't punishing the kids who were discriminating against my family. He taught me there were other ways to deal with people like that. One was to defend people. In the right way. I thought about college, but the financial burden that would put on my mom was too much. So I went to the police academy instead."

"Well, it worked out right. You're a good cop."

"You would have been a good cop, too, you know."

She shook her head. "I'm in the right place. It's tough sometimes, but this is where I should be. HEARTS fits me. Even if I do hate the damn name."

Laughing as he sat back, he pulled her with him. She rested her head on his chest, and he kissed her head. An unexpected sense of warmth spread through him. Not just lust—he could grasp his lust; this was something else altogether. That same damn nagging that he'd started feeling the first time he'd seen her. Like he'd been waiting his entire life for her to come into it. Running his hand over her hair, he pressed his lips to her head again. "I don't understand this," he whispered.

"What?"

"I feel like this is where we're meant to be. The moment I first looked into your eyes—"

"You mean after I released you and lifted you off the floor?" she asked lightly, clearly trying to lessen the intensity his words had draped over them, but he wasn't going to allow that. Not right now, not when he needed to say what he'd been thinking.

Brushing his fingers over hers, he pressed on. "Yeah. That's what I mean. HEARTS fits you, but *you* fit me. In a way I can't explain." He swallowed at the silence that followed his declaration.

Finally she leaned back and met his gaze. "You don't have to sweet-talk me, Jack. I'm here. I'm interested in... whatever is going on here. But I'm not interested in lies or hollow promises. You don't have to lie your way between my legs. Okay. Just know that."

He probably should have been offended by the underlying accusation in her words, but he wouldn't have expected any less from her. She wanted him to know where she stood. Ready and willing for the sex they both knew was inevitable. But despite her leaving the door open, he wasn't in this for a quick lay. He wouldn't turn one down, but he actually thought they deserved to give each other more than that.

"Those weren't pretty words to get you into bed," he said honestly. "That was me telling you something that I've been wrestling with all week. The fact that I feel it so intensely after just a week is terrifying, but at the same time, being with you feels right. Like this is where I should have been all along."

She lowered her face and inhaled slowly, clearly debating how to respond. Finally she met his gaze. "I don't get it, either. But I *do* feel it." She spoke quietly, as if saying the words aloud would somehow negate what she was feeling. "I'm connected to you in some way that I don't understand. It took me months to tell Alexa about my mom. The rest of my teammates don't even know what I witnessed. But I wanted to tell you the day we met. I wanted you to understand why I'm so hardened. I don't usually care what people think of me. Actually, I prefer they don't like me so they keep their distance, but... I wanted *you* to understand. I *need* you to understand."

She gave him what was probably the most flirtatious smile she could muster, and it lit him on fire. The half smile, the hazy look in her eyes, the slight blush on her cheeks—everything about her in that moment made him want her even more, which he hadn't thought possible.

He tucked her hair behind her ear and lightly traced his finger around the rim before sliding his hand to cup her face. "I do understand, Holly. And I still want you," he whispered.

Her smile widened. "Good. Because I'm going to take you."

He laughed quietly. Even in professing their desire for the other, she was pushing her dominance. And he was more than okay with that. Something about her approach didn't make him feel like he was being subordinate to her—

not that he had a problem with being the weaker half. Knowing she was letting him in when she seemed to keep everyone else out was an honor he intended to cherish.

He grabbed her arm and tugged. "Come here," he whispered.

She moved, straddling his hips and looking down into his eyes as he leaned back on the couch. His heart did a funny little thump as she touched his cheek, brushing her fingers over his whiskers while she searched his eyes. If she was looking for hesitation, she wasn't going to find it. He wanted her more than he could remember ever wanting anyone else.

He tightened his hold on her hips but didn't push. She wasn't one to be pushed. Finally, she dipped her head down and kissed him softly. He wanted so much more than just a light brushing of her mouth on his. He wanted to pull her in, devour her, but he knew her well enough to know he needed to let her set the pace. Even if her pace was driving him insane.

After several moments of teasing caresses with her lips, she pushed her tongue into his mouth. The sensation shot straight to his groin, and he rolled up into her, unable to resist the urge. She responded in kind, grinding against him. But then she broke the kiss, leaving him needing more.

In true Holly fashion, she grasped his hair to stop him from leaning up to catch her mouth again. She smirked as she sat just out of his reach. "I think I let you have enough control last night, don't you?"

He wanted to protest when she stood, but then she

tugged her shirttails from her slacks. Starting at the bottom —likely because she knew the seduction was absolute torture—she released the buttons along her shirt one at a time but stopped short of revealing her body to him.

"Are you trying to make me lose my mind?" he asked when she stood staring at him with a smart-assed grin tugging at her lips.

"Maybe."

She finally parted the front of her blouse, and heat rushed through his body. Damn, she looked good. He'd known from the way she'd assaulted him that she was in shape, but without her shirt, he could actually see the muscle definition. Her abs weren't cut into a six-pack, but she was toned and her stomach was taut, and he had a damned hard time remembering how to breathe as he took her in.

The material slipped from her body, and Jack sat forward to reach for her. In response, she lifted her low-heel-covered foot and rested her shoe precariously close to his erection. She cocked her brow in the way that made him crazy—a silent warning that he wasn't to even think about touching her until she was damn good and ready for him to.

He exhaled a mixture of disappointment and excitement. No woman had ever tried to control sex this way. He wouldn't have guessed being bossed around was such a turn-on. Sinking back, he swallowed, waiting for her next move.

"Unzip my boot," she instructed.

He did. Then she switched feet, putting her other foot dangerously close to his groin, and he eased that zipper down. She stepped out of her boots and then released the button on her gray slacks. She pushed her pants over her hips, where they joined her blouse, socks, and boots. And then she was standing before him in a lacy nude-colored bra-and-panty set with her breasts pushed high in the cups.

Shit. He swallowed hard as she moved to him.

"Don't," she warned when he lifted his hands to touch her defined thighs.

Dropping his hands back to his sides, he let his head roll back. "I'm beginning to think I don't like you so much anymore."

She made a show of looking at his erection. "Part of you seems to think I'm okay."

He blew out his breath. "I'm not finishing in my pants this time."

"No. You're not." Putting a hand on either side of his head, she leaned in and breathed in his ear. "You're not finishing *anywhere* until I give you permission."

"Jesus, woman," he said with a moan.

"Hands behind your head, Detective."

He stared at her for a few rapid heartbeats before complying.

"Good boy." She rewarded him by untucking his shirt.

He watched her face as she released button after button and then finally pushed his shirt open. She smirked as she brushed her hand over the dark curls of hair that surrounded each of his nipples. Pushing herself back, she stood and grabbed his shirt to pull him up. She certainly liked manhandling him. He'd remind her of that when it was his turn to take control—and he *would* have his turn.

Standing with her, he let her push his shirt off his shoulders. After she tossed it aside, she tugged his belt free. He toed off his shoes as she released the clasp on his slacks and eased them down.

"That's better," she whispered when he was standing in his underwear before her. Turning her back, she pulled her hair aside, revealing a tattoo of a bald eagle, wings proudly spread, between her shoulders. "Unhook my bra."

He closed the little bit of space between them, standing far closer to her than necessary to do the task she had requested. He inhaled deeply as he stood inches from her exposed skin. *Shit.* He would swear he could smell her excitement, and his body started aching with his need for her.

If she didn't give him relief soon, he was going to have to beg, and much like the night before, he wasn't above doing so. He took advantage of the need to slide the straps down her arms and pressed his body against hers. She gasped as he pressed his erection against her, and he smiled as he realized she was suffering as much as he was.

After dropping her bra, he put his lips to her ear. "Now what?"

"Now you finish undressing yourself."

He did as he watched her hook her thumbs into the waistband of her panties.

Please, he silently begged. A moan slipped from him as

she finally let the thin material drop. Jesus, she was gorgeous.

"Let me see the rest of you," he said softly.

She looked at him over her shoulder and offered him a coy smile. "Say please."

"Please."

She faced him, and he had to tighten his hands into fists to stop himself from grabbing the most perfect breasts he'd ever seen. Barely more than a handful but perky and topped with rosy areolas that surrounded pebbled nipples he was willing to beg to suck. He licked his lips and let his gaze drift down to the juncture of her legs, where she had a neatly trimmed patch of light pubic hair.

"How long before I can touch you?"

She grinned. "I'm not sure. But if you're good, I may let you touch yourself."

He groaned. "This game isn't as fun as it was a few minutes ago."

She tilted her head and made a point of looking at his crotch. "Again, your body disagrees with you."

He gasped as she touched him where she'd just been looking, rubbing her thumb over the tip. He held his breath as he jolted at the sensations she was sending straight to his groin. He didn't breathe again until she pulled her hand back. But then she put her thumb in her mouth and closed her eyes as she sucked the pre-ejaculate away and moaned that damned moan of hers that made him crazy.

"That's it." His warning wasn't even out of his mouth before he reached for her. He tugged her to him and dug one hand into her hair as the other went around her waist. Pulling her naked body against his, he kissed her hard and deep.

She responded just as desperately, moving her mouth and tongue over his. He lowered his hand, grasping her naked ass and pulling her closer to him. He wanted to feel more, touch more, but she put her hand to his chest and pushed him back.

"Condom?"

"Condom," he whispered as he tried to understand the word she'd said through his haze of lust. "Oh, right. Condom." He grabbed his slacks and reached into his pocket. Pulling out his wallet, he found a packet and grinned at her. "I'm not going to say I put that in there after our conference-room wrestling match, but I'm not going to deny it, either."

"Always thinking ahead," she said as he tore the packet open. "Wait. Let me."

"Holly." He didn't think he could possibly take the torment of her hands sliding over him again, but she snatched the condom from him and pushed him back onto the couch. Then she kneeled before him and his balls tightened. "If you put your mouth anywhere near that thing, I can't promise what will or *won't* happen." He was getting used to that mischievous light in her eyes, but this time he wasn't sure he wanted to see it. "I could come in your mouth."

"I hope not. Then who would screw me."

He closed his eyes and rolled his head back as she

tempted fate and lowered her head. Her breath caressed him intimately.

He exhaled slowly. "We're really going to have a love/hate relationship, aren't we?"

She laughed quietly before the warmth of her mouth surrounded him. He ground his teeth together and hissed as he fought the need to ram himself down her throat. Digging his hands in her hair, he fisted the strands in an attempt to control himself. She slid her mouth over him until he hit the back of her throat and then pulled her head back and sucked him in again.

"Oh, baby, you gotta stop," he warned after just a few seconds. "I mean it."

She leaned back and met his gaze as she licked her lips. After sliding the condom over him, she crawled up his body.

"Thank God," he breathed, knowing he was about to be inside her. Pulling her to him, he kissed her hard and shoved his hand between her legs, finding her hot and wet. He slid his fingers deep inside her as his palm rubbed over her clitoris. She broke the kiss and rolled her head back, exposing her neck to him. He kissed her there, licked her skin, nipped at her, all while pumping his hand in and out of her slick body.

She gasped and moaned as he cupped her breast. He captured her nipple between his lips and flicked his tongue over the taut flesh.

Her body tensed, her breathing intensified, and her

back arched, telling him all he needed to know. She was definitely enjoying his touch.

"Harder," she breathlessly demanded.

He shoved his fingers deeper and faster until she cried out and quivered around him. As her orgasm ended, he released her nipple and pulled his hand from her body. But only long enough to guide her down onto him. He wasn't about to let the waves subside. He wanted her to finish again and again.

A strangled sound erupted from her as he pulled her all the way down. Looking at him, she met his gaze, and all signs of mischief had left her eyes. She wasn't playing anymore. Neither was he. Gripping her hips, he guided her up and down as she rocked, and ground, and dug her nails into him, and called his name, and, holy shit, bit his neck.

He grunted as her teeth sank into his skin. He couldn't hold off any longer. She'd toyed with his body far too much for him to be able to control himself now. Thrusting his hips up as he pulled her down, he exploded into the condom as she threw her head back and cried out.

Her body spasmed for several seconds after he finished, and he took that opportunity to watch her breasts heave in his face. When she finally relaxed and looked at him, they shared a quiet laugh. He brushed her mussed hair back and pulled her in for a kiss.

"I knew that was going to be good, but damn," he whispered.

She moaned her appreciation before falling forward and curling into him. He instantly wrapped his arms around her. He suspected it was a rare thing for her to submit to such a vulnerable position. She didn't seem like the cuddling type, so he wasn't missing this opportunity. Kissing her head, he held her tight.

"This is perfect," she whispered.

"Yes, it is."

As he suspected, it didn't last. She leaned back and smiled at him before kissing him lightly and pushing herself up. "Shower?"

He pointed to the back of his apartment and sat, completely spent, while he watched her naked body stroll away. Sighing with complete contentment, he slowly pushed himself up and followed her. Hell, he realized, he'd follow her anywhere.

10

HOLLY NEVER REGRETTED WAKING up alone. She preferred it. Until this morning. Loneliness stung her as soon as she woke up enough to remember she'd left Jack's bed after a second round of amazing sex. Her body ached in all the right places, except for some strange twinge in her chest. Being alone had never felt as wrong as it did when she looked at the left side of the bed—the side Jack had been asleep on when she'd slithered from his bed and out of his apartment like a coward.

She had wanted to stay. She'd wanted to curl up against his bare skin and absorb his warmth. She'd wanted to listen to his even breathing and let it soothe her into her own deep sleep. She'd wanted to feel his arms around her as she woke instead of this emptiness that had hit her nearly as hard as she'd hit him when she'd slammed him to the ground in the conference room.

Staring at the ceiling, she debated sleeping in instead of

going for her morning run. Her mental tug of war inside her quickly died as she refocused on Jack. She dragged her hand down her body, her nipples tightening under her T-shirt as her body remembered every touch from the night before.

She'd taken control, refusing to let him put his hands on her, because she didn't want him to see her crumble and she was certain she would. He had a way of reaching her that no one had since her mother died, and that didn't make sense to her. She barely knew the man, but he knew her, saw through her, and that set her on edge.

The way he'd looked at her as she'd undressed before him had nearly done her in. He wasn't just seeing her body; he was looking into her soul, and she couldn't comprehend how he'd done that. She'd never been so damned bossy in foreplay, but taking control had been a hell of a turn-on. And she could see how much Jack had liked her assertiveness as well. She wasn't sure how far he'd let her take it, but she thought she'd taken it just far enough.

By the time he slid his fingers inside her, she was ready to explode. She squeezed her thighs together as her body started to tingle at the memory. Fucking him on the couch... because that was what they'd done...had been amazing, but when they'd gotten out of the shower and Jack had backed her to the bed, they'd made love.

It hadn't been the slow, sensual kind of making love. He'd been determined to regain some of his dominance, clearly trying to put them back on even ground in that area. He'd been on top, he'd set the pace, and he'd held her gaze as they'd finished together. He'd stared down at her, seeing inside her, taking a part of her that she hadn't been ready to give—that maybe she didn't even know was there to take.

For reasons she didn't understand, she felt incomplete waking up without him.

Knowing she'd never get back to sleep, she rolled out of bed and shuffled to the bathroom. After using the toilet and brushing her teeth, she went back to her bedroom to dig through her dresser for something to go running in. The weather was changing to fall, and she found herself in need of more than just shorts and a T-shirt for her morning run but not quite ready for sweats.

She caught her breath when someone knocked on her door. That didn't happen often. A glance at the clock on her nightstand verified that it was too early for visitors. Ten till six. Grabbing her robe, she slid her arms into the sleeves as she left the bedroom and padded across the hardwood floor to the front door. She peered through the peephole as she worked on knotting the sash around her waist. She gave up and smiled when she saw who was standing on the other side.

Releasing the chain lock and then the deadbolt, she opened the door and smiled at Jack. "What are you doing here?"

"Well, I had intended on taking you to breakfast, but since I woke up alone, I decided to bring breakfast to you."

She refused to feel guilty, but that didn't stop her from feeling embarrassed. "I didn't have clean underwear at your house."

"Something tells me you're the kind of woman who keeps an extra set of clothes—including clean underwear—in a bag in her trunk."

She lifted her brow, hoping to feign denial, but she did indeed have a bag in her trunk that contained not only a full set of clean clothes but toiletries as well. She could have stayed with him. She *should* have stayed with him.

He distracted her from her regret by lifting a bag from a fast food place not far from her house and a drink holder with two large coffees. She opened the door all the way and moved aside to let him in. He stepped across the threshold, stopping to kiss her before going farther into the house.

"So," she said as she turned the deadbolt, "since my number and address are unlisted, I'm guessing you abused your power with the police department to find me."

"There is a strong possibility you could be correct." He glanced around her entryway. "You don't have a security system?"

"I have a black belt in martial arts, I'm a United States Army veteran, and I carry a gun. I *am* my security system."

He wanted to argue her logic—she could see the disapproval on his face—but he had the sense to keep it to himself. She gestured toward the dining room that she rarely used. So rarely used, in fact, the table was covered with images of Julia Fredrickson and Penelope Nelson and notes and maps and clippings from the newspapers with stories about the missing women.

Jack took a few moments to look at the table and then

faced her. "I think we should eat on the couch. That certainly worked out well for us last time."

"I concur." She led him to the living room and dropped onto the couch.

He sat next to her, putting their breakfast on the coffee table. "So why did you sneak out?"

"I didn't sneak."

"Well, you didn't say goodbye, either." He held up two breakfast sandwiches.

She snatched the egg sandwich. "You were sleeping." The frown on his face let her know he wasn't buying it. "I wasn't sure if you wanted me to stay and if I did stay...what that meant."

"It would have meant that we'd had an amazing evening and slept soundly until morning." He ate half of a hash brown in one bite as he looked at her while she focused on sipping her coffee. "You think I'm coming on too strong."

"I didn't say that," she insisted. And he wasn't. He was coming on just right. She just didn't know how to handle everything he was stirring up inside her.

"You don't have to, Holly. I get you. I do. And I like you. A lot. But we don't really know each other, and you aren't comfortable staying at my place. I respect that. But I don't respect you sneaking out."

"Like I said, Tarek—I didn't sneak. You were asleep." She put her drink down, not wanting to debate the semantics of her leaving. "Look, I wasn't going to crash at your place after our first—whatever. But to be honest, I hated waking up alone. I really did."

"So did I."

"This case is stirring up things from my childhood that are better left in the dark. I'm not feeling quite myself these days. I don't know how much of what I'm feeling for you is tied to that and how much of it is genuine. Does that make sense?"

He nodded. "You were vulnerable after the bartender lead didn't work out and telling me about your past."

She lifted her brow at him, not sure if she should be amused or offended. "I was *vulnerable*?"

He shrugged slightly. "You were upset. I shouldn't have taken advantage of that."

She smirked. Amused. She should definitely be amused. "*Oh.* You took advantage of me?"

A grin tugged at his lips. He must have realized how ridiculous the notion was. No one took advantage of Holly Austin.

"Definitely," he said softly. He lowered his gaze, skimming over her bare legs until he stopped to unashamedly stare at her crotch.

Checking to see what had him so captivated, she smiled at the sight of her dark blue underwear peeking out from beneath her T-shirt. A fire started low in her belly and spread throughout her until her nipples hardened and her breath became shallow.

She tilted her head and looked at him. "You definitely shouldn't do that anymore." She spread her legs farther apart as he continued to watch. "I mean, if you respected me, you would never even consider taking advantage of me. Would you?" She ran her hand along her bare thigh and over her satin-covered crotch.

"Definitely not," he said, clearly fascinated by her fingers.

Leaning back, she spread her legs even more as she forced a pout to her voice as if she were a bombshell in a porno. "Men who take advantage of vulnerable women should be punished."

He finally looked at her face. "And to think I went out of my way to bring you breakfast."

"I got your breakfast right here."

She laughed as he moved faster than she'd ever seen a man move before. Her underwear was off and he had his face between her legs in seconds, turning her laughter into a deep moan. She dug her fingers into his hair as he pushed his tongue between her folds and tasted her. Closing her eyes, she dropped her head back and bit her lip hard as he nipped at her clit, sending shockwaves through her entire being.

Damn, he was good. Really, *really* good.

She inhaled sharply as he slid two fingers inside her, pumping as he flicked his tongue over the overly sensitive bud of nerves. She pressed his head deeper between her legs and rolled her hips up to meet him. A grunt started low in her chest and pushed its way out as an orgasm slammed through her. She hadn't even had enough warning to fully enjoy the overpowering spasm. Her body just tensed out of nowhere, making her want to scream.

She didn't know when or how he'd gotten his slacks to his knees, but when she finally caught her breath and looked at him, he had a condom packet pinched between his hands. She met his gaze and clenched her teeth to stop herself from begging him to hurry as he tore the foil open. She needed to feel him buried deep inside her, needed to feel his breath and hands on her as she fell over the edge again.

He got on his knees—still wearing his dress shirt and dark blue tie—and grasped her calves, resting them on his shoulders. Seeing him like that, a hunger in his eyes as his lips glistened from his taste of her, made it that much better when he shoved himself as far inside her as he could with one hard, solid thrust. He stared at her, a powerful and demanding look in his eyes, as he pulled out and slammed into her again.

She smirked, not really meaning to taunt him, but he must have taken it that way, because the determination on his face grew as he fucked her harder. She wanted to close her eyes and relish in the feel of him but refused to break his stare. She knew he wasn't trying to dominate her—not in the true sense of the word—but letting him feel like he'd won some small sexual battle between them wasn't something she was ready to do yet.

Instead, she tugged her shirt up and cupped her breasts as he watched. The fire in his eyes grew as the muscle in his jaw tightened. She clenched her body tight around him as he slid in and out of her.

"Shit. Holy shit." He breathlessly thrust harder.

She'd decided the victory was hers—she'd won—and closed her eyes as she let the feel of him overtake her. The sound of their bodies smacking against each other and the sound of him nearing his peak filled her ears. Pinching her nipples hard, she cried out. She thought she said his name, demanded he screw her harder, possibly even screamed, but she couldn't be sure. Her mind came completely undone as she finished, and she lost all sense of self until he eased her legs down and collapsed on top of her, planting a lazy kiss on her lips.

She licked his lips, tasting herself on him. That had never been something she'd cared to do before, but in that moment, it was so perfect. *He* was so perfect, and that caused a battle of emotions somewhere deep inside her.

Laughing softly, she wrapped her arms and legs around him. "Your suit is going to smell like sex."

"Good," he said in her ear. "I want that part of you with me all day." Planting several kisses along her neck, he finished the trail with a light peck on her lips. "You're spoiling me."

She ran her fingers over his permanent scruff. "I'm spoiling myself, Jack. You're just benefiting from it."

"I can live with that." One more kiss, and he pushed himself up.

She moaned as he left her body. Pointing toward the hall, she said, "Bathroom's that way."

By the time he'd returned, she'd put her underwear back on and was eating her now-cold breakfast.

He plopped down beside her and took a drink of his coffee. "What's your plan for today?"

"I'm going to call the cable provider as soon as I get to the office. I'm hoping they will tell me which of their employees had contact with Fredrickson and Nelson. If any of them match, I'll run a background check and see what I find."

"If any of them match, call me. I'll go question them."

"Jack—"

"Look, they probably won't talk to you. They won't feel obligated to. I have a badge I can flash at them."

"A badge that you'll be abusing if you flash it at them. Meyer told you to keep off his case."

"Let me deal with Meyer. He's worried I'll compromise the case because of my personal attachment, but I'm not an idiot. I know how to handle evidence and witnesses without tainting his investigation."

"I don't want you losing your job."

He brushed his hand over her hair. "You let me worry about that. If you find probable cause for us to look deeper into someone, then we're looking deeper into someone. I can't toss it at Meyer again, not until we have something solid. If I solve his case for him, he can't give me shit. Right?"

She frowned, seriously doubting his logic. "I don't know where to look after this, Jack. If we hit another dead end, I'm just not sure what is left."

"Let's turn our attention back to the businesses on the volunteer list," he suggested. "We got distracted from that, but someone from the shelter had to have given Julia a sticker. Someone took the photos of her with the dogs."

Holly raked her hand through her hair. "Maybe..."

"What?"

She hated to say it. She'd spent so much time convincing herself that Julia was perfect. "Maybe she has a lover who is a volunteer at the shelter. He could have gotten her that sticker and taken a bunch of pictures of her to send to her husband on Tuesday mornings to cover their tracks. To make her alibi seem solid."

He nodded. "So we start sorting through the business employees and see if one of them fesses up to knowing Julia."

"That's a long list of local businesses," Holly said.

Jack gave her a quick kiss. "Then I guess we'd better get started."

JACK WAITED FOR HOLLY TO JOIN HIM IN FRONT OF her car.

"Are you sure about this?" she asked as he started for the building.

"Yup."

"You could get in serious trouble for this."

"Yup." Even so, he opened the front door to the small office that Appleseed Landscaping company used. Holly met his gaze as she walked in, frowning her disapproval. She'd been doing that ever since he'd shown up at HEARTS and insisted he go with her as they hit the businesses on the shelter's volunteer list. He couldn't quite stop his gaze from dropping to her ass as she stepped into the building, but he recovered quickly, remembering they were there on business. The cable service provider wouldn't give Holly names, but they did confirm two different men had worked inside the Nelson and Fredrickson homes, eliminating them from their shrinking pool of suspects.

Almost every company on the volunteer list was happy to offer up the names of employees who took advantage of the opportunity to help the shelter. There were only a few who said that information wasn't available. Appleseed was one of them. The woman on the phone had clammed up as soon as Jack identified himself as a police detective.

Jack smiled at the woman behind the desk. Her name plaque confirmed she was the same person he'd talked to earlier. Seeing her in person made his heart pick up its pace, though. She perfectly fit the description for both Penelope Nelson and Julia Fredrickson. Early forties. Shoulder-length blond hair. Blue eyes. A glance at Holly confirmed that she had noticed as well.

"Hi, Susan," he said to the receptionist. "I'm Detective Tarek. I called earlier."

She gave him a nervous smile as she cast a glance at Holly. "Detective, I told you all I could on the phone."

He took note of her words. *Could.* Not *knew.* She'd told him everything she *could.*

"I know, and I appreciate that so much. My friend and I just happened to be in the neighborhood, so I thought I'd drop by. See if maybe you *could* tell me something else."

She exhaled as she glanced around. The lobby was empty, but muffled voices drifted from somewhere in the back of the building. "I'll lose my job," she said quietly. "My husband had to cut back his hours after hurting his back. I've got kids in college. I *need* this job."

Leaning on the partition between them, he held her gaze. "We've got two missing women. The only link we have—the only *hope* we have of finding them—is here. I just need your help finding out who may have volunteered at the shelter."

She licked her lips and glanced around again. "We have a small team. They all rotate the responsibility."

"Okay. That's a start. You happen to have a photo of this small team?"

She shrank back in her seat. "There's one on our website."

He looked at Holly. She was already tapping away at her smartphone. A moment later, she turned the phone to him. Two men fit the very loose description they had from the security footage. He took her phone, turned the screen to Susan, and pointed at one man.

"Who is this?"

Susan again scanned the room before quietly answering, "John Middleton. He's the owner."

"And this?"

"Vance Pearson."

The way she said the last man's name, how she lowered her gaze and almost whispered, set Jack on edge. "Have you ever had problems with Vance Pearson, Susan?"

She didn't respond.

He opened his mouth, but Holly put her hand on his arm and jerked her head, indicating that he should step away. The last time she'd dismissed him had been with Gary Nelson and Jack had been furious, but he understood this time. Women who had been victims of harassment tended to shy away from sharing details with men. He stepped away but not out of hearing range.

"Susan," she gently pressed, "tell me about Vance."

The woman scoffed. "It's nothing. You know how men can be."

"He's been harassing you?"

Jack glanced back, but when Susan caught him, clearly embarrassed, he turned his back, giving her as much privacy as he could without leaving. He wanted to hear what she had to say.

"He comes in, strutting around, hovering. He made me uneasy, but he never crossed the line until..."

"Until?" Holly pressed.

"About two months ago. We always took the shelter dogs to the dog park and let them run since they spend so much time in cages. While we were watching them, he cornered me. Started saying how much he wanted to..." She closed her eyes as her cheeks turned bright red. "I pushed him away, and he grabbed me like... I thought he was going to kiss me. Before he could...do whatever he intended, the dogs started barking at someone coming to the park, so I was able to get away from him. I went to my boss as soon as we got back, but he wouldn't do anything, so I told my husband. He brought me to work the next day and confronted Vance. My husband's a big guy. Vance was intimidated. He's kept his distance from me since, but I've caught him staring at me when he comes in. I've been looking for another job, but I can't quit until I have one. We've got two kids in college," she justified again. "We need my income."

"I get it," Holly said. "I do. Other than that one instance, has Vance ever threatened you or made you feel threatened?"

She hesitated. and even though Jack wasn't looking at her, he could tell there was more she wasn't sure about telling Holly.

"He's a charmer," Susan finally said. "He has this way of coming on to you without you even realizing it. Do you know what I mean?"

"Yeah."

"Before you know it, he's in your space, touching you, and you didn't even realize you'd done something to make him think it was okay."

"Hey," Holly said with a soft sternness, "you didn't do anything wrong."

Lowering her voice to the point that Jack had to hold his breath and focus to hear her, Susan whispered, "I thought he was just...being friendly. Friendlier than most. I was pretty comfortable around him, so I didn't...I didn't realize what he was doing. I refused to volunteer after that. I'm not sure who helped him then, but if he kept going to the dog park, he couldn't have handled it alone."

Julia. Jack realized Holly had come to the same conclusion as he had when she glanced at him. Somehow Vance had lured Julia into helping him and convinced her she was volunteering for the shelter. Handing her a sticker would certainly convince most, and—a tactic used on so many children—telling her that he had a puppy to show her would easily tempt her to go to his vehicle.

"Susan," Holly said again, "if he got out of line, that is not *your* fault."

"He came in one day and got real close, but I didn't think much about it because he was like that. Then he leaned down and whispered in my ear that he could see my nipples pressing against my shirt and he was glad I was as turned on as he was. It was freezing in here. That had nothing to do with him. I told him to back off. That he'd crossed the line. He just laughed. After that, he got it in his head that I liked him, so he always found a way to come in the office alone and say things he shouldn't."

"And your boss knew this was happening?"

She nodded. "John is Vance's uncle. He said Vance was just being a guy and I needed to toughen up." She frowned. "Vance gave me the creeps before, but after my husband confronted him, he really started to scare me. He looks *so* mean. I'm afraid to be alone with him."

"You think he's capable of hurting you?"

Jack glanced back in time to see her nod.

"Do you have any other information on him?"

She rolled her eyes back, not dismissing Holly but clearly debating. After a moment, she moved her mouse to bring her computer back to life, clicked a few times, and then the printer whirred to life. "Please keep me out of this."

"We will. I promise. I want you to do something for me. Do you have sick time built up?"

"About a week."

"Is your boss here?"

"No. He works with the guys."

"Call him. Tell him you're sick and you're going home. Then you call in sick tomorrow and the next day and every day after until you find a job."

"I've been looking."

Holly pulled a card out of her pocket and handed it to Susan. "E-mail me your résumé. You'll have a new job before your sick time runs out."

Susan gave her half a smile. "I don't know if—"

"I do." Holly gave her that look that Jack figured was rarely argued with. "Now, what about the other guy? The owner. What was his name again?"

"John Middleton. He keeps to himself. He's quiet. Other than him not standing up for me, I've never had any problems with him."

"Okay. Thanks. Make that call. We'll wait and walk you out." She joined Jack, and he smiled at her.

"How you going to find her a job, Hol?"

"I know people who could use the help, but I'll hire her

at HEARTS if I have to. She shouldn't be here. She shouldn't have to put up with that."

He wanted to touch her, silently soothe the anger that was alive in her eyes. "She won't have to anymore."

She looked over the papers Susan had given her. "She gave me his résumé. He never seems to stay at one job long. Wonder if his previous employers stood up to him when he harassed their secretaries."

"Administrative assistants," he corrected. He smiled when she cocked a brow but didn't look at him.

"Ready," Susan said, approaching them. She had her purse and a picture frame in her hand. Apparently she'd already cleared out the rest of her personal belongings.

They walked out into the warmth of the autumn afternoon and watched Susan climb into her car and drive away before turning to where Holly had parked.

Jack put his hand to the small of her back as they crossed the parking lot. "She's a perfect match to Julia and Penelope."

"I noticed." She pushed the button on the fob to unlock the car. "Think he's using them as a substitute for her?"

"From what she described, he has a healthy obsession with her. I doubt she even realizes how deep it runs. If he came that close to assaulting her at the dog park and harassing her at her desk on a regular basis, he could be capable of much worse."

Inside the car, she reached for the seat belt with one hand while the other turned the key in the ignition. "Can you run him through the system and see what comes up?"

"Yeah, and I intend to."

She glanced at him. "Discreetly, so you don't get fired?"

Touched that she was concerned, he put his hand to her knee and squeezed it. "You could always hire me at HEARTS."

She dismissed his suggestion with a laugh.

11

HOLLY SHOOK her head as she finished reading over the information Jack had managed to find on Vance Pearson. While she had spent the afternoon calling associates, looking for a job opening for Susan, Jack had dug deeper into their latest suspect. She had agreed to not talk about the case over dinner, but as soon as they tossed their trash, she dragged him to the bedroom.

He was probably thinking something else was about to happen. She just wanted to stretch out and read his research. Jack eased back against the pile of pillows he'd fluffed up against Holly's headboard and aimed the remote at the TV on the wall across from her bed while she read the report.

And what he had found was disturbing Holly deeply. "How do guys like this keep getting jobs? He clearly has a problem. Four jobs in less than two years, and he was let go from all of them?"

"Unfortunately, a lot of people still blame the woman for sexual harassment. *She shouldn't have dressed like that. She shouldn't have smiled like that. She should have a better sense of humor.* See it all the time."

What he said was true. The Army hadn't exactly been free from conflict between men and women. Nothing put men in the mood to break a woman down more than feeling threatened that she might out-man him, but most of the time the COs drew a line that wasn't crossed. Sexual harassment was taken seriously by her superiors. Women were equals. They didn't get favors or special treatment, but they sure as hell weren't going to tolerate men making them any less because of their genitals. If a female could pull her weight, she deserved to be there and would be respected for her contributions the same as any man. The way the modern world should be.

Focusing on Jack as he turned on the news, she wondered if he'd ever been so insecure he had to push others down in order to build himself up. He didn't seem that way. He seemed to take her independence for what it was—to take her for who *she* was—without issue. She was curious if the novelty of her strength would wear off, though. Too many men in her past had taken her on as a challenge, only to grow angry or bored when they couldn't make her subservient to them.

She needed a man who would, as her superiors in the Army had, treat her as an equal. So far, Jack had done that. But she had to wonder, how long would that last?

"What are you looking at, Princess?" he asked.

She narrowed her eyes. "One of these times you're going to call me that and I'm going to punch your balls all the way up to your navel."

"Sounds fun. Do I get to shove my fist into your genitals, too?"

She pretended to consider his words before shaking her head. "Tempting as that is, no, you may not."

He tore his focus from the television and met her gaze. His teasing smile faded into something more somber. "What's on your mind?"

"Who said anything was on my mind?"

"I actually have peripheral vision. I could see you staring at me."

"Peripheral vision, huh?"

"Yeah."

"Is that your superpower?"

He smirked. "One of them. You okay, baby?"

She drew a breath as she fondled her necklace and nodded toward the notes and photos spread across her comforter. "I'd be better if we could find them."

Jack rubbed his hand over her knee. "I know we've talked about this before, Hol, but the likelihood—"

"Yeah," she said, cutting him off before he could once again remind her that these women were probably already dead. She stared at Julia Fredrickson, dreading the day her husband found out what Holly and Jack already suspected to be true. She wasn't coming home.

"Hey," Jack said as he nudged her. "Answer that."

She looked at her phone, surprised to realize it was ringing. "Holly Austin," she answered.

"Ms. Austin. My name is Neil Adams. I found your card on my kitchen table."

She creased her brow. "How can I help you, Mr. Adams?"

He exhaled. "Do you know my wife? Susan?"

Holly instantly pictured the woman from the landscaping office. "Yes."

"Do you know where she is? She isn't answering her phone."

Holly checked the clock on her nightstand. It was close to nine in the evening. Sitting up, she shook her head as if the man could see her. "No, I don't."

He sighed again. "This isn't like her. She doesn't disappear without telling me where she is. Are you the woman who offered to help her find work?"

"Yes." She looked at Jack, who was clearly confused. After putting the call on speakerphone, she asked, "Mr. Adams, when is the last time you saw Susan?"

"When I left for work this morning."

Jack's face sagged along with Holly's heart.

"What time was that?" she asked.

"About seven thirty."

"She e-mailed her résumé to me at about noon. That's the last I heard from her. Do you know if she was planning to run errands?"

"Not that I know of, but she was pretty excited about getting a new job. She wanted to buy a few outfits. I told her to go for it. She deserved something new after the stress that asshole had been putting her through."

Holly closed her eyes. *Shit.* "Do you know where she would go?"

He exhaled loudly enough for Holly to hear his misery through the phone. "No. I never paid attention to where she shopped. How could I not know that?"

"Hey," Holly soothed. "That's not usually something men think about. Call a few of her friends. Ask where she might have gone to buy some new clothes. My co-workers and I will start looking for her now."

This time his exhale sounded a bit relieved. "Thank you."

She ended the call and looked at Jack. "Shit," she said under her breath and dragged her hand over her hair. "We're going to have to take this to Meyer. We have to bring the police in. If Pearson has her..."

Jack grabbed his phone. "I'll call him now."

"You stay out of it. Let me take the heat."

"No."

"Listen." She leaned forward to hold his gaze so he knew how serious she was. "I'll go to Meyer. Tell him what *I* have found and that Susan is now missing. You go to HEARTS and get everyone up to speed so you guys can start looking for this woman. You know I'm going to have to walk through fire to get Meyer to listen after the bartender was cleared. Who knows how long it will take me to convince him to go look for Susan. She doesn't have that kind of time. You guys get out there and start looking for her *ASAP*."

She tapped her pointer finger on the documents she'd been examining. After a moment, she looked at him. "Tell me we're going to find her."

He put his hands to her face and kissed her lightly. "We're going to find her. Now go."

J ACK GLANCED AT E VA IN THE PASSENGER SEAT OF HIS car. "Where to next?"

Jack and the HEARTS—minus Holly and Rene—had split up to search the list of shopping centers Neil Adams had texted to Holly. Holly, of course, was walking into the lion's den by going to Meyer. He was going to be furious, but Jack thought he'd listen to her. As egotistical as the man could be, he wouldn't risk Susan Adams's life to make a point.

Rene had taken her intimidating stare straight to the unlisted home address of John Middleton—owner of the landscaping business and jackoff who'd let Susan be sexually harassed. She was going to find out exactly what had happened, how to find Vance, and—as she said while admiring her .45—let him know what she'd do to him the next time he let one of his employees be harassed on his watch. Alexa reminded Rene of her rule to never go anywhere alone. She insisted she wasn't the least bit concerned—at least not for *her* safety.

Jack hoped she was kidding, but he doubted it. Rene didn't seem to have much of a sense of humor. He just pretended that he hadn't heard her underlying threat so he wouldn't be obligated to warn her against using her own brand of harassment.

Eva used the tip of her pointer finger to nudge the rim of her thick-framed glasses as she looked over the map on her tablet. "Let's hit the Target on Main and Beaker. That's closest. Turn right—"

"I got it." He sped out of the parking lot of the latest dead end and turned toward the next location.

She looked at her phone and frowned. "Still no message from Holly."

"She'll get Meyer on board. Don't worry." He sensed Eva staring at him and glanced at her. "What?"

"What's going on with you two?"

"Well, Meyer might act like he isn't in love with me, but really—"

"Holly," she snapped. "What is going on with you and *Holly?*"

He chuckled but didn't answer. He didn't think Holly would appreciate him adding to the gossip he had no doubt her office was tossing about.

"Okay. Beyond the obvious intense sexual attraction. What's going on?"

"Shouldn't you be asking Holly this?"

She lifted her hands, palms up, and looked around. "You see her anywhere? Me either. I'm asking you."

He shrugged. "I'm not sure we know each other well

enough for it to be more than attraction. I think she's pretty damn amazing. I'd like to think she has the same opinion of me, but I can't say for sure."

"So...sleep with her yet?"

"Private."

"Taking that as a yes."

He cast her a sideways glance.

"So that must also mean you know she lost her mom and her dad's a drunk."

He tightened his grip on the steering wheel, not appreciating her approach.

"Also taking that as a yes. So you know that she's fragile even if she would never admit it."

"Eva. Just say what you are trying to say so we can move on."

"Fine. If you break her heart, HEARTS will break *you*. And I mean that in every sense of the word. Your life will be shit if you hurt her. We'll ruin every minute of your life until we forgive you. And we don't forgive easily."

"Good to know. Thanks for the warning."

"I'm serious."

"So am I. And listen." He finally caught her gaze, but just for a moment—staring her down to make his point wasn't worth rear-ending the car in front of them. "Holly and I have known each other for like two weeks. I really like her. I do. But that doesn't mean we're in some deep, spiritual relationship. It means we're still feeling things out to see if we even want to see if there's some deep, spiritual relationship to be had. We're just floating right now."

"Floating?"

"Floating. Cruising. Testing the waters."

She seemed to ponder his words for moment before taking her laser-sharp stare off him. "I know people look at me with my laid-back style and think I'm too chill to kick ass. I'm not. I'm a brown belt in Krav Maga. Know what that is?"

"Martial arts of some kind."

"*The* martial arts to end all martial arts. Someday, someone will rise to power and rule the world with Krav Maga alone."

"You're a *Lord of the Rings* fan, aren't you?"

"Holly is my dear, dear friend," Eva stated.

"Anime?" he continued.

"I *will* be the first in line to inflict a severe amount of pain if you hurt her."

He pressed his lips together to contain his desire to continue with his sarcastic replies and simply nodded. "Got it," he finally said. "And for the record, Holly is just as capable of breaking my heart as I am of breaking hers. This isn't a one-sided relationship. You know that, right? Women can break hearts as easily as men."

He glanced at her and found her red-painted lips twisted into a frown and something like self-inflicted culpability flashing across her face. She didn't look nearly as threatening as she sat there wiping her glasses on her shirt. In fact, she looked a little sad.

"Hey," he said more genuinely. "I'm going to look out for Holly. I know we just started seeing each other, but I care about her. I have no desire to hurt her. And I don't think she has any desire to hurt me. We're just going to see how this thing plays out. Okay?"

"Yeah. Cool." She shoved her glasses back onto her face and looked out the passenger window. "Nice chat, Jack."

"Nice chat, Eva."

He pulled into the Target parking lot and screeched to a stop by the front doors. As before, he headed straight to the customer-service desk to flash his badge and ask to speak to the manager right away while Eva shoved a photo of Susan in front of every person she could find wearing a name badge.

Jack hoped to hell they got some kind of lead. Susan had last been heard from when she'd e-mailed Holly nearly ten hours before. If Pearson had snapped and taken her, that was more than enough time for him to hide her away and do whatever he intended. Nothing good, Jack knew. He just needed to get to her before Pearson did something so horrific Susan would never recover.

He couldn't imagine the kind of blame Holly would heap on herself if Susan were killed. She'd convince herself that Pearson had snapped because Susan left. And Susan had left because Holly insisted on it. She'd carry that with her for a long time, if not forever.

He had to find this woman for Holly's sanity almost as much as he had to find her for her own sake.

Showing his badge to the approaching manager and explaining the situation, Jack requested the man check the day's sales to see if Susan had made a charge at the store.

As he waited, he checked his phone. Still nothing from Holly.

Damn it.

"Detective?"

He looked at the manager.

"A sale for Susan Adams cleared at 1:32 this afternoon."

"I need to see your parking lot surveillance for that time."

"Yes, sir. Follow me, please."

As he did, he called Eva. She met them at the back of the store, where the management offices were tucked away behind a red door. Moments later, they were watching security footage on multiple screens.

"There." Jack tapped a screen. "That's her."

They watched as a man approached her. Same as before. White male. Face shadowed by a baseball cap. Only Susan didn't seem nearly as friendly as the last two women he'd approached. She turned on her heels as if she were going to run back to the store, but she didn't get a chance. He was on her, his hand gripping her arm...and there it was. The gun they hadn't been able to clearly see in the other camera footage.

This time, it was obvious he was threatening her. He steered her to her car, and a moment later the trunk popped open. She put her bags inside, and he slammed it shut. Even as they watched him walk away with her, Jack was calling Meyer. He no longer cared about getting his ass ripped for involving himself in someone else's case.

There was no doubt in his mind that Susan Adams's life was in immediate danger.

He frowned when Meyer didn't answer. He called Holly. "Hey." He didn't give her a chance to respond. "Target on Main and Beaker. We've got surveillance video of Susan being taken."

She must have taken the phone from her ear, because when she spoke, her voice was muffled. A moment later, though, she came back clear as could be. "We're on our way. And I'm sorry."

He smiled slightly, understanding that her apology was because there was no way he could hide his involvement now. Even if he left, the police would find out why the manager had shown him video. Because Detective Tarek had asked to see it. "Don't be. We're going to find her. That's the most important thing."

Hanging up, he looked at Eva. "They're on the way."

"Should you skedaddle?"

"Too late for that, I'm afraid. Can you play that again?" He and Eva leaned closer to the monitor, doing their best to compare the shadowy figure on the screen to the one in the photo they'd taken off the landscaper's website.

HOLLY STOOD RAMROD STRAIGHT, HANDS CLUTCHED behind her back, as she listened to Jack getting his ass ripped from behind the police captain's office door. They should be out there, looking for Susan, but Holly hadn't been permitted to leave the police department as they awaited Jack's arrival. She hadn't been arrested—yet—but the threat had been made. She wasn't scared to go to jail—Tika could get her out—but she couldn't waste the time.

Susan couldn't spare the time.

Holly had done her best to convince the captain Jack hadn't been involved in her continued effort to locate Penelope Nelson, which had led her to Susan Adams, but the captain wasn't having it. He insisted that Tarek had been warned. And that was what Jack was being told again.

"What the hell were you thinking?" Captain Reinhart yelled.

Jack's answer, which was spoken in a normal tone of voice, was indiscernible, but the fact that he had to sit there and answer twisted her gut.

"Don't give me that personal time bullshit, Tarek! You flashed your badge outside of our jurisdiction. That makes it my time!"

Holly exhaled slowly. Jack might have abused his power...*slightly*...but he'd only done so because no one believed these cases were tied together or that all these missing women could be tied back to Vance Pearson.

Three missing women. All with the same appearance. All taken in the same way. And their only lead was out there, and Holly had no idea if Meyer actually believed anything she'd told him.

When she'd asked if he was going to follow up on Vance Pearson, Meyer had just sneered at her and marched away, cursing her under his breath for interfering. She wasn't sure if it was because she was encroaching on his case or because she had found information that he hadn't. It was hard to tell with some people.

She relaxed her stance when her phone rang, but the name on her caller ID made her stomach knot. Joshua Simmons. Josh was the county coroner and Eva's ex-boyfriend. She'd warned both of them when it was obvious they were interested in each other that the agency came first. HEARTS needed Josh's brilliance and, in times like these, his connections to the police department. She'd asked him to keep an eye out for anyone fitting Julia's description. His phone call made every nerve in her body light with dread. "Hey, Josh."

"Holly."

His solemn tone made goose pimples rise on Holly's flesh. "What is it?"

"You said you wanted to know if..."

"You got a body that matches my case?"

"I'm headed to a scene right now. Two bodies. A third woman is barely hanging on. She's on her way to the hospital."

She swallowed the acidic taste of raw emotion that had risen to her throat. "Where?"

"Acer Park. Buried in the woods out there. Thought you should know. I'm heading there now. I'll tell you what I can."

"I'm headed that way, too. See you there."

"Holly—" he warned.

She didn't need him to tell her that he couldn't grant

her access to a crime scene. She didn't need access. She just needed to be there. "Joshua. If one of those women is my case...I should be there."

"You can't do anything. The police won't let you near the scene."

"I know. I just want to be there."

He was quiet for a moment. "It sounds gruesome."

She closed her eyes, silently thanking him for the warning. She didn't need it, though. Julia had been missing for weeks. Penelope had been missing for weeks. Neither had likely been alive recently. "I'll see you there." She looked at the office door, where Jack's muffled voice was drifting. Swallowing, she knocked on the door as she opened it. "I'm sorry to interrupt."

"You'd damn well better be," Reinhart snapped. "You're lucky you're not in jail right now."

"Captain," Jack said with a shake of his head.

"Don't you—"

"Three women were found at Acer Park. In the woods. One is still alive. The other two—they match the descriptions for Julia Fredrickson and Penelope Nelson."

Silence was like a weighted blanket, pressing down on all of them.

"Let's go," Jack said.

"Forgetting something, Detective?" Reinhart lifted his brows at Jack, who scoffed before taking his badge and gun from his hip.

"No," Holly started.

Jack waved his hand to dismiss her protest. Setting his

ID and protection on the captain's desk, he stared at his boss. "You know, maybe if Meyer had listened to us instead of pissing on the case folders and rejecting any outside information, those women would still be alive." He put his hand on Holly's arm and steered her from her office.

Once outside, she frowned. "Jack?"

"It doesn't matter," he insisted, but his tone implied otherwise. He was angry and maybe even a little worried about the outcome.

She opened her mouth, but he started moving faster, almost trotting out of the station. "This way," she said when he headed for his car.

He turned and stared for a moment before following. Climbing into her passenger seat, he slammed the door. "One of these days, I'm going to drive," he said, more to himself than to her.

"Doubt it." She backed out of the parking spot, and the silence closed in around her. "How long is your suspension?"

"Two weeks."

She frowned and heaved a heavy sigh. "Desk duty?"

"Nope. Unpaid leave."

Glancing at him, she said, "I can use some help at HEARTS. I'll have Sam set you up on payroll."

He looked at her and shook his head. "No thanks. Honestly, after all this, I need the break."

"But unpaid, Jack?"

"Yeah. Unpaid."

She was quiet for a few moments before softly saying, "I'm sorry. I tried to cover for you."

He nodded. "And what did the captain have to say about that? Besides that you should be in jail?"

"That pretty much covered it." She swallowed as they closed in on the park and the uneasiness in her stomach grew. "It's them, isn't it? Julia and Penelope."

"Probably."

"That means Susan is on her way to the hospital."

"Probably."

Reaching over, she grabbed his hand. Rare was her need for some kind of comfort, but the feeling rushed through her and she needed to connect with him. "We did everything we could to save them. Didn't we?"

Lifting her hand to his mouth, he kissed it.

But he didn't say a word.

12

JACK'S STOMACH twisted as he climbed out of Holly's car and looked at the area surrounded by yellow tape. The ME was just getting supplies out of his van when he looked over at them through thick-framed glasses. Holly trotted up to him, and Jack followed.

"Jack, this is Dr. Joshua Simmons."

Jack held out his hand, and Joshua paused in pulling up a white full-body suit. He shook Jack's hand briefly and then zipped himself into the protective clothing. Holly had said this guy was Eva's ex-boyfriend, and Jack couldn't imagine two people better suited for each other. Eva's midthirties, not-quite-out-of-the-hipster-stage look matched the coroner's perfectly. Though he was wearing a jumper, his stylish glasses and shaggy hair made Jack imagine him standing in skinny cords, a button-down plaid shirt, and an oversized grandfather sweater while sipping an organic decaf soymilk latte with a shot of hazelnut.

"Do you know what happened?"

"Kids hiking through a wooded area of the park tripped —*literally*—over what turned out to be a few shallow graves."

"Do you know anything about the woman who survived?" Holly asked. "She was here?"

Joshua frowned but didn't stop gathering the equipment he needed. "I haven't made it to the scene yet, but according to the call, he buried them alive. All of them. The kids heard her screaming and realized there was a survivor. They were still trying to dig her up when the PD arrived." He finally stopped moving and looked at Holly. "I'll know more by morning. Bring doughnuts—the kind with maple icing and bacon crumbles on top—"

"I know," she said, sounding irritated.

Joshua wasn't deterred by her attitude. "You can bring me coffee, too. You know what I like."

"I can't wait until morning."

"I'm sorry, Hol, but you'll have to. Two bodies? I'm probably going to be here all night." He nodded a brief farewell to Jack and then headed toward the bright yellow tape blocking any onlookers from getting too close to the scene.

"Come on," Jack whispered, reaching for Holly's hand.

She pulled out of his reach and shook her head as she watched Josh walking away. "I'm staying."

"Why?"

She looked at him as if the answer to that was so damned obvious. "Julia is my responsibility, Jack. I may not have saved her, but I will not walk away from her until this is done. I will not leave here until she does."

He started to argue—logically there was nothing they could do—but then he realized this wasn't logic. This was duty. A duty instilled in her in the Army. And a guilt instilled by sitting just a few feet away from her mother while she died. Accepting that she wasn't going to budge, he decided he wasn't either. How could he possibly leave her here all alone to roll the case over and over in her mind until she figured out how to blame herself? No. He would be right there, discounting every fault she tried to find in herself. "You're right," he said quietly. "We'll stay."

She returned her focus to the lights shining in the woods. "What did I miss?"

Yup. There it was. He almost laughed at how predictable she was in taking the blame. But nothing about this was amusing. Not the murdered women. Not Holly's deep-rooted need to blame herself. Not his inability to help her see that she really had done everything she could. "Stop," he said anyway. "Stop blaming yourself."

"Who else am I going to blame?"

"The lunatic who just buried three women alive. Let's start with him." His attention shifted from Holly's tightly drawn lips to the silhouette of a figure leaving the crime scene and headed their way. He recognized Meyer even though he couldn't make out his features. The man's cocky gait was unmistakable. "Meyer!"

Jack stepped around Holly and met the detective

halfway across the parking lot. Holly was right beside him when he stopped to get an update. Jack wasn't expecting to get any information, but he had to ask. Before he spoke, though, he reminded himself to check the innate need to give this dickhead attitude and to be humble. "Can you tell us what you have?"

Meyer shifted as he looked around the gathering crowd. Dark had long since fallen, but that didn't stop people's natural instinct to want to see whatever they could. The lighting—yellow fluorescent in the parking lot and bright white at the scene—mixed to give Meyer's naturally tan skin a green hue. Or maybe that was the distress of what he'd just witnessed.

"They were buried alive." His voice was strained and his shadowed eyes looked haunted. Yes, the green hue was a physical reaction to the crime scene, not the magic of bad lighting. "All of them. In what looked like a handmade coffin. The ME said they would have slowly suffocated to death."

"How do you know they were alive?" Holly asked.

Meyer took a long breath and looked around again. He swallowed so hard that his Adam's apple lurched in time with a gulping sound. "There were scratch marks and blood on the coffin lid. All the women's hands were cut up and nails torn from trying to claw their way out."

Jack swallowed hard, too, as the mental image filled his mind. *Shit.*

"From the looks of the coffin, he's reusing the same one.

He must dig them up after they're dead to put his next victim in."

Jack flinched at the thought, but he had to say what he was thinking. It could give Meyer insight into the criminal that he hadn't considered. "Think he dug up the coffin in front of them to let them know what was coming? A kind of psychological torture?"

Meyer puffed his cheeks out as he exhaled and squeezed his eyes tight as if that could somehow clear his mind. "Probably. A little mind-fuck before forcing them into their own grave. Sick bastard. We'll know more after we question Susan Adams."

"So it is Susan?" Holly asked, just above a whisper.

Meyer nodded. "She's pretty shaken, but she'll be okay. Physically, anyway."

Holly lowered her face, and Jack guessed she was once again blaming herself for what the woman had been through. Even if she would have allowed him to, Jack didn't try to comfort her in front of Meyer. Not because he didn't want to but because she wouldn't have appreciated the show of affection in front of another officer of the law. Jack knew her enough to know she'd fear that was a weakness in Meyer's eyes or assume Jack was letting her in on the case because he was screwing her. Knowing Meyer, he probably would.

Instead, Jack kept his focus on the case, putting the need to console Holly on the back burner for now. He did his best not to picture Penelope screaming for help as she clawed at the coffin, using up what little oxygen she had left, but he knew once he saw pictures from the scene, he'd have those images permanently burned into his memory. "So we definitely have a serial killer."

"We definitely have a serial killer," Meyer quietly agreed.

Holly finally spoke. "Can you confirm if it is Julia Fredrickson and Penelope Nelson?"

"We won't know for certain until their families identify their bodies."

She tilted her head at him, giving him that *bullshit* look she had perfected, and he exhaled loudly.

He put his hands on his hips and seemed to debate for a few more seconds before nodding. "It's definitely Nelson. The second victim is in stages of advanced decomposition. There's no way to visually identify her body."

"May I?" she asked. "It will help us both if you know for certain now instead of sometime tomorrow."

"She's too far gone," Meyer insisted.

Holly stared at him until he caved and led them under the tape and into the woods. Though it wasn't necessary, he warned Holly and Jack to watch their step. Then reminded them anything they saw was confidential and if he saw them on the news, he'd toss their asses in jail for interfering with his case.

Again.

"This is a murder case now," Holly said. "Trust me. I'm not going to do anything to stop you from nailing this asshole."

They didn't have to hike far before finding a crew of

technicians combing the area. Yellow flags marked what little evidence there seemed to be.

Just like Meyer had said, the coffin looked to be home-made, likely from plywood and lumber that could be found at any hardware store. Nothing about the box was fancy, but it was certainly sturdy enough to keep someone trapped inside. A young man with a jacket that identified him as a crime-scene investigator was using a pair of tweezers to pull something out of the wood. When he succeeded and held it up, Jack's stomach rolled at the real-ization that it was a fingernail.

They wouldn't know whom it belonged to until DNA could confirm, but Jack was certain it was one of the three women he and Holly had been on the search for.

Meyer stopped at the grave where Joshua was exam-ining Penelope Nelson but didn't say a word. In an unusual show of humanity, the detective seemed at a loss for words. Jack didn't blame him. This was one of the most horrific things he'd seen in all his years on the force.

He glanced at Holly to see her reaction. Stone-faced. But he could practically hear the gears in her mind racing. She was seeing the scene, memorizing every detail, calcu-lating what had happened to her client's wife. He also hoped she was finally understanding that she couldn't have possibly prevented Julia from dying. She'd been dead long before Holly had ever heard her name.

Josh glanced up but didn't acknowledge the three of them standing there before returning his attention to the woman in the ground.

Jack stared at the body, remembering how Penelope had always smiled and waved when she saw him stopping by to visit his mother. She had been a good friend to his mom, kind and generous and never treating her differently because of her religion or thick accent.

His mother was going to be devastated when he told her. His mother rarely cried, but he imagined he'd be holding her for some time to ease her tears when she found out Penelope was gone. He'd just have to do his best to keep the details to a minimum and hoped the news stations would do the same.

Joshua used a gloved hand and lifted Penelope's wrist, turning her palm up and examining her bloodied and bruised hands. She'd fought like hell to get out of that box.

"You okay?" Holly asked.

Jack nodded and put his hand to the small of her back. He'd been restrained earlier, but he needed to touch her now. Not only for his peace of mind but to remind her that he was right there, absorbing all this horror with her. "You?"

She drew a breath but didn't answer.

"I want to warn you again," Meyer said. "This next body.... It's bad."

Following Meyer to the second grave, she looked down, standing as still as the soldier she probably was calling upon to keep her from showing the emotion Jack didn't doubt was boiling inside her.

As Meyer warned, the body exhibited advanced decay. Though the coffin had been open since the discovery of the bodies, a sickening sweet smell hung in the air. The smell—unmistakable to those who'd experienced it—of human decomposition.

Jack had no doubt that the body before them belonged to Julia Fredrickson. Even though her sun-kissed skin was now discolored and her sockets were nearly empty, making it impossible to determine what color her eyes once were. Her once beautiful face was now a thinly veiled skull. What struck Jack immediately was the big diamond ring on her left ring finger. That ring had been in almost every photo of Julia Fredrickson that Jack had studied.

The only way to positively identify this body would be dental records or DNA, but Jack felt in his gut this was Julia. He glanced at Holly and knew she felt the same.

Holly closed her eyes. She was likely blaming herself for the condition of the woman lying in a shallow grave before them.

"I'm pretty sure that's her," Holly said. "That's Julia Fredrickson."

"You can't know that," Meyer asked.

"I've been staring at her picture for weeks. That's her."

"You have the contact information for the detective working her case?"

She opened her phone and read off the name and number while Meyer jotted it down in his little notepad.

He started to leave but stopped. "Go home, Ms. Austin. The detective will take care of notifying her family."

"I'm not leaving."

"You've done everything you can do here." He hesitated in walking away. "Look, I don't appreciate you sticking your nose in my case, but I don't appreciate shit like this, either." He gestured to the graves behind him. "You did good."

Holly frowned. "Yeah, well. I should have done better."

Jack caught Meyer's gaze when Holly walked away. "Did you catch Pearson yet?"

"Yeah. He's downtown. I'm going to go question him when I'm done here."

"Can I—"

"Don't push it," Meyer warned. "Besides, you're on leave, remember?"

Jack scowled and straightened his back. Meyer was undoubtedly loving that he'd been the one to put that ball into motion. "Yeah, I remember."

Without another word, Jack left the scene, hoping he could somehow get the images out of his head as much as he was hoping he could convince Holly to put the blame where it belonged. On the sick fuck who had kidnapped and buried Julia alive.

THE DRIVE FROM THE CRIME SCENE BACK TO THE police department, where Jack's car was still parked, was heavy with silence as Holly and Jack tried to process the reality of how their cases had ended. He had tried to ease her guilt, and she appreciated that, but it wasn't his place to try to prove to her that she couldn't have prevented this. She knew who was to blame.

Vance Pearson.

She understood Julia had been dead for weeks, probably before Eric had even hired her.

She understood all the things Jack kept telling her. But that didn't ease the knot in her stomach or lighten the cloud hanging over her heart.

"I don't know what to say to my mother," he said, breaking the heavy silence.

Holly squeezed the steering wheel. "Just...make sure she knows not to say something to Mr. Nelson until the police have notified him."

He nodded and looked out the passenger window.

"Eric Fredrickson is going to be devastated," she whispered.

"At least he'll have closure."

"I guess."

Parking next to his car, she faced him, finally seeing him instead of the scene that kept playing out in her mind. He looked as exhausted as she felt. His hair, though short, was disheveled. He tended to run his hand over his head when he was frustrated. He'd been frustrated a lot since those bodies had been discovered.

"They never had a chance, did they?" she asked.

"No, they didn't. Listen, Holly, Julia Fredrickson has been dead for weeks—probably since the day he took her.

You aren't to blame for this. Do you hear me? She was dead before you even got this case."

"Stop, Jack. Please. I know. I hear you. I do. But..."

"But you're still going to let this eat at you."

"I've got a lot to process."

Leaning across the console, he rested his palm against her cheek and gave her a soft, lingering kiss. "I have to go see my mother before she hears this on the news."

Holly squeezed his fingers in hers and pulled his hand from her face. "Give her my condolences."

"I will." He turned and leaned close to her. "Susan Adams is alive. Let's hold on to that."

She nodded as he climbed out of her car and shut the door behind him. She waited until he was in his car before pulling away.

Hold on to that. Good plan. But it didn't work long.

As Holly drove back to the HEARTS office, she remembered the first time Eric Fredrickson had met with her. The police had hit a dead end, and Eric was convinced they'd stopped looking. She reassured him they hadn't—they wouldn't, not yet—and agreed to help him any way she could to locate his wife.

That had been her mission in life for the last two weeks. Julia Fredrickson had consumed her. Holly thought she knew more about that woman than she knew about herself. She'd analyzed her habits, her friends, her accounts.

And nothing ever pointed to a shallow grave in a wooded area of a public park.

Holly frowned when she found the parking lot half-full. She needed to be alone, but she knew her team well enough to know they were about to start hovering. She sucked her lungs full of air and then pushed it out and forced herself to go in. She needed to file this case away, and she didn't want to put it off. She hadn't been helping with the other cases HEARTS was working. Not as much as she should have been, anyway. She needed to get back on board and start pulling her weight on all their cases, not just hers.

The chatter from the conference room quieted, and Eva stepped into the doorway.

"She's here," she said to the other women.

Holly headed her way. Eva stepped aside, and Holly entered the conference room. There were aluminum pans of food, but they were all covered, and a stack of plates sat waiting to be used. "You didn't have to wait for me."

"Jack called," Alexa said. "We're so sorry, Hol."

"He shouldn't have."

"He's worried about you," Eva interjected. "He knew you'd head this way. He didn't want you to be alone."

Holly gave a dismissive laugh as her eyes moved to the wall. There was a blank section where there had been images of Julia and Penelope. A cloud of guilt covered her. "That might not be Julia." Her statement was true. There was a chance. But she didn't believe it. Neither did anyone else. Looking around the room, they all knew as well as she did. That body that had been dead and buried for so long was Julia Fredrickson.

"You did everything—"

"I know." Holly cut off Eva's attempt to make her feel better. She didn't want to feel better. She deserved to feel like shit. Julia's and Penelope's families were about to be faced with a horrific truth. So no. Holly didn't deserve to feel better.

"Eat," Alexa said, reaching for a pan. She pulled the lid back, and the smell of pasta sauce surrounded Holly.

She realized she should be starving, but she wasn't. Her stomach was tense and she was certain her body would violently reject any food she attempted to put in there. "I just wanted to thank you all for your help with this case. I know it's taken a lot of my time, but now that it's closed, I can focus on the other issues we have on the table. And thanks for dinner, but...I'm really not hungry."

"Holly," Rene started.

With a quick shake of her head, she turned and nearly ran into Sam.

Sam gave her that same damned sorrowful look as she lowered a stack of papers in her hands. Holly's guilt grew as she recognized the missing person posters with Julia's face on them that Holly had had Sam plaster all over town.

"I think I got them all," she said softly.

Holly left her team to eat their late dinner.

She dropped into the chair behind her desk. She didn't want it to—did her best to fight the urge—but her gaze drifted to the framed photo of her with her parents. The image was old and faded now, but it was the only photo she had of the three of them together. She didn't even know why she kept it there. Part of her hated looking at it.

Seeing her mother smiling at her hurt more than it helped. Some kind of self-punishment, she expected. Seeing her now made Holly's heart shatter. She didn't want to hear her screaming, see her being pinned down in that small slit of space between the sofa and the floor, and she didn't want to smell the blood in the air. But all those memories came flooding back.

Closing her eyes, knowing she couldn't stop the visions from hitting her, Holly relived the night her mother died. From the sound of them laughing at an episode of *The Golden Girls* to the sound of the door crashing open. The man's voice telling her to shut up. He had a slight accent that Holly had realized when she was older was from Boston.

The first time she'd heard someone speak with that accent as a teenager, she'd had a panic attack. She'd made a note in her diary. Her diary, which she'd started after her dad put her in therapy, would later become her most cherished possession. Not because of her deep thoughts but because of her memories. Because of the details therapy was able to help her remember that she'd blocked out.

Assault on December 2, 1989

Approximately 8:10 pm

Caucasian male

Boston accent

Black tattoo of dagger on right forearm

Size 10 boot prints found outside

Police estimated 6 feet tall and 200 pounds

Raped

Stabbed 14 times; third was fatal

Other entries had greater detail. What she heard. What she smelled. How he enunciated words.

The police had never found her mother's murderer. Logic told Holly she never would either. But she'd never stop looking for the son of a bitch.

Leaning her head back, she closed her eyes and wondered if Alexa had been right. When this case initially came in, she insisted Holly not work it. She said it was going to hit too close to home, cause too much pain. And it had. And despite the watchful eyes of her teammate, she'd let it consume her. She'd thought more of her mother in the last two weeks than she had in the last two years. Yes, she wanted to catch the man who'd killed her, but Holly had stopped obsessing about the case years ago. It was always on her mind, somewhere in the back of her thoughts, but looking for Julia had somehow reminded her of what she'd lost. Maybe it was the look in Eric Fredrickson's eyes when he spoke of his wife. She'd seen that look in her father's eyes for too many years.

Haunted.

Hollow.

Accusing.

She didn't want to remember her father that way, but he'd never been the same after her mother died. Neither of them had.

Holly was lost in memories of her father when the sound of the entrance door slamming jolted her.

"Where the hell are you?" a voice boomed.

Holly sat straight up in her seat as her breath caught. She had no doubt the owner of that voice was searching for her.

13

JACK TRIED to shake the memory of his mother's quiet sobbing as he climbed from his car. As he'd suspected, Holly was at the HEARTS office. But from the look of the parking lot, so were all the other members of her team.

He opened the door, expecting to find them seated around the conference-room table eating a late meal and comforting Holly, as Eva had promised him they'd do. Instead, the women were all standing in defensive poses, two of them blocking the hallway to Holly's office as a man stood before them.

Jack's initial instinct was to rush in and save them all, but he suppressed the urge, knowing that he'd probably get his ass kicked as well. Holly tried to push her way through the women in front of her, but Rene and Alexa didn't move.

"She's dead!" the man screamed, and Jack finally realized it was Eric Fredrickson. "You promised to find her."

Holly finally squeezed between her protectors, and the rest of the women moved closer, ready to defend her if necessary. Eva, in all her hipster glory, raised her hands in some pre–kung fu move while Rene did her signature glare. Alexa rested her hand on the Glock on her hip—reminding Jack he no longer had a gun. Tika, looking just as intimidating as the rest, leaned down, as if she would tackle the man should the need arise, while Sam stood back, phone in hand, ready to call for help.

"Take it easy, ladies," Holly said. "Mr. Fredrickson has every right to be angry at me."

"Damn straight. You were supposed to find her. You were supposed to bring her home."

"We don't know if that was her," Holly said. Much like her team, she could see he didn't believe her.

"They showed me her ring." His voice trembled as he narrowed his eyes, "Julia is dead."

"Not necessarily," Holly soothed. "We'll know more after the—"

"They won't even let me see her body," Eric said with a tone that sounded broken.

"We did everything we could," Alexa offered.

Holly glanced over her shoulder and gave her a subtle shake of the head. Clearly, poking the bear wasn't going to solve anything.

"I'm sorry, Mr. Fredrickson," Holly said in a soothing voice. "I know I failed her."

"Failed her? Do you know what that animal did to her? Do you know how she died?"

Instead of pushing the theory that the body might not be Julia, Holly nodded. "I do."

He stepped closer to her, and the tension in the room rose. "I hired you to save her."

"I know."

"Why didn't you?"

She didn't answer. What the hell was she supposed to say? Jack couldn't think of a thing that could make this better for the man. He needed someone to blame, and Holly was standing there letting him dump that on her. It wasn't fair, or right, and Jack knew it would just compound the guilt she already felt.

Screw that.

"Mr. Fredrickson," he said without really knowing what he'd say beyond that.

The man turned, and the small amount of anger that Holly had managed to soothe seemed to reignite. "You..." He turned back to Holly, but he pointed at Jack. "That. That is the reason you didn't find my wife. You think I didn't see you? The way you two were ogling each other. The way you couldn't take your eyes off him. You were too busy fawning over your boyfriend to find my wife."

"No," Holly said quietly.

"It's your fault," he said in a voice that chilled Jack to the bone. "You did this. You fucking bitch."

"Okay," Rene said. "That's enough."

"We all worked this case," Alexa offered in a more sympathetic tone. Holly had said she was the nurturer. The comforter. She was proving it now. "We all tried to find your wife. We all failed her and you, but it wasn't for lack of trying."

"Well, I guess you should have tried harder." Turning, he stared at Jack, who was between him and the door.

Jack stood firm as Fredrickson moved across the lobby to him, their eyes locked, backs straight, and fists clenched. Jack definitely didn't want to fight a man who had just learned his wife had died, but like the women in the room, he wasn't going to take any shit, either. He'd put Fredrickson down if necessary, if for no other reason than to keep him from spewing more hate toward Holly.

Stopping in front of him, just inches away, Fredrickson clenched his jaw and angrily stared Jack down. He had a few inches on Jack but their builds were similar. He might not go down without a fight, but he'd fucking go down. No doubt in Jack's mind.

Thankfully, Fredrickson didn't push things that far. He stepped around him, intentionally hitting their shoulders together, before storming out of HEARTS. The door closed behind him, and the tension in the room eased like a switch had been flipped.

Jack walked to the door and flipped the lock, just to be sure, as Holly reassured her teammates she was okay. They left the lobby, and she tilted her head as she looked at Jack.

"Defending my honor again?"

"Someone has to."

She smiled slightly, but he could see it wasn't heartfelt. "How's your mom?"

"Devastated. How are you?"

"Devastated," she whispered.

Pulling her into his arms, he hugged her tight and kissed her head. He didn't care if she wanted him to or not; he was going to give her the comfort she didn't know she needed.

Or maybe he was going to take the comfort he didn't know *he* needed.

THE SILENCE IN THE CONFERENCE ROOM WAS THICK and heavy as Holly picked at her food. She really wasn't hungry, but between her team and Jack, she'd had no choice but to accept a plate. Though she knew her body was in need of the energy source, her stomach was too tight to eat anything. Looking around the table, she realized she wasn't alone in that. No one was engaging in their usual habit of gorging food while discussing the day's events.

As upset as Holly was over the discovery of Julia's and Penelope's bodies, she couldn't stop analyzing the other thing nagging at her. She'd never felt more protected than when her team and Jack had all stood at the ready, prepared to defend her if needed. Fredrickson had every right to be angry, and they had all respected that, but they'd stood their ground. For her. Protecting her.

She knew her father would have done the same; aloof as he'd become, he would have protected her if she'd ever needed it. Her battalion would have protected her.

But somehow, this felt different. This felt personal.

Real. This felt like family. Like she was finally accepting what they'd all been telling her for so long. That she wasn't as alone as she seemed. That she did have a place here that went beyond order and management and keeping the company moving.

This was her place. This was her home. Her family. They put themselves between her and perceived danger. And they didn't even know what made her tick. What she kept buried deep inside and hidden away like a dirty secret. How many times had Alexa told her to just open up? To just let the other women know so they could support her.

She glanced at Jack, who seemed to sense her eyes on him and gave her a slight smile. Telling him the truth had been liberating in a way. Letting him see that side of her had eased the weight she'd been carrying for far too long. Taking a breath, she looked around the table at the women who had become her family.

"My mother was murdered," she said, cutting the silence. "When I was eight. She hid me behind the sofa, but I lay down and pressed my cheek against the floor. I saw it happen. He...he raped her and stabbed her to death. I didn't help her, and that haunts me. Every day." She swallowed and blinked her tears back. "My father found her. That's why he drinks. To forget. But I can't forget. I can't forget anything about that night. And I can't stop blaming myself. Even if I was just a kid," she said before they could remind her of that fact. She sighed as she glanced around. Everyone was looking at her, but none gushed with the sympathy she'd feared. Their eyes were sad but understanding. They weren't pitying her. Just accepting that this was part of her.

Alexa squeezed her hand. "I still look for my sister. Sometimes I think I see someone who could be her, and I'll follow her until reality crashes in and I accept that she's dead. That she died a long time ago."

"I still replay the day I lost a team member," Rene said. "I could have saved her. If I'd been more aware of what was happening. If I'd been paying attention and realized what she'd been thinking. I would have stopped her before she left."

Eva sighed loudly. "Joshua broke up with me because of this job. Because I can't think of anything else when I'm working a case. Because he hates the danger. I chose this job over him. I don't know if I did that because I love the job or because I'm so terrified of losing him that I just pushed him away first. How screwed up is that?"

"It's not," Tika assured her.

"It's completely screwed," Sam countered. "Completely screwed. All of you are, really."

"All of us?" Tika asked, clearly offended. "What about you?"

Sam rolled her eyes. "Bitch, I'm perfect."

Everyone looked at her, but Holly was the first to crack. Just a slight chuckle, but it was enough to break the shocked silence and cause the other women to laugh as well. She wasn't in the mood to laugh, but damned if she could stop it from erupting.

"Screw you all," Sam said, though she was grinning.

Taking a breath, Holly grabbed Jack's hand and squeezed it tight. "Thank you. All of you, for being here tonight. I know you all have better things to do than sit around and watch me process this."

"Take tomorrow off," Rene said.

"I doubt it, but maybe I will come in late."

Jack stood, pulling her with him. "Don't worry, ladies. I'll take care of her."

Holly eyed him, and he shrugged.

"I don't have anything better to do with the next two weeks."

HOLLY JOLTED AWAKE WITH HER HANDS REACHING UP, scratching at nothing. Exhaling harshly, she let her hands fall as she realized she'd been dreaming. She didn't really remember what, but she didn't have to consider it long to come up with a logical conclusion.

She didn't think she'd ever get the image of those women out of her head.

Taking another deep breath, she looked to the other side of her bed. Jack was sleeping soundly, and an inexplicable sense of peace washed over her. The feeling didn't last. As soon as she started to roll into him, seeking the comfort of his heat, guilt kicked in.

Eric Fredrickson would never hold his wife again. She knew that kind of emptiness could never be healed.

Instead of rolling into Jack, she sat up, putting her feet

on the floor. She grabbed her robe as she passed the foot of the bed, wrapped the terrycloth around herself, and headed straight for the kitchen. Rather than pour a glass of whiskey, she grabbed the bottle and carried it with her to the dining room table, where she took a big swig.

Jack had wanted to box up the files and photographs, but Holly had refused. She should have let him. She should have told him to take it out back and burn it all. But she hadn't. And now she stood in the middle of the night, staring at the images of women who would haunt her forever.

Julia was dead before Holly ever got the case. That was what Jack had said. And he was right. Holly knew he was right. Pearson hadn't hung on to his victims. He hadn't kept them alive, at least not for long.

But why?

She couldn't be sure if they'd been sexually assaulted or abused in any way until she met with Joshua the next morning, but she hadn't seen any obvious signs of abuse—beyond being buried alive.

If they were replacements for Susan in Pearson's mind, why would he have been so quick to kill them? And so horrifically.

She picked up the photo of Susan she'd pulled from the landscaper's website.

"This doesn't make sense."

"That's not going to help," Jack said quietly, startling Holly.

She looked up. "The drink or the obsessing?"

"The talking to yourself."

She shook her head. "I feel like we're missing something."

"Like what?"

"I don't know. If Pearson was so damned infatuated with Susan, why did he bother with Julia and Penelope? Why didn't he just go for Susan? She was right there."

"Don't try to understand how minds like that work, Hol. You'll make yourself crazy trying."

"But we have to understand, Jack, or we won't be able to stop the next one like him."

He gestured to the bottle she'd forgotten she'd pulled from the cabinet. "How much have you had to drink?"

"Not enough."

Walking around the table, he picked up the bottle and swallowed a mouthful before setting it down and wrapping his arms around her. Resting his chin on her shoulder, he looked at the papers. "What doesn't make sense?"

"Why would he kill them so quickly? If they were a stand-in for the woman he wanted, why get rid of them so fast?"

"You don't know what his feelings are for Susan. Maybe she misinterpreted his interest in her as sexual when he really just wanted to put her in a box and hear her scream."

She stiffened at the image he'd just created and then reached for the bottle herself. She swallowed and exhaled as the liquor burned down to her belly. "Maybe Susan wasn't his fixation."

"Maybe not. Maybe she was a stand-in as well. Someone hurt him who he's trying to hurt back."

A chill ran through her at the thought of what he would have had to go through to turn him into something so damned demonic. Turning, she slid her arms around Jack's waist and buried her face in his chest. She couldn't remember the last time she'd actively sought comfort, but this case was getting to her. And not just because she hadn't saved Julia Fredrickson. There was pure evil in the way the women had died that she could have gone her entire life without witnessing.

Jack hugged her back and kissed her head, sending a bit of warmth to the parts of her that seeing those dead women had chilled. She leaned back and met his gaze.

"What's happening here?" she whispered.

"We're trying to make sense out of pure insanity in the middle of the night," he said back just as quietly.

"No. Here. Between us. What is this?" She closed her eyes as she realized how that must have sounded. "I'm not trying to trap you, Jack."

"I know. You're too independent to need to trap anyone."

"I just don't understand what we're doing."

"Me either."

She started to step away. "I'm sorry. I'm a bit unsettled."

Jack pulled her back to him. "With good reason. What we saw out there...that would unsettle anyone."

"I've seen worse. Soldiers ripped apart by IEDs. Kids caught in the crossfire."

"That was war, Holly. This isn't war. Julia and Penelope weren't at war. Susan wasn't at war. As far as what's happening with us, I don't know"—he kissed her again before leaning back—"but I like it."

She smiled at his confession. "Me too. I just worry..."

"What?"

"When this is over and we've come to terms with this case and moved on to another, are we still going to feel this connected?"

He cupped her face and brushed his thumbs over her cheeks. "I'm not going to make you promises about what the future may or may not hold, but I will tell you that right now, all I want in this world is to be with you."

Digging her fingertips into his hips, she inhaled slowly and then exhaled as much of the negativity clouding her heart as she could. She pushed away the images of what she'd seen in the park. She pushed away the reservations she had about letting her guard down. She let go of that last little bit of self-preservation that she always held on to— that bit of control she always refused to give up—and she let in the warmth that had been trying to surround her since the moment she'd met Jack.

Something about him felt so right, as if she'd been waiting for him all her life but never knew he was missing.

Pressing her lips to his, she let the light kiss linger. For once, she didn't want to consume him or bend him to her will. She wanted to be there with him, to feel him with her.

She wanted him to make her feel something beyond the need to be in control.

As he tended to do, he seemed to read her mind.

Following her lead, he kissed her tenderly instead of indulging in their usual fit of passion. He lightly ran his hand over her hair, touching her as if she might break. And part of her felt ready to. She'd forced herself to be strong for so long that letting even just a bit of that go exposed all the cracks she'd been hiding most of her life.

Some surge of emotion she couldn't quite explain welled inside her, causing her chest to tighten. Gasping from the shock of it, she turned her head from him, resting her forehead on his shoulder. He wrapped his arms around her, encircling her in the cocoon of his warmth, and she felt another layer of her strength give way.

"Jack," she whispered, surprised at how her voice cracked with that unnamed feeling taking over her.

He hushed her as he threaded his fingers in her hair. Gently pulling her head back, he met her gaze before he put his mouth to hers.

Holly clenched her hands into tight fists to fight the urge to take the lead. She needed to trust him to give her what she needed. Deep inside, she knew he could if she'd just let him.

Jack used her hair to again pull her head back, this time exposing her neck. Holly bit her lip, her nerves coming to life as he dragged his hands down her body. Gripping her thighs, he lifted her and carried her to the bedroom. Moments later, he eased her onto her bed.

Her instinct to grab him and have her way kicked in, but she gripped the blankets and forced it down as he moved his mouth lower, nipping at her flesh along the neckline of her tank top. He slid the strap down, freed her breast, and flicked his tongue over her nipple before lightly sinking his teeth into the nub. The sensation was like a lightning bolt straight to her groin. She gasped, and he repeated the move as he reached between her legs.

Twisting her hands in the sheets, she let go as he easily brought her to climax. She had barely caught her breath before he put his mouth on hers, and then he was pressing against her and easing deep inside. She inhaled as he moved, slowly loving her, and she realized that was the sensation. Love. She felt loved. For the first time since she could remember.

From the protective circle the HEARTS had made to Jack's gentle touch—this was what had been missing all her life. This sense of love.

The feeling rolled through her and tugged at her heart. She knew he didn't love her—he couldn't possibly; he barely knew her. But he could. Someday. And she could love him. And they could have something she'd never had before, and the possibility rocked her core.

Breathing his name, she clung to him as he made love to her. She closed her eyes, riding the sensations he was bringing out in her. He brushed her tears away when they fell and whispered in her ear that everything was going to be okay.

And she believed him.

14

HOLLY PULLED her suit coat a bit more tightly around her as she entered the chilly morgue. She called out to Joshua, but he didn't respond. She didn't have to ask why. He was bouncing his head to whatever indie folk music was blaring from his earbuds as he studied the file he had sprawled on the desk. She smirked when he jolted as she dropped a box of doughnuts in his line of sight.

He yanked the earbuds free. "I hate when you do that."

"It's not my fault you try to block out the sounds of silence by destroying your hearing."

"I never listen to my music higher than seventy decibels."

She tilted her head at the sheer nerdiness of his response, but he was too busy digging for his breakfast to notice. Easing his coffee down, she looked at the table where the body everyone had accepted to be Julia

Fredrickson was covered with a white sheet. "Have you had a chance to examine her yet?"

"Just a preliminary."

"Sexual assault?"

"Hard to tell with her body in the stage of decomp, but we did collect evidence from the second body. I'll know more after further testing."

Holly's stomach knotted and her throat tightened, but she forced her face to remain neutral and her mind to stay in the present as she ignored the echoes of her mother's screaming bouncing through her memory.

"And by the estimated time of death, she was in that coffin not long after disappearing."

Creasing her brow, she looked at Joshua. "So he kidnapped her, assaulted her, and almost immediately buried her alive?"

"That's what I'm guessing, but I haven't done a full examination, Holly. This is all preliminary."

She lifted her hand before he could go off on one of his tangents about how detailed his work needed to be. "I know. I get it. We assumed Penelope was a replacement for Julia, but if she'd been dead that long, there was quite a bit of time before he broke down and took another victim."

He set his doughnut aside, wiped his fingers on his pants, and flipped to a page in the file. "He buried her with the intent of her suffering. She had no life-threatening wounds."

"We saw in the video she went with him willingly,

under duress perhaps, but he didn't physically assault her to get her into his vehicle."

"But do you believe she got in the coffin willingly?"

"Maybe he drugged her. Do you have a tox screen?"

"Pending."

Of course it was. He hadn't even had the bodies for twelve hours yet, and he'd slept for at least a few of those.

"Sorry. I wasn't pressing—"

"Yes, you were. And it's okay. I get it. Eva said this case is taking a toll on you."

Holly tilted her head again. "I thought you two weren't talking."

He shrugged. "We check in on each other every now and then." He sighed when she lifted a brow at him. "Okay, she just wanted me to know that you were taking this case to heart and if I could speed things along, it would help you out."

She offered him a slight smile. "It would."

"I'm sorry you're dealing with this. Hell of a case."

She nodded. "Yeah. This one's going to stick with all of us for a while. Will you call me when you get anything new?"

"Of course. Thanks for breakfast."

She snagged one of the doughnuts. "You're welcome."

JACK DROPPED THE REMOTE CONTROL ON THE PLUSH carpet as he stared up at the ceiling. This sucked. He should be out trying to solve a case, not watching the cable news channel cycle stories over and over. Then the image of Penelope Nelson flashed through his mind and reminded him how he'd failed to solve that particular case.

Sitting up, he rested his forehead in his palms and exhaled heavily. He couldn't sit here all day doing nothing. He'd lose his mind. Checking his watch, he decided he had just enough time to shower before going to HEARTS to drag Holly out to an early lunch.

He had no doubt she was reliving the scene from the park the night before as well.

Pushing himself off the sofa, he headed for the bathroom and started the shower. While the water warmed, he trimmed his facial hair and rinsed the sink. As much time as he was spending at her place, he wondered if he should buy a backup to keep in her bathroom.

He smiled as the idea struck him. It was probably a bit soon to be thinking along those lines, but being with her was as natural to him as breathing, and they'd easily fallen into whatever it was they were doing. Jack shook his head as he stepped into the shower and rinsed off. He'd actually already taken a shower with Holly before she left for work that morning, but that'd been more about pleasure than cleanliness.

He stuffed some spare clothes into a bag, intent on staying with her yet again, and headed for the door. He didn't even bother getting his toothbrush—he'd already left a spare at her place. The realization of that made him laugh softly. He suspected she hadn't noticed or else she would have pushed back—made him take that little bit of himself home. Or maybe she had and by not saying anything, she was saying everything. Maybe she felt as content in this newfound companionship as he did.

Tossing the straps of his bag over his shoulder, Jack made sure all the lights were out before leaving. He trotted down the stairs and out of the building to his assigned parking spot. Opening the trunk with the push of a button on his fob, he dropped the bag inside and started whistling as he anticipated where to take Holly for lunch.

"Detective Tarek?"

Jack spun, his defenses on high alert as he came face-to-face with Eric Fredrickson. He instinctively reached for his hip, but there was no gun. Before he could defuse what he suspected was about to become an ugly confrontation, pain shot through his head. White light flashed before his eyes, and then everything went black.

HOLLY FROWNED AS SHE ENDED THE CALL WITHOUT leaving a message for Jack. It was early yet, but she'd hoped he'd come over and look over a few cases with her. He didn't have to tell her he was upset about being on unpaid leave from the police department. She knew he was, and she wanted to stop him from spending his time fixating on that.

He was right. She could use him at HEARTS. And she

could use the distraction from dwelling on her disappointment at losing a client.

"Losing a client?" she whispered to herself. "You didn't lose her, Holly. She died."

"Hey," Eva said, sticking her head into Holly's office.

Holly hoped Eva hadn't heard her talking to herself. The last thing she needed right now was a mental health check. Hell, she'd probably fail at that, too.

"Fredrickson is back. He wants to see you."

Holly frowned. She'd known she'd have to face him again sometime, but she wasn't quite ready yet. "Great."

"He's calmer today."

She nodded and reached into her desk drawer for an envelope. She'd written a check from her personal account to repay him for the money he'd wasted by entrusting her to find Julia. She wasn't going to take that money from HEARTS when it was her fault, so she'd decided to tighten her personal belt for the next few months and repay him herself.

Her stomach knotted as she entered the lobby. She didn't know if the police would have given him details by now. Did he know his wife had likely been raped before being buried alive? Holly remembered her father's reaction to the news. He'd broken down. And she didn't think he'd ever put himself back together.

She was a kid, so she didn't know how much that had to do with losing his wife, but considering he'd had Holly enrolled in self-defense classes within a few weeks of her mother's death and he had constantly warned her to never go anywhere alone, she suspected his wife's rape had just as much, if not more, impact on him.

She imagined Fredrickson would take the news just as hard.

Before he even spoke, she noted how nervous he appeared. He looked disheveled. A streak of dirt marred his forehead, and his hair—which was usually immaculate even when he'd been stressed over his missing wife—stood on end in several places. He dragged his hand over his head, and Holly noticed the dirt under his fingernails.

"Mr. Fredrickson?" she asked hesitantly.

He finally noticed her and wiped the same dirty hand over his face. "I, uh... I shouldn't have come here like I did last night."

"It's okay. I know how upset you are."

"Do you?" he asked quietly. "I, um...I haven't been able to think of anything except how she died. How frightened she must have been. Locked in that coffin. No way out. How painful it had to be to die like that."

Holly lowered her gaze. She'd imagined Julia's last moments more than once herself. "I'm so sorry. I want you to know that we did everything we could—"

"But it wasn't enough, was it?"

Ouch.

"Hey," Eva started, but Holly lifted her hand and stopped her.

"I wish things had ended differently," Holly said.

"You mean you wish you'd found her before she died alone in a box, wondering when help would come."

"Yes," Holly said after taking a moment to process the intent of Fredrickson's jab. He had to know Julia had been dead long before he'd even hired Holly. She wasn't going to argue with him, though. He was grieving and didn't need to be pushed at the moment. "Yes, I wish I would have found her sooner."

"So do I."

"Mr. Fredrickson, I know losing someone you love to a senseless act of violence is difficult—"

"Do you?"

"Yes. I do. And the next few days, as you make arrangements for her, are going to be incredibly difficult. My team and I...well, if there is anything we can do, anything you need assistance with—"

He scoffed. "Let me guess. You'll do your best to help me. Just like you did your best to help Julia."

She lowered her head for a moment, letting his anger roll off her shoulders before meeting his gaze again. "I know it's hard to see right now, but someday I hope you will realize that I did do my best for Julia."

"Too bad it wasn't enough." Looking into Holly's eyes, he drew a breath. "I hope you do better for him."

Holly creased her brow. "Who?"

Fredrickson pulled something from the pocket of his shirt and held it out to her. She set aside the envelope she'd been holding as she accepted the one he handed her. As he did, she noticed the sweat stains that left the material around the man's armpits a few shades darker than the rest of his shirt, along with more streaks of dirt.

She hesitated before taking what he was offering, giving herself a few seconds longer to take in more of his distress. Finally, she lifted the back flap and pulled out the contents. The photos inside caused her chest to grow tight. Fredrickson must have been following her and Jack for days.

The pictures showed them in a pub. Leaving HEARTS. Going into Jack's apartment building with beer and pizza. Jack leaving Holly's house early one morning. Walking out of Susan's office.

But it wasn't until the image of Jack lying with his eyes closed in a car trunk that Holly's defenses kicked in. She tried to hide her panic as she looked at Fredrickson. Suddenly the sweaty, dirt-covered appearance of the man made sense, but Holly steeled her mind against what was obvious.

Eva, who had been looking over Holly's shoulder, demanded, "What have you done?"

He ignored Eva as he stared Holly down. "At first I wanted you to know what Julia went through. How she suffered because of your failure. But after seeing the way you looked at that man, I realized killing you was too easy. No. You don't deserve to die for what you've done. You deserve to know what it's like to *live*. Without *him*." He pointed at the photo of her walking out of HEARTS with Jack.

He had his arm around her shoulders and they were smiling. She remembered that night. That was the night he'd taken her to his apartment with one thing on their minds. And it wasn't the pizza and beer they'd picked up on their way to his place.

Swallowing the horror rising in her chest, she looked at Fredrickson. "Detective Tarek has done nothing but try to help you."

"No. He did nothing but distract you when you were supposed to be finding my wife."

Eva turned to Sam, who had been watching the exchange from her desk with wide eyes. "Go get the others. Now, Sam."

Sam scurried off as Holly looked at the image of Jack in the trunk of a car. "This man... We aren't married. He's just a friend."

A wry laugh left him. "That's not how a woman looks at her friend, Ms. Austin. You're in love with him. A fool could see that."

"No. I barely know him. I—"

"Bullshit!"

Holly lifted her hands, clutching the photos in one. "Listen. I'm the one who failed."

"Oh, I know. I know you did. And now you're going to get what's coming to you. I did some research, Ms. Austin. Do you know how long it takes to suffocate to death after being buried alive? Do you know how long my wife suffered? Four hours. She was fighting for her life in that box for as long as *four* hours." He stared at her for a long moment before he looked at the watch on his wrist. "When's the last time you spoke to your boyfriend?"

The tension in Holly exploded, and she slammed the

photos onto the partition in front of Sam's desk. "What have you done?"

Rather than answer, Fredrickson smirked as he pulled a gun from his pocket.

Eva lifted her hands as if that act could stop what was about to happen. "Don't!"

Her plea was futile. Fredrickson put the gun to his temple.

"Four hours, Ms. Austin," he said. A shot rang out as he fell to the floor.

Holly stood stunned for what seemed an eternity, but it was only seconds before she pulled her phone from her pocket as Eva called 911.

Alexa appeared, gun pulled, ready to fire back, but then her gaze fell on Fredrickson. "Oh, shit."

"Find his keys," Holly said. "I think he took Jack. Go check his car."

"I'll help." Eva followed Alexa outside.

Holly tapped the screen on her phone to call Jack. No surprise. Her call went straight to voice mail. "Hey, Jack, call me. Right now. I need to know you're okay."

She hung up, not expecting the call to come, but she had to try. Her second call was to the police but not to report Fredrickson's actions. She dialed Jason Meyer—the detective who had taken great pleasure in getting Jack suspended.

"Meyer, it's Holly Austin."

"I can't talk right now."

"It's about Jack. I think something may have happened

to him." The silence on the other end of the line added to Holly's tension. "Meyer?"

"I'm outside Jack's apartment. Someone reported witnessing a kidnapping."

Holly closed her eyes and exhaled. "Was it Jack?"

"The description fits. The witness said the man was hit over the head and shoved into his trunk as he was putting a bag in. Jack's car is missing."

She looked at the office door when it opened.

Alexa shook her head. "He brought Jack's car, but he's not in the trunk."

"Did you hear that?" Holly asked Meyer.

"I got it. I'll send someone over. What else do you know?"

"Eric Fredrickson came into my office about ten minutes ago. He showed me some pictures of Jack and said he hoped I did better for him than I did for his wife, and then he blew his brains all over my lobby."

"Son of a bitch. We were trying to figure out why this guy was so careless."

"What time was he taken?"

"About ten thirty."

Holly looked at her watch—11:58—and did her best to push the rising terror down as she did the math. He'd had plenty of time to bury Jack and get to her office to taunt her.

She ran her hand through her hair and exhaled slowly, determined to remain calm so she could help Jack. "If Fredrickson did what I think he did, we don't have a lot of time. Sometime in the last hour and a half, Jack was buried alive. Fredrickson said he read someone buried alive can only last about four hours, Meyer. We're already running out of time. I'll get my team—"

"Hey, I'm actually the detective here, Austin. I got this. You stay put. I'll send someone over."

Holly exhaled slowly. "Sorry, but I'm not sitting this one out."

"Austin—"

"I'm heading to Fredrickson's now. With any luck, Jack is there."

After ending the call, she noticed Rene kneeling over Fredrickson. She looked up, and Holly flinched at the look in her eyes. It wasn't often Rene appeared shaken, but she did now.

"His hands have blisters."

"From digging," Holly whispered. She swayed as fear rolled through her. Gripping the partition to steady herself, she immediately recalled how bloodied and bruised Penelope's hands had been from her futile attempts at saving herself. She pictured Jack screaming and clawing in the darkness, knowing he'd never escape. No one deserved to die like that, and imagining that for Jack made the world drop from beneath her.

Rene stepped over the body and grabbed Holly's shoulders. "Keep it together. Jack needs you."

She nodded and swallowed hard. Pushing away images of Jack with empty eyes and bloody hands, she inhaled deeply and forced her mind to clear. "Right. Sam, hack into

248 / MARCI BOLDEN

the DOT and see if you can find traffic cams. Maybe the feed can lead us right to Jack. Tika, you go with Rene to Jack's apartment. Maybe he's asleep and didn't hear the phone. If he isn't there, you check his mother's. I'll take Alexa and head to Fredrickson's. Eva can stay and handle the police. She was a witness to Fredrickson's suicide. Eva, call Joshua and confirm Jack has four hours of oxygen. You all stay in touch, got it?"

She didn't wait for confirmation. She rushed out and yelled for Alexa to follow her.

She was starting the engine when Alexa slammed the door. "You really think he buried him alive?"

"I noticed how disheveled he was before he even spoke. Sweaty, dirt streaks. Rene noticed blisters on his hands. So yes, I think he buried Jack alive."

"Holy shit."

"Yeah," Holly breathed and pressed harder on the accelerator.

THE FIRST THING JACK NOTICED WAS THE THROBBING in the side of his skull. He'd definitely hit his head on something, but he couldn't recall what. The second thing he noticed was the smell filling his senses and nearly drowning out everything else.

Dirt. Wood. Sweat.

He kept his eyes closed, not wanting to alert anyone that he was awake, as he listened for signs of his surroundings. Nothing. Silence. Absolute, unnatural, unsettling silence.

He lifted his eyelids with caution so as to keep his conscious state a secret. At least until he realized he was surrounded by complete darkness. Not a pinpoint of light was visible. Finally, confident he wouldn't be seen, he moved.

His elbow struck a wall, causing a deep *thunk* to sound. He jerked his hand in response and found another barrier just inches above him. His heart did a funky flip-flop in his chest as he lifted his left arm and went through the same routine. Elbow against one wall. Hand hitting another.

The space he was in couldn't be more than two and a half feet wide, and there was just enough room above him to press his palms flat against the cool surface—which he suspected was wood based on the smell. He refused to believe what his mind was telling him and attempted to scoot down, ignoring the pain his movements sent through his head. His feet touched the bottom after sliding just a few inches. He pushed his way in the other direction until his head hit the top—maybe five or six inches. *Maybe.*

A coffin. He was in a coffin.

He tamped down the urge to panic as he recalled the scene at the park—gray skin, cloudy eyes staring at nothing, a coffin with claw marks, bloodied fingers and knuckles. He knew it wouldn't help, knew it was a waste of oxygen and energy, but in that moment, Jack couldn't stop himself from screaming and banging and begging for help.

15

HOLLY IGNORED SPEED LIMITS, traffic lights, and the angry honking of other commuters as she sped to Fredrickson's house. The tires on her sedan screeched to a halt in front of the one-story. Foregoing the legalities, she ran onto the porch and tried the door. It was open. She wasn't expecting that. She hesitated as she looked at Alexa, who appeared just as put off by the unlocked door.

That was too easy. Like walking into a trap. Pulling their guns from their hips, they eased into the house. After a quick glance around the living room, Holly stepped in first. "Anybody home?"

Silence.

"Hello?"

Nothing seemed out of the ordinary. Moving through the house—the small but tidy living room, a galley kitchen —they came to the bedrooms. The first was the master and, like the rest of the house, was clean and organized. The next room, however, caused Holly's stomach to twist into knots. A large whiteboard—just like the one they used at HEARTS—hung on one wall. Beside images of Holly and Jack printed on regular paper, likely from the printer that sat on a small desk in the corner, was a list of almost all the places they'd visited since meeting.

"What the hell?" Alexa breathed. She stepped to the board before looking at Holly.

Holly swallowed. "Check the rest of the house. I'll see if anything here indicates where he might have taken Jack."

Alexa disappeared, and Holly tuned out the sounds of her rushing through the house, opening and closing doors, as she looked over the images of her and Jack. The irony of the detective and the investigator being followed without realizing it wasn't lost on Holly. One of them should have noticed at some point.

Maybe Fredrickson was right. Maybe she had been too distracted by Jack to do her job.

No. She refused to believe that. She'd done all she could. So had Jack. And her team.

Pearson was to blame.

And now, Fredrickson was to blame. And only Fredrickson.

She scanned the images. The notes. Nothing indicated where Jack might be. She was wasting time standing there.

She was heading toward the back door when Alexa emerged from what appeared to be the basement.

Alexa shook her head. "Nothing. Let's check outside."

"Look for any signs of a disturbance," Holly said as she

did the same. From the patio, she scanned for any obvious signs of misplaced sod but found none. There was, however, a shovel tossed aside, which made her stomach lurch. Grabbing the shovel, she started stabbing at the ground as she walked, checking for loose dirt.

The yard wasn't huge, but halfway through she couldn't help but feel that she was again wasting precious time. Every breath she took was one breath closer to Jack's last. *If* he was still breathing.

She'd come to the conclusion that he wasn't in Fredrickson's backyard before she even made the last pass through the grass, but she couldn't simply stop. She could be wrong. But she wasn't. The last patch of dirt was just as hard as the rest she'd checked.

"Damn it," she yelled as she threw the shovel. "What did you do with him, you bastard?"

She raked her fingers through her hair as she closed her eyes and tried to clear her mind of anxiety long enough to think. She pictured the clues she had obsessed over while working the case. Every photo. Every scrap of paper. Everything she knew about Eric Fredrickson.

Nothing came to mind.

She was hitting as much of a roadblock now as she'd hit while looking for Julia.

"Check in with the office," she said to Alexa as she walked the backyard, thinking of all the places Jack might be. She looked at the perfectly trimmed landscaping, and helplessness collapsed down on her. She'd failed her mother. She'd failed that kid in Fallujah. She'd failed so many times. And now she was about to fail Jack.

Alexa stepped to her as she slid her phone in her pocket. "He's not at home or his mom's. The police said the witness accounts match Fredrickson's description, and his car was in the parking lot at Jack's apartment complex. Sounds like he hit Jack over the head and got him in the trunk before speeding off."

Putting her hands to her face, she fought to stay in control. "I don't know what to do." Her breath rushed from her as if she'd been sucker-punched as an image of Julia's dead, milky eyes flashed before her. "The park. He took him to the park where Julia was found."

"DON'T PANIC," JACK WHISPERED. EVEN SO, HORRIFIC images banged around in his brain, reminding him exactly how he was going to die. Even worse, he realized, was wondering if Holly was somewhere facing the same fate. Was she in a box just like this? Maybe just feet away. Had Fredrickson taken Holly, too?

Closing his eyes, he inhaled a shaky breath. "Don't panic."

Putting his palms against the wood, he pressed with all his strength, not the least bit surprised when the surface didn't budge. He bent his knees as much as possible and tried to lift his legs at the same time he pushed with his hands. Not so much as a millimeter of movement.

He curled his hands into fists when the urge to claw at the wood took over. That wouldn't work. He had the images of two dead women burned into his memory to prove that wouldn't work. But he understood completely why they'd tried.

The air was getting thick, humid. Sweat was breaking on his brow.

He needed fresh air. Cool air. He needed light. He needed sound. He needed to find Holly and make sure she was safe.

He had already screamed. Had already pounded his fists on the wood. But that didn't stop him from doing it again as fear overtook logic and the image of himself lying in the woods next to Penelope Nelson filled his mind.

HOLLY JUMPED OUT OF HER CAR AND RAN TOWARD THE wooded area where the graves had been discovered. She doubted Fredrickson could bury Jack alive in the light of day—surely the police were still in the area—but she had no other ideas at the moment.

"That's a crime scene," Alexa called as Holly slipped under the yellow police tape. "Holly! You could get arrested if you go in there!"

She ignored Alexa's warning and cursed as the damp leaves shifted under her feet, causing her to slide as she tried to climb a hill. Instinctively, she reached out, letting even more harsh words erupt as the branch she grasped to maintain her balance cut into her palm.

Using the leverage and ignoring the pain, she yanked herself upright and regained her footing. Moving forward, marginally more cautious of where she was stepping, she finally stopped at the graves. Three holes still clearly visible, but no sign that another grave had recently been dug and filled.

"That doesn't mean he isn't here," she whispered.

"Hey," a man yelled, and she was confident he was screaming at her. "Get outta there!"

She ignored him as much as she'd ignored Alexa. She kicked at fallen leaves and twigs, looking for any sign of a newly dug grave. "Jack?" she screamed on the off chance that he could scream back. "Jack?"

Moving farther into the woods, she searched for any evidence of a struggle—broken branches, drag marks through the mud or fallen leaves, scraps of cloth that could have gotten caught on the surrounding trees, mounds of dirt large enough to hide a body.

Nothing. Everything looked in place—as in place as it could in a wooded area.

She moved toward the bike path that bisected the area. Putting one hand up, she stopped two bicyclists and pulled out her phone.

"Have you seen this man?" she asked, opening the camera app. A second later, she was showing them Jack's image—she'd snapped the photo to put in her' phone contacts so his face popped up whenever he called her.

Neither had seen him. Nor had the next rider, or the one after that, or the joggers she stopped, or the man walking some strange mixed-breed dog that was the size of a Great Dane but had the head and curled tail of an Akita. Spinning slowly, seeing nothing but trees on either side of her, Holly exhaled slowly and finally let the sinking feeling of defeat start to settle around her.

Alexa finally caught up to her and grabbed her arm. "Come on. Let's head back to the office. The police are waiting for you."

Using her cell as they headed back to the car, she called Meyer, who answered on the second ring. "Anything?"

"No. You?"

"No. I'm at the park. I thought maybe..."

"Yeah. We had the same thought. A K-9 unit is headed there now."

"I didn't find anything." Swallowed when her voice cracked. She raked her fingers through her hair, debating what to do. "Have any other suggestions? Ideas? He's not at Fredrickson's house. If he's here, I haven't found him. Where else would he take him? Did you find anything in his car?"

"Fredrickson's car was clean. We're checking Jack's now."

Holly closed his eyes. "We might not—"

"We'll find him. Why don't you go to the station? Look through the files. See if we're missing anything."

She laughed wryly. She could almost hear Jack lecturing

her for obsessing over what little information they had on the case. "I know those files front to back. I don't need to look at them. This isn't about Pearson or the other women he took. This is about me. He blames me. He took Jack to hurt me."

She ended the call and closed her eyes as she envisioned Julia's body in the morgue. This time, she imagined Jack on the table beside her. "We need to get back to the office," she said quietly.

Every step she took toward her car felt heavier and heavier. This was real. This was happening. Jack had been buried alive, and there was nothing Holly could do to save him.

At the car, she turned to Alexa. She tried to fight the fear, but it hit her hard and she couldn't stop the tears from filling her eyes. Reaching into her pocket, she pulled out her car keys and put them in Alexa's hand.

Alexa looked at them like she didn't quite understand what they were.

"I can't..." Holly said. She swallowed hard when a sob threatened to rise in her throat. "I just can't. Not right now."

"Okay," Lex said softly and pressed the button to unlock Holly's car.

For the first since she could remember, Holly slid into the passenger seat and let someone else have control.

♥

JUST BREATHE. IN SLOWLY, OUT SLOWLY. DEEP, HOLD, absorb, release.

No. Shallow is better. Shallow. Don't use too much air.

Jack's head hurt. He could no longer determine if the pain was because of the welt he'd felt on the side of his head or the lack of oxygen he was sure he was suffering by now.

He'd spent the last few minutes trying to convince himself Holly was out there. She was looking for him. She was going to find him.

But the reality was, if she wasn't in a coffin beside his, she probably didn't even know he was missing.

"She was dead before you even got the case," he'd told Holly.

And now those words of comfort applied to him.

He'd be dead before Holly even knew he was gone.

Swallowing, he closed his eyes tightly as sweat rolled off his forehead. Slamming his now-tender hands against the wood, he exhaled heavily. No. He refused to believe that. She was too smart. Too aware. She was out there looking for him. She had to be.

And if she were trapped in a box like him, then HEARTS would be out there. They would be looking for her. And they wouldn't give up.

Please, don't let them give up.

16

HOLLY JERKED the door to HEARTS open and headed straight for Sam. While Alexa had driven them to the office, she'd taken some deep breaths and pulled her head out of the pity pool. She needed to get, and keep, her head on straight. Jack's life literally depended on her keeping her cool. "Did you get anything from the traffic cameras?"

Sam opened her mouth, but Detective Meyer spoke for her. "No. And she won't. We don't hack into the Department of Transportation, Ms. Austin."

Holly turned and gawked at him. "One of your detectives has been kidnapped and presumably been buried alive. I think we can make an exception today, don't you?"

"We're working on getting a court order."

"A court order?" Holly nearly screamed. "That could take hours."

"We do things right."

She scoffed and shook her head. "Yeah. We'd hate for

that dead guy to challenge how we found his victim in a court of law, Meyer! Jack is running out of time!"

"I know that."

She raked her hand over her hair. "Fine. I'll head back to Fredrickson's. Maybe I missed something."

"I have a team there."

She stared at him for a moment. "Then I'll go back to the park."

"The K-9 unit is there. You'll stay here."

"I'm not going to sit here and do nothing—"

"You will let the police handle this."

Eva put her hands on Holly's shoulders and gently pulled her back before she could tell Meyer exactly where she wanted him to go. Only then did Holly realize she was standing nose-to-nose with the detective. She imagined the look in her eyes was as threatening as her posture.

Exhaling, she let Eva pull her away.

"Listen," Eva said quietly. "Sam's not the only one with mad computer skills. Rene went to see Joshua. He might be able to help."

Holly took a deep, calming breath. "Did you ask him how much time Jack might have?" When Eva didn't respond, the knot in Holly's stomach tightened. It was already closing in on one o'clock.

Eva stuttered for a moment. "There's no exact length of time. It depends on the size of the...coffin and how much room Jack takes up and how much he breathes."

Holly gave a soft laugh. "Joshua answered in mass and dimensions, didn't he?"

Eva gave her a weak smile. "I got him to translate it for me."

"And?"

She nodded a bit. "Four hours give or take. There are variables."

Holly looked at her watch and then closed her eyes. "It's been almost two and a half hours since he was last seen. How long do you think it took Fredrickson to bury him?"

"I don't know," she said softly.

Holly glanced around the lobby. "Has anyone called his mother?"

"Tika and Rene brought her back here after verifying he wasn't with her."

"Where is she?"

Eva nodded toward the conference room. "She's taking this hard."

"I imagine so. I should... Shouldn't I?"

"She's asked for you a few times."

Holly drew another breath before heading for the conference room. Tika sat with a small woman in the white uniform she'd likely been wearing at the bakery where she worked. A light blue hijab covered her hair.

Tika looked up and her eyes lit with hope, but Holly gave her head a slight shake. Patting the woman's hand she'd been holding, Tika nodded toward the door. The woman turned, and the fear in her eyes struck Holly's heart. She'd seen that look in her mother's eyes right before she'd died. In the child lying in the street in the warzone. In so many others' eyes.

"You must be Holly," she said, her voice lilting in a thick accent.

She nodded and somehow found the strength to sit next to the woman. "I'm sorry to meet you under these circumstances, Ms. Tarek."

She touched Holly's cheek and her eyes filled with tears, but she sat a bit straighter and held them in. "He will be found. I believe that. Don't look so scared."

Holly wished she could share in Jack's mother's confidence, but she had no idea where to look for him. No idea what she could possibly do to save him.

At the feel of Ms. Tarek's gentle tug, Holly leaned in and hugged the woman. She smiled slightly as she found the same internal peace in her arms that she'd found in Jack's. He must have somehow gotten the ability to soothe pain from his mother. And now that peace was about to be lost.

She felt the need to cry well inside her.

She wasn't a crier.

As the feeling filled her, she pictured Jack in her house, in her bed, in her kitchen. She tried to cling to every moment she'd shared with him. Every bit of peace she'd felt in the last few weeks. She'd never feel that way again, and going home to an empty house every night would just magnify how much Fredrickson had made her pay for her failure.

Opening her eyes, she slowly leaned back, and things clicked into place in her mind.

"What is it?" Ms. Tarek asked.

"I know where he is. Tika, go get the others." Pushing herself up, she trotted back to the lobby but found it almost empty. "Where's Meyer?"

Sam shrugged. "He didn't say where he was going, but I think he got permission to work with the DOT to look at the traffic cameras."

"I don't think we're going to need that after all."

"You know where Jack is?"

She looked around at the women surrounding her. "He wanted to hurt me, right? Fredrickson. He made this personal. What could be more personal than killing Jack in a place where I can't escape what happened? I think Jack is at my house."

"Son of a bitch," Rene breathed. "Let's go."

Holly turned when she noticed a woman much shorter than her standing next to her. "Ms. Tarek, you stay here. I'll call as soon as I know anything."

"Absolutely not. If you are looking for Jakeem, I am going with you."

Holly only hesitated for a moment. She wasn't going to argue. "Ride with me."

The women jumped in cars and sped away, with Holly taking the lead. Tires squealed as they turned corners far too fast and screeched as they stopped in front of Holly's house. She jumped from the driver's seat, not bothering to close the door as she ran for the gate that led to her backyard. She immediately started skimming for signs of a fresh grave.

He had to be there. He just had to.

"There," Rene yelled.

Holly beat her to the lumpy, disturbed grass and dug her hands in. She exhaled with a mixture of relief and horror when it easily gave way. Tugging the loose sod away, she swallowed the lump in her throat. "Somebody get the shovel out of the garage. And call 911."

Ms. Tarek dropped to her knees and started pulling at the dirt as well. Hands were moving faster than Holly could keep track of. Then a shovel was in her face. She grabbed the handle and told everyone to move back. She didn't even bother to look where she was tossing the dirt; she just needed to move it as quickly as possible.

And then she heard what she'd hoped for and feared. The sound of the shovel hitting something solid. Ms. Tarek sobbed again, and Holly shoveled harder and faster to clear enough earth to uncover the coffin. As she continued moving the dirt, Rene and Alexa started working on brushing the top clear to determine how to open it.

"We need a hammer or a crowbar or something," Alexa said.

"In the garage," Holly panted. "By the workbench."

"Jakeem," Ms. Tarek yelled. "Can you hear us?"

Holly didn't stop digging, but she did notice the lack of response.

By the time Eva came back with a hammer in hand, Holly had unburied the coffin and they could hear the wail of sirens growing louder. She snatched the hammer and shoved it between the lid of the box and the side, grunting as she pried the nailed surfaces apart.

She had to do this in several spots before the top inched up enough for Rene and Alexa to get their fingers wedged in to start pulling the lid.

And then her heart lifted at the most beautiful thing she'd ever seen—Jack's fingers slipping through the crack they'd made.

"We're coming," Ms. Tarek said. "We're coming, Jakeem."

After several more pries with the hammer and tugs from Rene and Alexa, the wood cracked and nails gave way and the top pulled back enough for Jack to stick his arm out. Ms. Tarek grabbed his hand, holding it as Holly and the others finished prying the top off.

Holly smiled, and the tears she'd been fighting finally won. Reaching into the coffin, she grabbed his arms and pulled at him. "Come on," she said when he squinted at her. She had no doubt that seeing the afternoon sun was stabbing at his eyes—he'd been in the dark for so long.

He gripped her, and she pulled him enough to roll him from the grave. Sweat soaked his brow as he gasped for air. His mother wiped his head as she cried and prayed in a language that Holly could probably decipher if she listened closely enough, but in the moment she didn't try.

"You're okay," he said. Clinging to Holly's hand, he smiled. "You're okay."

Brushing his soaked hair from his face, she waited for

him to open his eyes a bit more. "You're okay, too," she promised him. "An ambulance is coming."

"I thought he might have buried you, too. I thought..." His words faded as he relaxed on the ground.

"Jakeem," his mother cried.

"He's okay," Holly whispered. "He's okay. He just needs some fresh air." With one hand on Jack's, Holly slid her arm around his mother's shoulders and held her as she cried.

Jack opened his eyes, just a crack, and gave her a weak smile. But it was enough to fill her heart.

[17]

JACK GRINNED at the sound of two women whispering so as not to wake him. His mother was telling the tale of how he'd nearly gotten suspended for defending her honor, and Holly was reassuring her that he'd done the right thing even if it had gotten him in trouble. They were making him out to be some kind of hero. Who was he to interrupt?

"Look at that smirk," Holly said after a few moments of silence. "Someone is enjoying being the center of attention."

"He always did," his mother offered.

He finally opened his eyes. "That's not true."

They both smiled at him, and as his mom reached out to take his hand, he noticed how their hands were also entwined. His heart filled with some strange sensation— he'd call it happiness if he weren't so scared of jinxing the feeling.

His good feeling faded and he exhaled heavily at the guilt he saw in Holly's eyes as she looked at him.

"Stop it," he insisted. "You didn't do this."

"I've been telling her that," his mom said. "She's like you. She doesn't know how to listen."

"Hey," he said, focusing on her. "I'm in the hospital. Be nice to me."

Surprisingly, she didn't have a witty comeback. She scooted closer and then leaned down and kissed his forehead. Usually he'd remind her he was too old for that, but today he'd let it slide. Today, he'd definitely let it slide.

"I'm going to get some hot tea. Would you like some?"

"Yes," he whispered. "I would."

She looked at Holly, who shook her head, and then his mother eased out of the room.

Jack took Holly's hand and tugged until she finally moved closer to him.

"I'm so sorry," she whispered, her voice thick with emotion.

"Don't."

"He hurt you because I failed."

"No."

"Yes, Jack. He came to the office and confronted me. He told me what he'd done and why."

Damn it. He was going to have to beat her over the head with the truth for months—if not years—to get her to hear him. "He was grieving, Hol. He was lost in his grief. No sane person would do what he did to me out of payback."

She lowered her face and shook her head. "This was my fault."

He pulled her closer until he could put his hand on her face and look directly into her sorrowful eyes. "You saved me."

"I got lucky."

Exhaling heavily, he frowned. "I don't have the energy for this fight."

"We're not fighting."

"We're going to be if you don't shut up and kiss me."

She smirked but then put her mouth over his. Kissing her was almost as amazing as that first deep breath he'd taken after she pulled him from the coffin. He figured nothing would ever be quite that good. But this...this was close.

The door creaked as it was pushed open, and Holly leaned back. Jack was expecting his mom carrying in a hot cup of tea, but Meyer stepped through the doorway, taking a moment to look from Holly to Jack and back again.

"Is this a bad time?" Meyer asked.

Holly sat all the way back, and Jack shook his head. "I'm not really ready to answer questions," he said. "Besides, it sounds like you have a pretty good idea what happened."

"We do." The son of a bitch actually looked a bit guilty. "Good thing your girlfriend isn't much for following the rules, huh?"

Jack filled with pride. "Must be why I like her so much."

She chuckled and shook her head at his joke.

"Look, um," Meyer started, "I'm not here about what happened to you. We know who was responsible for that. We're examining the evidence in the Adams case, as well as the other two victims. Hearing Adams's report of what happened to her—well, I don't think Pearson was working alone, and he's not giving up any information. Not even when we offered him a deal."

"He doesn't deserve a deal after what he did to those women," Holly snapped.

"If there's another psycho like him out there, we'll gladly shave a few years off his sentence to find him. We don't want his partner starting this shit again. Look, I know I didn't give you enough credit while you were looking for Fredrickson."

She glanced at Jack but had the sense to keep her sarcasm to herself.

"But...if you have any idea who he might be working with, I need to know. I need anything you've got."

"What's Susan Adams saying?"

"Pearson confronted her in the parking lot. She said it sounded like he'd been following her for some time. Her neighbors confirmed seeing a vehicle matching his several times over the last few months. He must have been stalking her. So when he followed her to the store, he waited for her to emerge and confronted her. He took her to his house and tried to convince her they belonged together."

Holly swallowed. "Did he rape her?"

He nodded, and she felt like a knife had sliced her heart open.

"Okay?" Jack asked softly.

Holly nodded and focused on Meyer again.

"She fought him," he said. "That made him mad, and she thinks he knocked her out. When she came to, she'd already been buried."

Holly took a moment to process his words, certain he'd left out more information than he'd given. "What part of that makes you think he had help?"

"Look, I know those woods aren't well travelled, but they are within a public park. People come and go all the time. Hikers, dog walkers... Anyone could have stumbled upon him not only digging the graves but carrying an unconscious woman from his truck to the woods. That's something someone would notice, right?"

"So you think he had a lookout?" Jack asked.

"I think he had to have. I just don't think he did all this on his own. Did you have any inclination that he was working with someone?"

Holly shook her head. So did Jack. They had been pretty certain Pearson was their man. They had never really considered that there were two of them.

"I can review my files, though," Holly offered. "I may have missed something."

"Would you mind?" Meyer asked.

"Not at all." Leaning down, she kissed Jack softly. "Be good."

He smirked. "Or what?"

She simply cocked a brow and stood upright. "Would you like me to bring you back some dinner?"

"I never turn down food."

"I'll call you when I'm headed back." She headed for the door, promising to call Meyer if she found anything in her files.

Jack drew a breath when the cop who'd gone after his badge simply stood there. "Need anything else?"

"I talked to Captain. As soon as you're out of here, he's going to reinstate you."

Jack nodded. "Sounds good."

"Sorry I was such a prick, but really, Tarek. Stay out of my cases going forward. Got it?"

Jack chuckled. "Yeah. Got it."

HOLLY TOSSED A FILE ASIDE AND SHOOK HER HEAD, frustrated at the lack of evidence pointing to anyone other than Vance Pearson. The police had questioned his uncle, John Middleton, but from what Meyer had told her, he was as shocked as anyone by the charges.

"I thought you'd be at the hospital with Jack," came a voice from the door.

She exhaled slowly so she didn't seem as startled as she was by Alexa's sudden appearance. Damn, she was more on edge than she'd realized. "I was. The police think Pearson had an accomplice. I was going through our files to see if I had anything that might assist in finding him."

"No luck, huh?"

She shook her head. After taking a deep breath, she dug up the strength to say, "He raped them, Lex. He raped all of them."

"I'm sorry, Hol."

She nodded slightly, knowing Lex was consoling her for the pain of Holly's childhood more than the horrors these women had faced.

"You stepped in and did your best to stop this from happening to Susan."

"I think telling her to walk out is what got her hurt in the first place. I think I pushed his final button."

"No. You saw the danger and tried to protect her."

Lifting her hand, she scowled. "I don't want to debate this right now."

Alexa didn't push. "How is Jack?"

Holly's mood instantly brightened. "He's good. Soaking up the attention."

Alexa moved into the room as a smirk spread across her face. "Look at that smile. You look happy."

Holly tried to force her mouth back to a neutral line but ended up chuckling. "He's a good guy. I like him."

"And he's adorable."

She nodded slowly. "Yes, he is."

"And he thinks you are *the* shit."

"Well, I didn't say he was smart."

"He's obviously brilliant." Alexa sat across from her. "It's about time you found someone."

"You know we've known each other for just a few weeks, right? Hardly qualifies as finding someone."

"Disagree. You two fit."

"I keep hearing that."

"Because it's true."

Holly pressed her lips together and drew a long breath.

"And there it is," Alexa said softly. "The self-loathing we've come to know so well."

"Don't start on me."

"Don't start on yourself. You deserve happiness. You've punished yourself long enough for things you couldn't control."

"I know. I know I can't protect everyone. I just don't know how to stop trying."

Eva leaned in the door and cupped her ear. "I was just passing by, but...I'm sorry. What was that? Did Holly Austin just acknowledge that she can't save the world all on her own?"

Holly met her gaze with a frown. "Not you too. Okay. One of you is enough."

Eva dropped into the seat next to Alexa. "I'll stop when we finally break through that thick skull of yours."

"It's not that thick," Holly said, causing her co-workers to look at each other with sarcastically raised brows.

They all laughed, and Holly took a deep breath. For a few moments, her heart and soul had stopped aching. She had these women—and Jack—to thank for that. But again, that was starting to feel like such a weight on her shoulders.

She cared about them. She did. All of them. Why was that so damned hard to swallow?

Alexa leaned forward and tapped on her desk. "Hey. Stop. Stop thinking." She looked into Holly's eyes as if she were seeing her innermost thoughts. Hell, maybe she was. "Let it go. Let go of the past so you can move forward, hopefully with Jack...because his mom's cooking is *amazing*."

"Hell, yes," Eva agreed. "If you dump him, he's mine. Just for the food."

Holly smiled. "I might wrestle you for him."

"From what Sam says, he likes when you wrestle."

She shook her head. "What is going on with you two? You are being really hard on me tonight."

"You're finally in a good enough mood to put up with it," Eva said.

Silence lingered for a few moments before Holly narrowed her eyes at her. "Since we're picking at each other... We've been talking about Joshua quite a bit lately. He had a pretty heavy hand in this case after the bodies were found."

Eva scoffed. "It's not like I didn't know we'd cross paths sometimes."

"Are things still amicable between you?"

"Joshua wouldn't have it any other way. Peace and love and harmony and all that."

"Wanna tell us the real reason you pushed him away?"

"No."

Alexa snorted a half laugh. "I still think he broke up

with her because she put a can in the plastics recycling bin."

"He got over that," Eva muttered.

Holly smiled, feeling her stress ease even more as she bantered—actually bantered—with her friends. "I love how you ladies keep pushing me to be more open, but none of you want to do the same."

"Baby steps, fearless leader," Eva said. "Go back to the hospital. We'll look through the files. If we see anything, I'll call you. *Go*," she said when Holly didn't move.

"You two planned this, didn't you?"

Alexa simply smiled. "Go."

Holly grabbed her keys and her phone and then pushed herself up and walked around her desk. She wasn't overly affectionate with her teammates—Tika was the hugger of the group—but she did put her hand on Lex's shoulder as she passed. "Thanks. I'll see you tomorrow."

As she headed out of the building, she called Jack. "What do you want for dinner?"

"You," he deadpanned.

She smiled. She couldn't help it. "That's dessert, silly. What *food* do you want for dinner?"

"I stand by my previous answer. But considering I just got a pizza and some burgers from some guys at work, I'd say we're both covered on the food side of things. Get back here. I miss you."

"I'm headed your way." She pressed the button on her fob as she ended the call. She was almost to her car when a figure stepped from the shadows. Her defenses kicked in, and she was immediately aware of everything all at once. The parking lot, though well lit, was too dark to make out his face clearly, but he smelled of alcohol seeping from his pores. Beer, to be exact. She knew that smell. She'd grown up with that smell.

"Holly Austin?"

"Who's asking?"

She put her hand on her gun and was unsnapping the holster with her thumb, but he was faster. By the time she realized he was lifting a Taser instead of a gun, she was already feeling the jolts shoot through her.

18

Jack tried to be discreet as he looked at his phone, but his mother caught him anyway.

"It hasn't been that long," she said.

"Almost half an hour. HEARTS is just a few blocks away, Mama. She should be here by now."

His mom shrugged. "Go ahead. Call her. You know you want to."

Not that he *needed* permission to call Holly, but he accepted his mother's and dialed the phone. He wasn't expecting his call to go to voice mail, but it did. So he texted: *Where are you?*

He set his phone aside to impatiently wait for her reply. "Why don't you eat while we're waiting for her?"

"Why don't *you* eat?" his mother asked.

"Because you raised me to be a gentleman, and a gentleman would wait for his lady to join him before eating."

She smiled. "I like her, Jakeem. She has *umph*."

"*Umph?*"

"*Umph,*" she said with a decisive nod. "She's a strong woman. She will be a protective wife and mother. Like a lioness."

"Whoa. Mama, I told you before—"

She lifted her hand. "I know what you said. But I also know what I see. And I see love beginning to blossom. She was so scared for you, and when she found you"—she lifted her hands and rolled her head back—"the sun couldn't compare to the smile on her face. Or on yours."

"Well. She had just saved me from certain death. That tends to bring a smile to a guy's face."

"So does falling in love."

"Mama," he said with a shake of his head as he looked at his phone in case he hadn't heard Holly respond. She hadn't. So he called her again. And she still didn't answer.

"She probably went home to freshen up."

"She would have told me."

His mother watched him for a moment before pulling a card from her purse. "This has the office number on it. Call. Maybe she got caught up."

Jack lifted his hand. "I have that number in here." He dialed and waited.

"Thank you for calling HEARTS. This is Eva."

"Eva. It's Jack. Is Hol around?"

"No. She left a bit ago. She was going to grab some dinner and head your way."

"Yeah," he said softly. "I told her to forget the dinner and head on over. Someone sent pizza."

Eva was quiet for a moment. "She's not there yet?"

"No."

"Hang on."

Sounds in the background indicated Eva was walking across the lobby. The door opened and, within moments, closed.

"Holly?" she yelled, her voice echoing through the lobby. "Hey, Hol! You here?"

Several more moments passed with muffled voices in the background and then the distinct sound of Eva picking up the phone. "Her car is here, but she's not." She didn't hide the stress in her voice well at all. "I'm checking the surveillance camera. Just one second."

Jack swallowed. Something was off. He felt it in his gut.

"Shit," Eva whispered. "Jack. Someone took her."

As Holly came to, she took a moment to assess the damage to her body. The Taser hadn't knocked her out, but she sure as shit felt the aftereffects rolling through her chest as she breathed. No, that son of a bitch had hit her over the head when she was defenseless from his first attack.

Coward.

Damn, her head hurt.

Taking a deep breath despite the pain it caused, she let

the cool air awaken her senses a bit more. Something tickled her nose, and she smelled the earth beneath her.

That scent rocked her the rest of the way awake. She hadn't been able to stop smelling that since pulling Jack from the ground. The dirt had caked beneath her nails and ingrained itself into her senses. When her entire body jerked, she realized she was being dragged across the ground. Taking in the landscaping around her—particularly the yellow tape—she also realized she was in the park. Being pulled toward the holes where Julia and Penelope had been buried.

Oh, hell no.

She was plotting her escape when whoever had hold of her dropped her feet and pulled a handkerchief from his pocket, wiping the cloth across his forehead.

She moved, intent on jumping to her feet and running, but her muscles didn't quite agree. She pushed through it, biting back the need to grunt out in pain, and had just made it to her feet when the man turned. He reached for her, but Holly was able to lean back before he could grab her hair.

Still off balance, she had to stumble several times before regaining her balance. About the time she did, she had to lean away again to miss his next swing. This time, she recovered more quickly. Her focus moved to his face, and he smirked.

Middleton.

She and Jack had given him a pass after finding out Pearson had been sexually harassing Susan. Stupid.

He swung again, and this time, she dove in toward his waist instead of leaning away from him. The move took him by surprise, and it was his turn to stumble. Holly took advantage of his shock by sweeping her leg under his. He fell, landing with a thud, and she fell with him.

She pressed her palm into his throat as she sat back, cutting off his airflow while she reached for her gun with her other hand. Her holster was empty.

Looking at him, she was about to demand to know where her gun was when she was answered by a loud pop and a searing pain shooting through her thigh.

She cried out as Middleton pushed her off. Grasping her wound, she cursed the blood seeping through her fingers. A quick glance down confirmed it was a through-and-through, no real damage done. But it hurt like hell. The scent of her blood hit her hard, and her stomach rolled. As always, the memories came at her fast. Her mother dead. Bleeding. Lifeless.

Grinding her teeth, Holly pushed the past away and focused on Middleton, glaring as he sat up and rubbed his throat.

"Stupid bitch," he muttered. He stared back at her, and Holly realized he probably was the more frightening of the two. His eyes weren't just angry—they were crazy. *He* was crazy.

Standing, he aimed the gun at her, and Holly's brain suddenly switched gears.

She was eight again. Peering beneath the couch. Dust

tickled her nose, but she refused to sneeze. The bad man would hear her.

Her mom was screaming. And the man hit her. But not with his fist. With a gun.

When her screaming turned into crying, he set the gun down. Holly had seen that kind of gun before on the TV. A revolver. He had a revolver. But he'd stabbed her to death. What kind of sick bastard would do that?

"You sit your ass right there and don't you move," Middleton said, pulling her from her memory. "Or I'll shoot your other leg, too."

He slid the gun into his waistband and grabbed her ankles again.

As Middleton neared the open graves, Holly considered her options, noticing a box off to the side. It wasn't the same coffin Jack had been buried in. Or the one used on Julia, Penelope, and Susan. Those coffins were at the police station.

This was a new one. And she suspected he'd made it just for her. She looked around, seeking any signs of people, but the park would be empty this late at night. If there were others around, she wouldn't have been carried into the woods by a madman. Besides, she wouldn't give this asshole the satisfaction of hearing her scream. He would never get her in that box—not alive, anyway.

Biting her teeth together when he dropped her wounded leg, she swallowed the pain and steadied her voice. "What happened, big guy? Not enough hugs in your childhood?"

He didn't answer. He was focused on moving the coffin into the hole in the ground.

She had to distract him. Buy time. Give Jack enough time to realize she was missing. It wouldn't take them long to realize where she was. Or so she hoped. "Mommy didn't love you. Or maybe she loved you too much and not the right way."

He turned then, pointing at her. "Shut your mouth, whore!"

"She touched you? Or she didn't touch you? Which was it?"

He stared at her for a moment before strolling back over and smiling as he loomed over her. "She screamed so loud. When I pushed her into the well. I listened to her scream for hours before I pushed the side in on her to shut her up."

Holly swallowed. "You killed your mother?"

"You look just like her, you know. Golden hair and crystal-blue eyes. I bet you're a whore, too."

"You killed her because she was a whore?"

He stroked his hand over her hair. She tried to jerk back, but he fisted the strands and forced her to look at him. "She would drink from the liquor cabinet and screw men right in front of us when Daddy wasn't home. I got brave once. Told her I was going to tell. She chased me. But I knew where to go."

"And you pushed her down the well?"

His smile widened. "And she screamed so loud. Begged

me to let her out. Promised she would do whatever I wanted."

Holly's heart pounded against her ribcage. She could barely control her breathing, but she had to stay calm. She was certain that Middleton, crazy as he was, knew to get rid of her phone, but if she was lucky, the tiny tracker Rene had forced her to wear was still safely in her pocket. Sam was probably online finding her right now. No, better than that, they were on their way to her. *Right now.*

"I bet Julia begged, too," Holly said, hoping to keep this lunatic talking.

"Yup."

"And Penelope?"

"And Susan. Susan." He closed his eyes and took a deep breath. "She screamed almost as loud as Mama."

"Pearson brought them to you?"

Middleton grabbed the coffin and dragged it to the hole, where he dropped it in. "Vance is an idiot. All he cared about was getting Susan in bed. When she wouldn't give in, he tried to find a replacement. Started hitting on clients. Julia was too nice to notice, and by the time she did, he had it in his mind she wanted him." He chuckled. "So the dumbass just took her. He came to me. Said he messed up."

"And you offered to get rid of her."

He grabbed the lapels of Holly's jacket, lifting her to her feet. She ground her teeth to stop herself from crying out at the pain shooting down her wounded leg.

"Somebody has to clean up his messes."

"Why? Why you?"

"I've been cleaning up after that boy all his life. As soon as he realized how easy it was, he couldn't stop himself from taking that other girl. He might like taking 'em." He pressed his lips to her ear. "But he knew I liked killin' them."

Holly swallowed. No way was he getting her in that coffin. No way in hell. He yanked her, and she threw her head forward, crashing her forehead to his nose. He howled and released his hold on her. She reached for the gun in his waistband, but he recovered and twisted her arm until she dropped to the ground.

He used his grip on her to drag her toward the box. He'd only managed to pull her a few feet when a body jumped over her and tackled him. He was on his back, cursing, before Holly recognized it was Jack punching Middleton in the side.

It was the second time in one day when seeing Jack had made her the happiest she'd ever been in her life. But then Middleton threw his head back into Jack's face and Jack fell away.

"Gun!" Holly screamed as Middleton reached for her Glock.

Jack dropped his hands, focusing on Middleton as the man pulled the gun from his waistband. He aimed the gun, ready to fire on Jack, as Holly pushed herself up, gripping the shovel handle as she went. She swung, and a sickening crack filled the air as the flat side of the blade connected with Middleton's skull. Jack lurched forward, grabbing the gun as the man fell.

Looking up, Jack gave Holly a crooked smile. "Are you ever going to let me be the hero?"

She smiled as warmth spread through her chest. "Not a chance."

19

Jack didn't mind having HEARTS around, but he didn't particularly care for feeling like he was being edged out. He and Holly had been released from medical care and were at her house, where he was perfectly capable of taking care of her. If the mother hens would let him.

Her wound wasn't even that bad. Not really. Yes, she was sore. Yes, she needed to take it easy. But she was going to be fine. She was already planning to go back to work—desk duty at least. They didn't need to hover.

"Are you pouting?"

Jack glanced at Rene standing in Holly's kitchen door. "No."

"I'm pretty sure behind those black eyes and taped-up broken nose, you're pouting, Detective."

"Why would—"

She walked into the kitchen, cutting his question off

with that stone-cold stare of hers. "We just need to reassure ourselves that she's fine, and then we'll go."

"She is fine."

"We know."

"So why do you need reassurance?"

"Because we love her, too." She lifted her brow before he could refute her inclusion of him.

He smirked. Holly did that same brow-cock shut-the-hell-up move. He wasn't going to deny that he cared about her. Not anymore. That was obvious after all they'd been through. But he wasn't sure they were ready for the L-word just yet. And Jack was fine with that. And if he read Holly right, she was, too. They were in a good place. A solid place. Building a foundation. A life. With each other and all the people in their lives.

Including the one staring at him like she knew every damned thing there was to know.

"Sorry," he said, suddenly feeling a bit embarrassed about his lack of empathy for her friends. "It's just that we've barely had a moment alone since all this happened."

After the police had arrived and arrested Middleton, Jack and Holly had ended up back at the hospital and hadn't been alone since.

"You're right. You haven't. Between us and your mother, you two have had a revolving door on this place. I'll round up the troops."

"I wasn't kicking you out."

She grinned. "You couldn't if you tried, Detective." With a wink, she left, and Jack finished drinking the coffee he'd been staring into when she'd caught him internally griping.

By the time he'd rinsed his mug and headed out of the kitchen, Holly was hobbling along on her crutch behind the rest of the women, telling them she'd be at work the next day and not to worry about her. She closed the door behind Tika and collapsed against it.

"Do you hear that?" she asked.

"What?"

"Silence," she whispered as she hobbled toward him. "Blessed silence."

He smiled as he rested his hands on her hips. "Nice, isn't it?"

"Amazing." Resting her cheek on his shoulder, she took a deep breath before rolling her head back. A quiet laugh left her. "You look so terrible."

"Well, you're walking like Igor."

She laughed more heartily, and he had no choice but to smile.

Running his hand over her head, he gently tugged at her messy bun. "What should we do with all this quiet time?"

Mischief lit in her eyes before she whispered, "Eat more of your mom's basbousa."

Chuckling, he put his arm around her back and let her lean on him as he guided her to the sofa. "Would you like coffee with your cake?"

"Yes, please."

Easing her down, he kissed her forehead. "You know

she's never going to stop cooking for you now that you've gushed about her food."

"I hope not. She's spoiling me rotten, and I love it."

"Me too," he said before kissing her head again.

She moaned when her phone rang. "That thing hasn't stopped for days."

"People are worried about you."

"Reporters wanting me to answer questions, you mean." She looked at the caller ID and then to Jack. Confusion filled her eyes. "It's my dad."

"Answer it."

She hesitated before pressing her thumb into the screen. "Hello?" She lowered her face. "Hey. No, I'm fine, Dad." She nodded as if her father could see her. "Yeah. That'd be fine. Um, next week sometime, though. I'm still recovering. Okay. See you then." She hung up and stared at the phone for a minute.

"He wants to see you?"

"Yeah."

"Why are you so shocked?"

She met his gaze and scoffed. "Because he sounded sober."

"Maybe he was."

"Maybe."

He stared at her while she stared at her phone. Her mind was always going, always trying to put pieces together, always trying to anticipate what to expect. He didn't blame her after all she'd been through, but he hated that she was always so suspicious of everyone. She never took anyone or anything at face value. He was going to have to work doubly hard to make sure she knew how he felt about her. But he was okay with that. She was worth it. She was definitely worth it.

"You okay?" she asked when she caught his gaze.

He inhaled slowly and realized he'd probably never been more okay in his life—despite the broken nose Middleton had given him—than in that moment as he looked into her curious blue eyes.

Okay, so maybe his mom and Rene were right. Maybe they were there; maybe the L-word wasn't as far away as he imagined.

"I'm great, Hol." He smiled and tucked a strand of hair behind her ear. "I'm more than great."

Normally Holly would hate being catered to, but she had to admit, she'd been eating it up the last few days. Somehow she'd come to terms with her place in this life—in HEARTS and with Jack.

They'd only been together a short time, but things with him had felt right from the beginning, and their joint near-death experiences had seemed to cement their places with each other. Okay, his near-death experience and her quasi-confrontation with death.

However she categorized it, knowing that she and Jack had come far too close to losing each other seemed to push her beyond whatever emotional block she'd put in place years ago. Tika had rushed into Holly's hospital room and given her the customary hug, and instead of simply tolerating it, Holly had hugged her back and clung to her. She'd needed that comfort, and she'd allowed herself to accept it.

And when Ms. Tarek—or Najwa, since she now insisted Holly call her by her first name—had done the same, Holly had hugged her as well. She felt a bond to Najwa that ran much deeper than amazing food. The woman felt like a mother to her. Not *her* mother, but *a* mother. And that was the closest Holly'd had for a very long time to feeling like she had a family. And Jack was a part of that. As much as Eva, Alexa, Rene, Tika, and even Sam.

This was her family now. And she had refused to feel that until she'd come so close to losing them all.

That train of thought led to where all her thoughts seemed to lead these days. To the night her mother was raped and murdered in front of her. She'd added her memory of the revolver to her journal, but now she was beginning to question the validity. She'd been under duress when that flashback had happened, and in all these years, she'd never recalled the man having a gun. Why would she remember that now? Maybe she hadn't. Maybe her mind was playing tricks on her. Honestly, she had no way of knowing for certain.

"Those are some pretty heavy sighs you're letting out," Jack muttered.

"I thought were you asleep."

"Your heavy breathing is keeping me awake."

"Sorry," she whispered.

He dropped his arm on her waist when she started to lift the blankets. "Where are you going?"

"I don't want to disturb you."

"Too late." Moving closer to her, he kissed her shoulder. "What's wrong, Princess?"

She smiled at his nickname. One day she'd kick his ass for that, but today definitely wasn't the day. Turning, she hissed as pain hit her thigh, but she pushed through and turned to face him. Even in the barely lit bedroom, she could see the medical tape across his nose.

"We are a sorry pair right now."

"I think we're okay. Considering the alternatives."

Tilting her face, she put her lips lightly on his. "I'm done thinking about the alternatives. What Fredrickson did to you. What Middleton tried to do to me. It's over. I'm letting it go."

He lifted his brows. "You? Let something go?"

"Hey," she chastised. "Let me have this moment."

Putting his hand to her face, he cupped her cheek. "You take as many moments as you need, babe. We have all the time in the world."

Covering his hand, she smiled. "I feel that way, too."

His kiss was so delicate it melted her heart. Whatever last bit of resistance she was holding to faded, and she felt her soul open to him. Then, as he leaned back and looked into her eyes, Holly realized what the feeling was. Love. This was the moment. The moment she fell in love with this man.

"What is it?" he asked, stroking his hand over her hair.

She swallowed and blinked as unexpected tears filled her eyes. Damn it. She'd turned into a crier. "There is something I can't let go of, Jack. That I'll never be able to let go of. Since I was a teenager, I've been keeping a journal with what I remember about the night my mom died. Everything I can remember, no matter how big or small. If I remember it, I write it down. I know the odds of finding that bastard are low, but...I have a file at the office. Would you look at it? Would you help me try to find him?"

He brushed his thumb over her lips. "Of course. I'll do everything I can."

"Thank you."

"You're welcome."

She inhaled slowly. "First, I need you to do something else."

"What?"

"Help me get all these thoughts out of my head. I can't stop thinking about losing the people I care about, and I'm about to lose my mind. I need you to make love to me."

He seemed surprised by her request. She'd never put sex in the context of him having any kind of control, and his reaction confirmed that he'd noticed that, too. She might not have said what was on her mind, but she was certain he'd read between the lines of her meaning. He always managed to do that somehow.

Jack lightly ran his hand over her thigh. "I don't want to hurt you."

"So be gentle."

She rolled onto her back, pulling him with her and biting the urge to hiss when her muscles cried out against the movement. If he knew she was in pain, he'd stop. Just one more thing she adored—no, *loved*—about him.

He kissed her slow and deep, and she let him. She let him take the lead as she followed, determined to allow herself to enjoy not being in control for a change. That was something she was going to have to work on for a while, but she'd taken the first step with Alexa the other day by letting her drive, and now she was taking the first step with Jack... by letting him drive in a different way.

She had to open up and trust. Her friends, her lover, and herself. Now that she'd accepted that, she was finding letting herself care about them a bit easier than she'd thought it would be.

Holly smiled at Jack as he eased back and carefully started removing her underwear—paying special attention as he slid the cloth over her bandaged wounds. Then he tossed the material aside before discarding his boxer briefs.

"This is going to be very interesting," he commented.

"Why?"

"I haven't quite figured out where to put your leg so I don't hurt it."

"You're overthinking this."

"Am I?"

She nodded and gestured for him to return to her side. He stretched out, and she kissed him as she ran her hand down his side, lightly brushing over his skin. She smirked and he gasped when she teasingly touched his erection.

Spreading her legs, stopping only when the muscles in her wounded thigh protested, she tilted her hips and guided him toward her opening. He held her as he moved forward, slowly entering her. She held her breath, bit her lip, and held his gaze as their bodies fully connected.

He gently ground into her and kissed her lips as they made love. She held his face as she deepened his light kisses. As her pleasure grew, she felt the need to climb inside him, to let him consume her. She held him more tightly, wrapping her arm around his shoulders, as her body tensed.

Wrapping her leg around his, ignoring the pain, she pulled their bodies closer together.

"I got this," he said when she inhaled sharply. Holding her hip, he ground into her.

She gave in and let him carry her with him as he got closer and closer to the edge. Looking into his eyes as he made love to her, she felt her doubts fade as warmth filled her. For the first time in longer than she cared to remember, Holly didn't feel the need to hide her heart.

STONEHILL SERIES:

The Road Leads Back

Friends Without Benefits

The Forgotten Path

Jessica's Wish

This Old Cafe

Forever Yours

THE WOMEN OF HEARTS SERIES:

Hidden Hearts

Burning Hearts

OTHER TITLES:

California Can Wait

Seducing Kate

A Life Without Water

Unforgettable You (coming soon)

ACKNOWLEDGMENTS

My heartfelt thanks to the professionals who helped clarify, explain, and guide me through the proper process of missing persons investigations.

Jill Goffin, Private Investigator, Assured Private Investigations (Appleton, Wisconsin)

Greg Gourd, Retired Crime Scene Investigator, Des Moines Police Department (Des Moines, Iowa)

Mandy Pagliai, Retired Senior Police Officer, Des Moines Police Department (Des Moines, Iowa)

Noreen Walker, Retired Deputy Superintendent, Chicago Police Department (Chicago, Illinois)

ABOUT THE AUTHOR

As a teen, Marci Bolden skipped over young adult books and jumped right into reading romance novels. She never left.

Marci lives in the Midwest with her husband, kiddos, and numerous rescue pets. If she had an ounce of willpower, Marci would embrace healthy living, but until cupcakes and wine are no longer available at the local market, she will appease her guilt by reading self-help books and promising to join a gym "soon."

Visit her here:
www.marcibolden.com

f facebook.com/MarciBoldenAuthor

🐦 twitter.com/BoldenMarci

📷 instagram.com/marciboldenauthor